SWEET TEMPTATION

"Damn and blast," Evan muttered.

"Whatever is the matter?" Katherine asked.

"I simply cannot like Miss Page being separated from the party as she is."

Katherine smiled. "I know we disagree on Mr. Wooding's character, but with me he has been perfectly gentlemanly in conduct. I have no doubt he will be attentive to Miss Page, who must be nearly twenty years his junior, but nothing that would be considered improper."

"She is a complete innocent."

At that, Katherine stared. "And I am not?"

He smiled at her ruefully before whispering, "You do not kiss like one."

She was utterly shocked and oddly enough not in the least offended, though she knew she should be. "What a completely disgraceful thing to say."

Evan held her gaze forcefully in his. "Accept it as a compliment. One day, you will make a most excellent wife for a very fortunate fellow."

But not for you. The thought swept through her mind with painful force. *But not for you.*

A
BRIGHTON
FLIRTATION

Valerie King

ZEBRA BOOKS
Kensington Publishing Corp.
http://www.zebrabooks.com

ZEBRA BOOKS are published by

Kensington Publishing Corp.
850 Third Avenue
New York, NY 10022

All Kensington titles, imprints, and distributed lines are avail-
able at special quantity discounts for bulk purchases for sales
promotions, premiums, fund raising, educational or institu-
tional use.

Special book excerpts or customized printings can also be created to fit specific needs. For details, write or phone the office
of the Kensington Special Sales Manager: Kensington Publishing Corp., 850 Third Avenue, New York, NY 10022. Attn. Special Sales Department. Phone: 1-800-221-2647.

Zebra and the Z logo Reg. U.S. Pat. & TM Off.

First Printing: December, 2000
10 9 8 7 6 5 4 3 2 1

Printed in the United States of America

To my daughter, Sarah, with love.

*Love is such a mystery,
I cannot find it out . . .*

—Sir John Suckling

One

Brighton, England, 1817

Katherine Pamberley saw a familiar, predatory look in Captain Evan Ramsdell's eye as he found her among the waves. He was just descending from his own bathing machine and did not hesitate to dive straight into the cold water, clearly heading in her direction.

Not again! she thought, her heart beginning to race.

She had been swimming past yet another of the large wooden sea-bathing machines on the beach at Brighthelmstone when, much to her horror, she saw Captain Ramsdell emerge from the very next one. She was a strong swimmer, but she knew from several previous encounters with the captain that he was muscled quite powerfully and would no doubt be able to capture her if he so desired, which apparently he did!

Panic flooded her. She gave a strangled squeal as she turned in the opposite direction, and with the strongest strokes she could manage in the turbulent surf, headed back toward Mrs. Alistair's bathing machine some hundred yards distant. The last view she had of Captain Ramsdell was of his back as he dove a second time into the surf, wearing only a muslin shirt and blue breeches.

Unfortunately, the flannel gown which she wore as the traditional sea-bathing garb of Young Ladies of Quality was weighing her down and made any serious progress an absurdity. Her heart beat furiously as she struggled against the gown as well as the relentless pull and tug of the ocean's drift, which happened to be flowing in the captain's decided favor.

She did not want Captain Ramsdell to catch her, for if he did . . . well, she knew precisely what would happen and she meant to avoid yet another passionate encounter at any cost.

She had gone little more than fifteen yards, however, when she heard his laughter behind her and felt his arm strongly about her waist. Her drew her into the surf until she was neck deep in the water. He pulled her close, and his lips swiftly covered hers, just as they had several times in the past.

She struggled only briefly, then, as several times before, simply closed her eyes and surrendered to the incomprehensible joy she felt in kissing a man whom she was neither betrothed to nor even remotely interested in wedding! Her arms found their way about his neck, and he laughed quite happily against her mouth as a wave descended on them. The water pushed them in a circle, then ebbed and began drawing them both toward the open sea.

Katherine held him fiercely for reasons she doubted she would ever fully comprehend. He seemed to have some strange, inexplicable power over her. Was it love? If not, how was it possible he had merely to look at her and she would fairly collapse into his arms?

A massive wave suddenly crashed nearby, and the resulting foam-crested, turbulent water had the happy effect of knocking her from his arms. She was awakened abruptly to the horrid impropriety of kissing Evan Ramsdell yet again, and that while sea-bathing in publIc where anyone might be witness to such a scandalous indiscretion.

"Oh, you beast!" she cried, letting the water take her yet farther from him.

He threw himself toward her in another swift dive and came up in the waist-deep water directly in front of her. "You enjoy my kisses," he said. "Confess it is so."

She fell back into the water and kicked away from him. "Does that make the experience a proper one?" she asked, trying to reason with him. She glanced around, grateful that the two machines nearby were deserted. She then realized this was exactly why Captain Ramsdell had felt at ease to torment her as he had.

"I do not give a fig whether it is proper or not," he responded, standing with water dripping from the muslin shirt, which now clung provocatively to his masculine frame. He was a picture of earth's vitality and strength. His wet black hair gleamed in the bright sunshine, and his eyes were a startling blue, as clear as a summer's day. His skin was sun-bronzed, for he had served many years on the Iberian Peninsula in Wellington's army. He had been toughened by years of service, which gave him a boldness lacking in all the other men she knew or had known over the course of her two and twenty years. He had had many adventures the likes of which she would never fully understand yet which made him mysterious and, yes, desirable, especially for a young lady who had spent much of her youth imagining herself doing battle with England's enemies, astride her favorite gelding, Prince.

Her gaze took in the way he stood defiantly against her and against what was proper and decorous. She had the most unreasonable impulse to rise in the water and throw herself upon his chest—again!

From the first, he had intrigued her as no other man had. The day her home, Lady Brook Cottage, had burnt to the ground, he had ridden up on his horse, like a knight of old, offering his help. Even then, she had known a decided tugging in the vicinity of her heart at just the sight of him.

Yet last summer, he had evinced but the smallest interest in her, forcing her to take a long look at herself, forcing her to admit that she needed to make a great many changes, which she had. Perhaps these changes had caused him to undertake so wicked a flirtation when he'd arrived in Brighton. She simply did not know.

He began advancing on her again, and perhaps would have assaulted her once more had not the voice of her friend Lydia Alistair reached her from many yards distant. She turned around and saw Lydia waving wildly at her. Another moment, and Mrs. Alistair had joined her daughter on the sea-bathing machine and was waving too.

Oh, dear! Katherine was afraid Mrs. Alistair might discover that she had been in Captain Ramsdell's company unattended—again. She waved back and watched as Mrs. Alistair disappeared inside the bathing machine.

"I must go," she said urgently. "Mrs. Alistair calls me."

The mere mention of her hostess's name gave the captain pause. "Very well," he said. "Another time, then, and we will finish our *discussion.*"

"Our discussion!" she cried. "What a wickedly absurd man you are. No, we shall never finish this discussion. You must leave me in peace, Evan Ramsdell, if you have even a modicum of honor."

Since he merely smiled maddeningly upon her, quite unmoved, she turned to go, his low, throaty chuckle following her.

Twenty minutes later, while climbing the stairs on the way to Mrs. Alistair's town coach at the top of Russell Street, Lydia held Katherine back from her mother's hearing and whispered, "I told her you were conversing With Miss Framfield, who I knew to be bathing farther down the beach. She believed me, for she cannot see at all well at that distance."

"Th-thank you," Katherine stammered. She would have continued the conversation, for she felt distressed by this most recent encounter with the captain, but Mrs. Alistair bade the girls to hurry along since Mrs. Nutley was expecting her on the Steyne within the hour.

Two mornings later, Katherine was in her bedchamber completing her toilet when her thoughts returned to Captain Ramsdell. She was trying very hard to make sense of the entirely oversetting encounter with him, but she could not. He had begun flirting with her from the earliest days of his arrival in Brighton, and she could not account for it, at least not in its entirety.

He had spent the summer prior in residence near the smoking ruins of Lady Brook Cottage, as had his brother, Lord Ramsdell, because of the spate of weddings which took place at the time. Lord Ramsdell had married her eldest sister, Constance, while his ward, the Honorable Charles Kidmarsh, had wed the youngest Pamberley sister, Augusta. Celeste soon followed and was wed to dear Sir Henry Crowthorne within three weeks afterward, so it had seemed provident to the captain to remain with his brother until all three weddings had taken place.

Katherine had come to know Captain Ramsdell a little since he shared with her a great passion for every manner of horseflesh. For the first time in her entire existence she had met a man who had actually interested her, particularly since he had served in the army as a cavalry officer. The knowledge that he possessed a handsome estate in Worcestershire at which he enjoyed his passion for breeding horses had confirmed her notion that here was a man who might make her a proper husband.

However, she had not been in his company but a half dozen times before she realized he was completely disinterested in her. Whenever she would attempt to engage him in conversation, his attention would drift as though he was bored with her company. How lowering! How utterly vexing!

However, she was not one to repine. Instead, she permitted the situation to work in her in such a way that she began to consider everything about her existence, past, present and future. What she found upon reflection was rather disturbing. Her opinions on any subject seemed ill-formed, she did not possess a great deal of information with which to converse, and beyond her love of horses, she did not know what she liked or disliked to any degree of certainty.

That winter, with three of her sisters married and no longer living at Lady Brook, and with Marianne intent on planning for her first London Season in which she hoped to set the town ablaze with her presence, she was left with a great many solitary hours in which to regard herself in the looking glass.

After serious contemplation, she realized she was no longer content to make the stables at Lady Brook the center of her existence. She began to read, to improve her mind, to discover her most secret thoughts and hopes, to alter the cut of her hair, her clothes, and to plan a new life apart from the comfort and safety of Lady Brook Cottage. She forgot about Evan Ramsdell and turned her attention to creating a world just for herself, making herself much more open to experience, challenge and knowledge.

By March, she had made arrangements to take up residence in Brighton in the home of her friend Lydia Alistair. Though she was able to visit Lady Brook on occasion, she soon came to think of Brighton as her home. She was even contemplating the unthinkable— taking a house for herself, and why not, for she had attained her majority and Lord Ramsdell's generosity had made it possible for her to have a quite handsome quarterly allowance.

She had brought her favorite gelding, Prince, with her from Berkshire and spent part of every day on horseback, either on the Steyne with Lydia mounted on her skittish mare, or galloping about the downs, particularly near the hamlet of Hove or in the vicinity of the White Hawk Downs where the annual August races were held.

She was never more shocked than when Evan Ramsdell suddenly appeared in Brighton. He was not one to frequent places where the *beau monde* congregated. Last summer, he had more than once expressed his dislike of the annual London Season and certainly thought places like Bath, Brighton, Tunbridge Wells or any of the other "watering holes," as they were known among the *ton,* were utterly frivolous.

So why then was he here? Given the wretched fact that he had kissed her no less than four times since his arrival, she thought it possible he had come for the strict purpose of tormenting her. She knew this to be ridiculous, of course, yet she could scarcely explain his conduct otherwise.

With any other man, she would have believed him utterly besotted. With Evan Ramsdell, she believed only that he enjoyed torturing her with the passionate sweetness of his assaults. She might even have tumbled in love with him had he been more agreeable. However, his propensity to disapprove of her at every turn completely obliterated any of the finer sentiments which often stole into her heart when he was near.

So, what is love then?

Katherine frowned at herself in the gilt-edged looking glass tucked in the corner of her bedchamber. The question had been plaguing her ever since her sister Marianne had tied the connubial knot earlier in the summer. Marianne had found love, as had the rest of Katherine's siblings. Why, then, had Cupid been so absent in her own life?

Will I ever know what it is to love? she thought curiously. *Will I ever love a man, any man, so much that I would desire above anything to be a wife to him?* These were mysteries to her.

Ah, well . . .

Other than Captain Ramsdell's reprehensible conduct, she was supremely content to be in Brighthelmstone. As she continued to regard herself in the mirror, she was yet again astonished at the changes a scant few months at the seaside watering hole had wrought in her. She was no longer the young lady who had secluded herself in the stables of Lady Brook Cottage, happy only when caring for her favorite gelding. Instead, she saw a Lady of Quality, a young woman intent on cutting a dash among Brighton's *haut ton,* a modish female so at odds with her former appearance, countenance and bearing that she could only wonder yet again that she had altered so very much.

Gone was her straight hair, and in its place was a whirl of brown curls dancing over the crown of her head and spilling in a complete riot of ringlets to her shoulders. Gone was the faded blue ballgown she had worn spring after spring to the local Berkshire assemblies, and in its place was a gossamer white muslin confection trimmed with lace and embroidered with fine blue stitching cross the bodice. Gone was the brown complexion of a lady who never protected herself from the sun, and in its stead was a creamy visage. Indeed, she was not in the least the creature Evan Ramsdell had met summer last at Lady Brook.

From the doorway, a melodious voice called to her. "I vow, Katherine, you become prettier every day."

At that, Katherine turned to greet her friend. "What do you truly think, Lydia?" she queried. "And no nonsense."

Lydia's eyes shimmered with sudden tears. "Do you know, I always thought you the most beautiful of all your sisters, but you never allowed yourself to shine. Now here you are, gowned and coiffed like a princess, and I will tell you truly, you beat even Marianne to flinders."

Katherine was dumbfounded. "Oh, pray do not say such ludicrous things to me!" she cried. "No one is prettier than Marianne."

"You are!" Lydia cried, her loyalty clearly knowing no bounds in this moment. She rushed forward and embraced Katherine tightly. "Indeed you are, which is why the Prince has singled you out so frequently when we dine at the Pavilion."

"What humbug!" was all she could think of to say in response. "Though I must say I am grateful for your attempt at flattering me, I only wish to know *why*, wretched creature!"

Lydia leaned back and squinted her eyes into a smile. "I meant every word I said. However, there is one thing you might do for me this morning, if you are of a mind."

"Ah-ha," Katherine murmured.

"If you must know, Mama wishes to go directly to Fisher's instead of sea-bathing, and if you will but lend your voice to mine, we will soon be rolling into the sea on the Prince's own bathing-machine. *Please* speak with her. Do! For I wish nothing more than to tell Miss Framfield that the Prince kept his promise to you, allowing us to make use of his machine, besides which I meant to tell you that Rudgwick has just now returned and informed my maid that His Royal Highness has already gone to his yacht and so will not be making use of his machine, not that he does much anymore. I have heard it said that he has been dipped but once in twelve years and only uses the machine when he needs to be taken to the boat which then transports him to his yacht."

At last, Miss Alistair drew breath.

"What a ridiculous speech, Lydia!" Katherine cried.

"You know very well I desire to sea-bathe more than anything, for it is one of my favorite occupations. Why do we not have our maids accompany us, instead of your mother? She could therefore have a comfortable coze with her friends at Fisher's whilst knowing that our propriety has been secured. Then we may be pounded by the waves in our very trying flannel and be as happy as larks, or seagulls, if you wish."

Lydia chuckled, then wrinkled her brow as some new thought struck her. "What if *he* should arrive as he usually does? What will you do then? Captain Ramsdell will not respect our maids as he does my mother's presence, which he tends to ignore anyway, just as he did the other day."

Katherine lifted her chin slightly. A very odd sensation coursed through her, something strangely reminiscent of taking a hedge at full run. "I am perfectly capable of managing Captain Ramsdell, thank you."

"B-but, Katherine," Lydia stammered. "The last time he kissed you, *again,* for you had let the sea take you past two bathing machines."

Lydia had told her that she had watched Captain Ramsdell kiss her from the vantage point of the bathing-machine and had been in the worst agony that her mother would see them as well. Katherine had apologized profusely for placing her good friend in such a wretched predicament.

"I will not stray from the vicinity of our machine today," she stated firmly, turning back to the mirror. "I was a perfect ninnyhammer on that particular occasion, and I promise you I shall not be so careless a second time."

She plucked at her soft brown curls, pretending to arrange them and wondering all the while if Lydia would notice the trembling of her fingers.

Lydia drew up beside Katherine and slipped her arm about her waist. "Are you . . . that is, Katherine, I have wondered for some time now if perchance you have fallen in love with Captain Ramsdell?"

Katherine met her friend's gaze in the looking glass. "What on odd question!" she cried.

"Yet not a wholly unreasonable one, and though I do not mean to be impertinent, sometimes when I have seen you together I have felt certain that . . ." Her voice trailed off as she stared meaningfully at Katherine in the mirror.

"Certain about what?" she asked, unsettled.

Lydia frowned. "I recall quite vividly the first time you saw Captain Ramsdell. You forgot your conversation entirely, you spilled tea on your amber gown, and then muttered something about your heart aching suddenly."

"I remember saying no such thing!" she cried, her cheeks warming. "That is, I remember spilling my tea, but only because I was so startled to see Ramsdell's brother in town. Surely I did not speak of my heart aching."

"Perhaps my memory is at fault," Lydia responded smoothly. "However, a sennight later, when you were dancing with him, you missed your steps, not once but thrice, and your complexion was so high even Mama thought your heart had been won at last."

"Lydia, I fear you are greatly mistaken. If my complexion was high and I missed my steps, it was because he was telling me that I had become absurd—vain, useless and absurd. Yes, those were his words."

"Oh," Lydia drawled, deflated. "I . . . I had no idea he spoke to you so cruelly that night. Yet you bore it so well. I vow had a man spoken to me in that manner— nonetheless in so public a place as a ballroom, for heaven's sake!—I should have swooned!"

Katherine turned away from the looking glass and strove to keep her cheeks from turning a fiery crimson. She had not told Lydia the entire truth. Captain Ramsdell had not been completely at fault. He had begun the exchange by recommending that she take care not to let so much attention from the *beau monde* turn her head. Because he had appeared so disapproving, *again,* she had taken exception to his suggestion and retorted that she did not feel he need be concerned with her on that score. His response had been, "I should hate to see you become one of these vain, useless and rather absurd creatures which tend to gather in such places as Brighton."

Perhaps he had not meant his remark to be unkind, but she found herself severely disappointed that instead of praising her for the numerous improvements she had undertaken since the previous summer, he could only hint her away from behavior which she already found abhorrent.

Lifting her chin, she had responded archly, "Is that all you will say, Captain Ramsdell?"

"Why, yes. I merely wished to hint you away from an idle mode of existence which I am convinced would make you unhappy."

"How kind of you!" she had exclaimed facetiously. "Though why you feel you must needs tend to my affairs so carefully, I cannot imagine. However, might I offer you a hint as well?"

"If you wish for it," he had responded, a frown settling over his features like a flock of birds descending on a favorite tree.

"Though you are in every respect a gentleman, I have noted that you seem to me the sort of man who is continually above being pleased. You may wish to examine your conduct and see if I am not speaking the truth, for I do not know which would be worse, to be a vain, useless creature or to be above being pleased."

"I am no such thing," he had responded, his frown deepening.

"Nor am I vain and useless."

"I did not say you were."

"Then we are speaking at cross-purposes, and since I

have missed my steps more than once because of this conversation I beg you will allow me to concentrate more fully on my feet."

He had obliged her, clamping his lips shut and guiding her through the remainder of the waltz if not gracefully then with a marked rhythm which could not leave her in doubt of the three-quarter beat to the music.

Lydia disrupted these hapless recollections by saying, "I see that I have distressed you, and I am sorry for it."

Katherine sat down on the edge of the bed. "Whatever happened then," she said, "or since, hardly matters. I am convinced Captain Evan Ramsdell will soon leave Brighton and we shall be as content as kittens playing in the sun."

"I am afraid that is unlikely," Lydia said woefully. She, too, took up her seat, on the side of the bed beside Katherine.

"Why is that?" Katherine asked.

"I was speaking with his good friend Mr. Keymer last night and it would seem they are both here not just for the pleasures of the season but in service to the Prince of Wales."

"In service to Prinny? Whatever do you mean? What service could either of these men perform for him?"

"Mr. Keymer would not tell me. Indeed, I believe he felt obligated to keep his concerns a great secret."

Katherine could make no sense of this. She could not imagine in what way so curt and disobliging a creature as Captain Ramsdell might ever be of service to a man commonly referred to as the First Gentleman of Europe.

She shrugged and released a deep sigh. "I suppose there is nothing for it, then, but to endure his company. I do not mean to repine, however, for I have no intention of permitting Captain Ramsdell to diminish even the smallest portion of my pleasure this summer."

"Indeed, you should not!" Lydia exclaimed.

"Come," Katherine said. "Let us lay our plan before your mother and see if she will permit us to sea-bathe with only our maids in attendance."

Two

An hour later, Katherine descended the cliffs from the top of Russell Street to the beach below with Lydia following closely behind. Her mother had acquiesced readily to the scheme provided both her daughter and Katherine remained with the woman in charge of dipping.

Once Katherine reached the sand at the base of the stairs, she lifted her head and sought out the Prince's bathing machine. The beach was rather crowded, but when she discovered the location of the machine, she cried out, "Oh, what bad luck! Lydia! Do you see who is waiting by the ladder?"

"Captain Ramsdell!" Lydia cried. "How does *he* merit use of the Prince's machine?"

"I can only suppose it must have something to do with what Mr. Keymer told you last night," Katherine replied, completely dashed.

It was all of a piece, she thought heatedly. Captain Ramsdell seemed always to be where he was least wanted. From the time of his arrival in Brighton, he had somehow managed to insinuate himself into every exalted household on the Steyne, not to mention the Marine Pavilion. How had he so quickly and easily won the favor of Brighton's *haut ton*? Even if he was connected in some manner to the Prince Regent, his popularity in the finest drawing rooms was not so easily explained except that he was one of the handsomest men she had ever known. He carried himself splendidly, as a distinguished cavalry officer would, and commanded notice whenever he but sauntered into a room.

Only yesterday during morning services, when he had entered the Prince's Chapel, she had noted with some rancor that more ladies turned to stare at him than at any other gentleman who crossed the threshold.

She had had much difficulty in keeping her thoughts centered upon the morning's message, which dealt with that which was kind, loving and just, particularly since the good captain had chosen to situate himself directly behind her and to occasionally make quite odious remarks to the gentleman next to him concerning the height of a certain bonnet which obliterated his view of the curate.

She had seethed, then seethed a little more. He seemed utterly intent upon making her life a misery.

Now here he was, preparing to climb into the Prince's bathing machine! And he had known quite well she meant to sea-bathe this morning, for she had told him so only last night during the Promenade on the Steyne.

She should have made an effort to control her temper, but she was all out of patience with Captain Ramsdell.

She walked swiftly to where he stood, or at least as swiftly as she could with a brisk wind whipping the muslin of her skirts between her legs and the dips and rises of the sand twisting her ankles. He was speaking to the dipper, along with his good friend Mr. Keymer.

When she reached the Prince's machine, she immediately addressed the captain. "Why are you here this morning?" she cried. "You knew very well I meant to bathe at this hour. Do you mean to steal the Prince's machine from me—from *us?*" She gestured to Lydia, who she suddenly realized had not followed her but had remained near the stairs, along with their servants. Lydia's complexion, even at that distance, seemed quite heightened.

Mr. Keymer smiled crookedly. "Miss Alistair does not seem inclined to bathe."

"She is merely intimidated by Captain Ramsdell's presence," Katherine explained, "her nature being much more retiring than my own."

"So it would seem," Mr. Keymer stated, turning his gaze toward Lydia.

Captain Evan Ramsdell had wheeled abruptly upon hearing Miss Katherine Pamberley's voice. He had completely forgotten she meant to use the Prince's machine this morning, though he could now recall that she had told him as much last night. Why he had forgotten, he was not certain, except that during the Promenade she had been coming the crab with him because he had pressed her about her association with Mr. Wooding who he knew to be a hardened gamester. She had not taken kindly his hints that she desist from encouraging her association with Mr. Wooding.

As for this morning, he had not intended to come to the beach at all, but had ventured forth on Mr. Keymer's insistence that they make use of the Prince's recent offer.

"For we would not wish to be backward in any attention," Mr. Keymer had said. "Particularly when we have not been especially successful in flushing out any hopeful assassins."

Evan had concurred. "Deuced business," he had said, "chasing ghosts in this small seaside town. I suppose a little sea-bathing might be a welcome diversion after all."

The discussion had then fallen to the latest rumors that an assassination attempt was forthcoming. The subject was a wretchedly serious one for which the men reviewed again what else they could possibly do to uncover a plot, if indeed one actually existed. For a fortnight now, they had been stymied on all counts.

In truth, Evan did not feel well equipped for the job,

which had been thrust on him a month past by his brother, Lord Ramsdell. Evan had told Ramsdell as much at the outset. His brother had listened to him intently, and though he had said he quite understood Evan's concerns, it would be a great favor to him if he would go to Brighton anyway, just to look around a little and see what he might discover. The Prince's usual spies had been able to do little in the past several months, which meant they were undoubtedly well known to the element intent on harming the future King of England. In the end, Evan of course had agreed to go.

As for Katherine, well, her countenance was so enflamed with outrage that he should be at the Prince's machine that he could not keep from teasing her. He smiled in just that manner which he knew always served to set up her hackles quite prettily. "But, Miss Pamberley," he began with a pretense to innocence, "you have forgotten entirely that we did not finish our conversation the last time I found you bathing in the sea. I recall our discourse having been remarkably *passionate,* yet interrupted most unhappily, and I have since hoped for an opportunity by which I might bring to a point the particular discussion at hand."

He watched her lips part as a small whoosh of air passed between them. Her cheeks darkened and she blinked rather rapidly so that he was left in no doubt that she fully comprehended his meaning.

"The *point* which you hoped to make," she stated coldly, "could never be of any particular interest to me, so you may save your breath."

"What a whisker," he said, feeling very much in command. "As I recall, the *opinions* with which I graced you on Saturday morning were received quite warmly."

The bloom on her cheeks began to flame. Mr. Keymer cleared his throat and stepped away with a mumbled intention of finding a pretty seashell or two for his young sister.

When he was out of earshot, she did not hesitate to speak her mind. "What a rogue you are!" she cried beneath her breath. "Does your brother have even the smallest notion that you are become a scoundrel? What would he think of your quite wicked flirtations?"

"And what of you, Miss Katherine? You did not especially struggle in my arms on Saturday morning. Indeed, you seemed to *embrace* the experience quite vigorously. Why should I then cease offering my kisses when the occasion would appear to demand it?"

"Because you are a gentleman?" she queried facetiously.

"You know, I think the difficulty here," he said, lowering his voice and drawing quite near her, "is that I served in the army for so long a time. I fear that a great deal of my *gentlemanly* conduct has gotten quite lost in all my years of service. The charge of a front line, the sound of cannon, the smell of gunpowder—these memories have blurred my thinking. Time becomes something to savor, and a flirtation the only worthwhile object of the day. I saw a pretty-enough face, and wished for a kiss. You obliged me, quite passionately—especially on the several occasions prior to Saturday—and I could not help myself. I shall do so again, if the opportunity permits."

"You, sir, are a libertine!"

"No, there you are greatly mistaken. A libertine does not especially differentiate between the females of his acquaintance. I have kissed no one but you since my arrival in Brighton and intend on kissing no others, at least not until you have tired of my advances, which you do not seem to have, or am I mistaken?"

Katherine stared into Captain Ramsdell's extraordinary blue eyes and found herself stunned. Something deep inside her began to quiver alarmingly. She had never thought for a moment that he had actually singled her out. She had thought, perhaps stupidly, that he had had no special interest in her and was sharing his charms where he would. Knowing he was being quite particular in his attentions somehow made everything worse, yet at the same time far better!

"This conversation is become utterly absurd," she said quietly, attempting for a dignity she was far from feeling. She truly did not know how to address him when he meant to be so very bad. "I . . . I came to bathe along with my friend Miss Alistair. We had hoped to be dipped within the hour that we might meet Mrs. Alistair at Fisher's before noon."

"Are you asking me to delay my own plunge?"

"Yes," she stated.

"You had only to ask, Miss Pamberley. I should oblige you in anything—well, nearly anything—for you are my brother's sister-in-law. You have only to approach me with a mote of kindness and I will undoubtedly oblige you, or is it that you are still in the boughs because I offered my opinion concerning Mr. Wooding?"

"Why must you speak of him now?" she cried.

"Yes, still in the boughs," he stated, maddeningly.

She rolled her eyes. "Captain Ramsdell, I am not in the boughs, I merely think you are mistaken in your—"

He lifted his hand. "No, no, I do not mean to brangle with you again on that head. I hereby relinquish the Prince's machine to you, for I do not intend to torment you further." He bowed and wished her an abrupt good day, then moved past her to join Mr. Keymer, who was examining a large shell he had found some twenty feet away.

Katherine could only watch him, fuming, as he strolled in the direction of his friend.

A minute more and Lydia joined her. "Your complexion is grown quite pink, *again*," she observed. "Whatever did he say to you this time?"

Katherine grimaced. "Nothing to signify, I assure you."

She heard Lydia sigh. "Mr. Keymer is wearing a new coat. He looks very fine today. Do you not think so?"

Katherine cast a glance toward the gentlemen. Because Captain Ramsdell chanced to turn toward her at that moment and found her looking his way, he offered her that wretched smile of his which always served to set her teeth to grinding. She turned away from him and responded to Lydia's query. "Mr. Keymer does indeed appear to advantage today. However, I think he would appear to even greater advantage did he not keep such poor company."

Later that morning along the Steyne, Katherine sat beside Mrs. Alistair and Mrs. Framfield perusing the *Brighton Herald* and enjoying herself prodigiously. The ladies frequently met before noon in order to read the newspapers and to exchange bits of gossip. Miss Framfield and Lydia were within Fisher's Circulating Library across the piazza.

Mr. Wooding approached the ladies, removing his glossy beaver hat. They all smiled and inclined their heads to him.

"Mrs. Alistair, what a fetching bonnet you are sporting this most excellent summer day," he said.

Mrs. Alistair, who was quite up to snuff, responded with an amused smile, "The summer day is fine indeed, Mr. Wooding, but my bonnet is quite spoilt because the feathers have been singed. I set it too close to a candle Wednesday last—you remember the day it rained late in the afternoon and the sky grew quite dark?" He nodded, and Mrs. Alistair continued, "Our good Rudgwick was so kind as to light a few candles, and I was exceedingly careless. Mrs. Framfield only just now made it known to me."

Mr. Wooding nodded in his serene manner. "Regardless, the design is flawless, and I am a stickler in such matters." Which was true, for Mr. Wooding was considered an arbiter of fashion.

"Then I am much obliged for your good opinion of my poor hat. But here is Miss Pamberley, and I know her to be a favorite of yours. I was just exchanging with Mrs. Framfield, Cook's receipt for sole with lemon and will leave you to entertain my young friend."

He took up her hint and made his elegant bow to both ladies. After begging of Katherine whether he might be seated, he took a chair beside her. Whatever Captain Ramsdell's opinion of Mr. Wooding, she found his company amusing, delightful and quite elegant.

He was rather tall and carried himself with the aplomb of a great statesman. He had wavy brown hair distinguished by feathers of gray at the temples. He was always dressed to perfection and no less so in this moment in a dove gray coat, starched white shirt points, a black silk waistcoat, black pantaloons and glossy black boots. But it was his eyes which always gave pause. They were round and quite expressive and had been compared to Lord Byron's rather soulful expression.

He was not a horseman of any merit, however, nor was he as well muscled as, say, Captain Ramsdell. Perhaps it was for these reasons Katherine did not feel in any particular danger of losing her heart to him. The man she would love, or so she believed, must have a great passion for horses. Mr. Wooding did not and saw his stable of hacks as beasts whose sole function was to carry their master from one destination to the next. She had tried to instruct him on the beauty and proud heritage of the horse, but he confessed he had been bitten by her protégés far too many times to have even the smallest interest in them beyond what was required for transportation.

If Captain Ramsdell found fault with her associations with Mr. Wooding, she did not care. She found his company delightful, and because he was so well known to the Prince, he moved in the first circles just as she did.

She accounted him, therefore, a friend, but nothing more.

"Where is Miss Alistair?" he queried, glancing along the piazza in front of Fisher's.

"She is within. Miss Framfield desired to read the subscription books to see if there were any new acquaintance in town upon whom she might pay a morning call. I have not heard the bells ringing in at least three days, so I must presume that of late only less-exalted persons have arrived." One of the first events which greeted Katherine when she came to live in Brighton was the intermittent sounding of the church bells. As in the city of Bath, when personages of renown arrived, the church bells were set to pealing. Lord and Lady Chiltingham's bells were the first she heard.

Mr. Wooding lowered his voice. "And Miss Framfield does desire to meet persons of nobility, does she not?" he said, turning his head so that only she might hear his naughty words.

Katherine bit her lip. Miss Framfield was notorious for setting her cap for every gentleman of rank and fortune who but crossed a Brighthelmstone threshold, and with such abandon that only a nodcock would be unable to determine her purposes.

"Hush," she whispered, opening her eyes wide by way of rebuke.

He merely chuckled and leaned back in his seat. "What news?" he inquired, gesturing to the copy of the *Herald* which lay open on the small table next to her.

"Ah. The Prince is in excellent health, Lady Hertford is in residence, and it appears that the mackerel season is nearly at an end." She picked up the newspaper. "Did you know, Mr. Wooding, that the mackerel begin their journey to our fair island from the Bay of Biscay, pass by Dieppe, appear again at Mount's Bay and are finally taken up in our fishermen's nets about the middle of April? Although it would seem they are never found along the Cornish coasts."

He nodded, as though contemplating earnestly the information she had just extended to him. "I had a mackerel at Lady Chiltingham's two nights past. It was atrocious."

Katherine flipped the paper. "There, you see! You have proven the information true. The mackerel season is ending."

"Either that, or someone who also dined at Lady Chiltingham's has since spoken to the editor."

Katherine could only laugh.

"Anything more?" he inquired, smiling.

"Why, yes. Sole should be edible until late September."

Mr. Wooding laughed heartily, which gave her great pleasure. When his laughter dwindled to a series of chuckles and finally ceased altogether, she met his smiling gaze and found that he was watching her with admiration. "Do you know how pretty you are, Miss Pamberley?"

She was slightly taken aback. Mr. Wooding's compliments were generally more studied. The circumstance of this particular compliment having burst from his lips so impulsively lent more credence to his opinion than if his speech had been ten times longer. "Thank you, Mr. Wooding," she returned brightly. "You are very kind to have said so."

Was he flirting with her? she wondered. He did not seem to be, but then she was not as adept as most young ladies her age at knowing the difference between general conversation and a serious attempt at flirtation. Marianne would have known the difference. Constance, too. Even Lydia was more attuned to the finer aspects of masculine conduct. Katherine, however, was not as accustomed to society and to flirtations as her siblings or as Lydia. Perhaps that was why she was not as adroit in handling

Captain Ramsdell as she ought to have been. She was, in this sense, woefully inexperienced.

"I was wondering," he began softly, the chattering of the ladies nearby keeping his discourse on an intimate tone, "if you mean to attend Mrs. Nutley's ball tonight. When I asked sennight last, you, or rather, Mrs. Alistair, was as yet undecided."

Katherine smiled. "We are to attend," she said quietly, then lowered her voice even further. "You see, when I last spoke with you, Mrs. Alistair had quarreled with Mrs. Nutley about something or other, but they have since resumed their friendship. To not attend I fear would be to invite a war."

"Then I shall see you at the ball."

"I depend upon it," she responded.

"May I secure the first waltz?"

"You are such a fine dancer, Mr. Wooding, that I shall accept of your offer with gratitude. I usually have to mind my steps, but I find that under your guidance I can be at ease."

"Ah, yes. The young lady who, until only this year, had forsaken the ballroom in favor of the stables."

"Was any lady more foolish?"

He smiled at her in the most disarming manner. She was enchanted by him, for he was undoubtedly the most charming gentleman in Brighton of the moment.

She might have continued in her contentment had not her gaze been caught by movement near the horse-railing some few yards away. She turned and found that Captain Ramsdell was regarding her with lifted brows and a rather condemning expression on his face. He nodded ever so slightly to her, then turned his horse away.

The effrontery! She desired above anything to give Evan Ramsdell a proper set-down, and if only she could, she believed she would be the happiest young lady on the seacoast.

Three

That evening, Katherine stood on the threshold of Nutley House on the Steyne and viewed the gilt-encrusted relief work of the ornate entrance hall with the same faint contempt she always viewed it. There was an ostentation about the decor of the house which seemed to afflict her nerves. Unfortunately, gilt seemed to be the single expression of Mrs. Nutley's aesthetic eye, and Katherine could never enter her house without wanting to bring a large paintbrush and a bowl laden with white paint to take some of the glitter from every chamber.

Mrs. Alistair's criticisms were not so uncharitable of her friend's home, for to some degree she was of a mind with Mrs. Nutley in matters of wealth and display. What amused Katherine most was to listen to Mrs. Nutley and Mrs. Alistair together as they complained vehemently about the want of taste in the Prince Regent's choice of architecture and decor at the Marine Pavilion. Katherine had been to the Pavilion several times and had found herself charmed immensely by Prinny's unusual choices. She believed the style of the Marine Pavilion was beyond the comprehension of Mrs. Nutley and even Mrs. Alistair.

Having come to be in the Prince's society for several weeks, Katherine had formed a sense of who her future sovereign truly was. In all his conversation, in his belief that he had been engaged in military action against Napoleon, in his use of Oriental tones in his decor, and in his vibrant brass band, she had come to see him as a boy who had not been permitted to live a life of adventure as he so obviously had desired. Even the Duke of Wellington had seen service in India before he came to command the British Army in the Napoleonic Wars. In the end, she had concluded there was much to pity in the rigorous demands of royal life. If the Pavilion had become a reflection of what the Prince Regent's life could never be, how better to give expression to such a need than in the creation of a fantastical home on the southern seacoast of England?

Otherwise, he seemed to truly enjoy the life he was given, and he appeared to delight even more in blessing his friends with his patronage and presence whenever he could. There was even some talk that he would be attending Mrs. Nutley's ball this evening, if but for a brief hour.

Mrs. Nutley greeted Mrs. Alistair as a frightened bird might. She approached all three ladies with her arms fluttering rapidly. "Oh, my dears, my dears! Have you heard that the Prince may grace my ballroom? I was never more ecstatic nor more frightened! I wonder if the champagne has been iced properly. But the dining hall at the Pavilion is always so hot! Perhaps Prinny prefers his champagne to be served directly from the buttery. I vow I shall perish before the night is through!"

Katherine watched Mrs. Alistair open her mouth to give some manner of reassurance, but Mrs. Nutley had espied more newly arrived guests and flitted away as swiftly as she had come, calling out, "There you are, my dear Lady Chiltingham! My dear Lady Beavan! You must tell me, for you are both on intimate terms with His Royal Highness, does he prefer his champagne chilled or . . ."

Katherine ceased listening. The sounds of the orchestra in the recesses of the house were calling to her. In the past several months, among the many changes she had made, she had discovered a true love of dancing. In the past, as a dutiful daughter of Lady Brook Cottage, she had attended the local Berkshire assemblies as was considered proper but always with less than delight. She would dance only that which did not set the tabbies to gabblemongering—a rather paltry four dances—then retire to a chamber in which she might find some friend or other who would be willing to tell her the latest gossip about who had crammed his horses recently and taken a fall, or which of the bloods of the neighborhood had been able to drive the mail coach during the last month.

Now, however, as she drifted toward the ballroom with Lydia beside her, she had no thought but to seek out the best dancers on the floor and to drop large hints that she meant to wear out her slippers that very evening if the gentlemen would so oblige her.

Before she could enter the vast chamber, however, Mr. Nutley appeared at the juncture of the hall and ballroom, his expression slightly harassed. "There you are, Miss Pamberley! You must tell me at once! Oh, how do you do, Miss Alistair. Ah, I see my wife is fairly shouting at Lady Chiltingham. What the devil is amiss with her now?"

Katherine could not restrain a smile. "She is in the unhappy state of not knowing whether His Royal Highness prefers his champagne tepid or chilled."

"Bah! What foolishness! He will drink it however it is served and not complain once, for he is a gentleman. Well, I have my answer, at any rate. I had meant to ask you whether my wife was presently distracted so that I might slip from the ballroom. I see that she is. If the Prince should come, tell him he might find a friendly face or two in the billiard room." With that, he smiled, bade the ladies to flirt vivaciously through the night, and headed toward his billiard room.

Before he disappeared through the doorway, however,

he turned back abruptly. "You, Miss Pamberley, and Miss Alistair, are welcome to join us at any time." Katherine watched him smile fondly upon her and felt a rush of pleasure at the sure knowledge that Mr. Nutley, whose company she enjoyed prodigiously, somehow approved of her.

"Thank you, Mr. Nutley," she responded warmly. "You are very kind."

He waved and hurried on as one engaged on a critical mission. She could not help but reflect how her rapport with Mr. Nutley had become established. She recalled in particular one evening during the Promenade on the Steyne when Mr. Nutley had explained his preference for her company. "There is no nonsense about you, Miss Pamberley. I daresay you would not adorn your wainscoting with gilt!"

To have agreed with him on that count would have revealed her opinion of his wife's sense of taste, which she felt would be an ungracious act, so she had remained silent, though she did venture to offer him a smile.

"You are right not to complain, but your smile tells all. You have a very pretty smile. I only wish I had had a son to cast in your direction. Alas, four daughters! Each of them sillier than their mother." He had sighed heavily, and when his wife had called to him in her shrill voice to lend her his arm, he had excused himself to perform his husbandly duty.

She had watched the couple for a time, thinking their union to be a perfect example of marital disharmony. Theirs had been a *marriage of convenience,* for Mrs. Nutley had been an impoverished daughter of a viscount in Staffordshire and he the son of an enormously wealthy tradesman.

Mr. Nutley had had little interest in gathering the *beau monde* about his heels, but performed his part in his wife's social undertakings in the same manner he had married her, with decorum, honor and duty. His pleasures were simple—a chamber in which to retire in peace whenever he wished, a jar of his own brand of blended snuff, a decanter of old brandy, a newspaper each morning and his billiard table. He wished only to conduct his life as far from his wife's social machinations as possible.

In addition to a home in the country and a townhouse in London, Mr. Nutley had built for his wife a traditional blue and buff house on the Steyne to suit her notions of rank and prestige, while for himself he had designed and maintained an excellent billiard room, which had had the good fortune to draw to his home a wide circle of male acquaintances—and an occasional lady—of similar pursuits and understanding. To be in Mr. Nutley's billiard room was the true honor of Nutley House on the Steyne, though Mrs. Nutley continued blissfully ignorant in her belief that her fine balls and soirees were the sole reason the *ton* flocked through her doors on a warm summer's eve.

Katherine wondered if she ought to visit the billiard room first or the ballroom, but knowing that Lydia had little interest in either Mr. Nutley or his sanctuary, she permitted her friend to draw her to the threshold of the ballroom.

She could not help but note the many heads which turned in their direction. She smiled to herself, thinking that her sisters would certainly be shocked that Katherine Pamberley, who had spent so many hours of her life in the stables, was actually admired in a ballroom.

She wished her sisters could see her now, dressed fashionably in a gown of patterned white silk, beaded in a delicate floral pattern over the bodice. A three-quarter overdress, which fastened just below her bosom, was of gold silk and tended to billow behind her when she made strong movements in a quick-paced reel. All was in fetching contrast to her brown curls which dangled to her neck and past her shoulders. A gold circlet held her locks in a Grecian manner.

She caught the eye of several of her favorites, and before but half a minute had passed, nearly a dozen gentlemen were descending upon both young ladies. Lydia was herself an exceptional dancer, and between the pair of them, they were soon secured of half the dances for the entire evening, though Mr. Wooding, of course, had the first waltz. She was then carried off by Mr. Yates and enjoyed the next two country dances with him.

Mr. Wooding approached her again and with his most charming smile led her onto the floor. He was an elegant dancer, and nothing was more pleasing than the manner in which he took complete command of the movements of the dance and whirled her expertly this way, then that, all about the floor. She was laughing by the time the orchestra played its last note. He then requested a country dance for later in the evening, after which he handed her to Mr. Sawyer for the minuet.

She found herself in a happy state as the dance began and might have continued so had she not become aware that Captain Ramsdell had arrived. How could she fail to notice his arrival when he was so quickly besieged by admirers? Miss Kelly, whom she could abide but half, had immediately seized his right arm, and Miss Hadlow, a very forward young lady, had pushed her way to stand on his left. Katherine felt overcome by the strangest desire to pull any number of locks of hair. She gave herself a strong shake and reverted her attention to her partner, Mr. Sawyer. He was a spotted youth with the wonderful grace of a stage dancer.

When the movements brought them together, he whispered, "Do you intend to brangle with the captain tonight?"

"Whatever do you mean?" she queried, startled. The steps of the dance separated them.

He drew near after a moment. "You always do, you know." His smile was sympathetic, yet quite amused.

She felt a blush warm her cheeks. "I do not quarrel

with Captain Ramsdell by design. He is merely quite provoking." She did not know what else to say, for she was deeply embarrassed. Was it true that even in a ballroom she had so taken to quarreling with Captain Ramsdell that even Mr. Sawyer had become aware of it? And if he was cognizant of their turbulent relationship, then surely a score of others were as well.

Mr. Sawyer, seeing her discomfiture, changed the subject, and the remainder of the dance concluded a little more comfortably.

Afterward, she made every effort to ignore the captain and was succeeding quite charmingly until she happened upon the entrance to Mrs. Nutley's small music room. On the opposite side of the chamber, Captain Ramsdell was leaning rather close to a young lady quite unknown to her and speaking in a low voice. The young lady's color was rather heightened when suddenly she burst out laughing. He had been telling her a joke, evidenced by his sudden smile and apparent delight in her amusement. Katherine could not remember Captain Ramsdell ever having told her a joke.

She was about to leave the room and make her way back through the gilt and red receiving room when he chanced to see her. "Miss Pamberley," he called. "Do allow me to present a friend to you. Miss Page is recently arrived in Brighthelmstone and has begged to be made known to you."

"Of course," Katherine murmured, crossing the chamber to them. Captain Ramsdell made the introductions.

"How do you do?" Katherine murmured politely.

"Very well, thank you," Miss Page responded. She was a small young woman with large brown eyes and white blond hair. "I have just come from Worcestershire, where of course I have been acquainted with Captain Ramsdell for several years, for he is a good friend to my father." She turned to smile sweetly upon the captain, and Katherine felt her heart lurch as he responded with an equally warm smile. Was he in love with her and she with him? Not that it mattered, of course, for she had no true and lasting interest in Captain Ramsdell. The captain would marry one day, and why not to such a sweet innocent as Miss Page appeared to be? Only, was he in love with her?

"How do you like Brighton?" Katherine queried politely.

Miss Page heaved a heavenly sigh. "I adore the sea and I have yet to find any activity more pleasing than being dipped."

Despite her desire to find fault with a young lady whose company Captain Ramsdell obviously enjoyed, Katherine could not help being charmed by this admission. "I am quite of a mind with you," she responded. "I sea-bathe every morning, as Captain Ramsdell knows quite well, and should enjoy being dipped with you if you should care to accompany me and my dear friend Miss Alistair."

"I should like that very much," Miss Page responded enthusiastically.

Katherine arranged to take up Miss Page in a hackney on the following morning and would have taken pains to know her better, but Mr. Horsfield arrived to claim Miss Page for the quadrille. Katherine was therefore left in the captain's company. She did not know what to say to him, since Mr. Sawyer's words were still burning in her ears. Fortunately, he begged to know if she wished to dance the quadrille with him.

She would have assented, as a point of ballroom decorum, but another notion struck her, something she rather thought he might enjoy. "Would you, instead, be willing to escort me to the billiard room?"

"The billiard room?" he queried in what she felt was his habitually censorial tone.

Sharp words rose to her tongue. However, Mr. Sawyer's previous remarks concerning how frequently she brangled with Captain Ramsdell snipped the speech off as if with a pair of particularly sharp scissors. Instead, she summoned her most even voice. "I wish to go to the billiard room because Mr. Nutley invited me to do so. I find him an estimable gentleman and I desire to honor his invitation. Do you care to escort me?"

He was frowning as he watched her. "I vow," he said quietly, "those are by far the kindest words you have spoken to me in the past fortnight, even the past month."

She did not know what to say of a sudden. She had thought he had been solely at fault in their frequent battles, but it would seem she was not entirely guiltless either. "Captain Ramsdell, I—"

"Please," he said, "I beg you will call me Evan. We are nearly brother and sister-in-law, after all. At least, will you do so when we converse privately? I find 'Captain Ramsdell' to be a trifle too formal given the connection of our families."

She was startled and met his gaze fully in order to determine just how serious he might be. There was not even a hint of disdain in his expression. Indeed, he was smiling in rather a friendly manner.

"If you wish for it," she said.

"Yes," he stated in his direct manner.

"Very well. As I was saying, *Evan,* I have not meant to speak so acerbically to you on previous occasions, and I do beg your pardon."

"Will wonders never cease? Is Katherine Pamberley actually apologizing to me?"

Impulsively, she laid a hand on his arm. "If you speak in a sardonic manner, I shan't promise how long I can command myself. I believe it is your curt remarks which send me into the boughs so frequently. If you would promise to try to temper such a mode of speech, I will endeavor to speak to you with greater civility."

He glanced down at the hand still pressing his arm. She would have withdrawn it, for she became conscious of how inappropriate such conduct was, but he prevented her by covering it with his own. The shock of his touch turned the moment upside down for Katherine. She felt queasy suddenly, in the nicest way possible, and her heart began to thrum against her ribs. How could a man's touch, *a mere touch,* cause her to feel as though she had just been racing across a fine stretch of turf on the back of her favorite gelding?

"You have rebuked me very sweetly," he said. "I shall do as you have said." He then curled her arm about his. "I should be happy to take you to the billiard room."

The trek across the length of the large house was conducted in silence. Katherine did not know why Captain Ramsdell—Evan—might have found nothing to say, but she was feeling far too much to be able to utter even a single word. The moment the heat of his hand penetrated her own, she had felt incapable of speech. All she could think was how much she enjoyed his touch.

Was this love, or one of the hallmarks of love? she wondered, glancing up at him. She did not know.

Once arrived at the billiard room, Evan did not release her arm. At first, she had desired to be rid of him in order that her heart might settle back into its normal rhythm, but in the end she found herself grateful for his company since there were no other ladies present. She felt decidedly uncomfortable, as though she were venturing into the sacred halls of White's or Brook's in London.

Mr. Nutley's billiard room was a fine chamber, fully half the size of the ballroom. Several tables for card play were arranged at the southern end of the room; another table graced the center from which brandy, sherry, champagne and a number of wines were dispensed by two footmen with great and careful rapidity. Two long windows, identical to the ones in the ballroom, opened onto yet another pretty garden. On the north side of the chamber, the billiard table reigned supreme. It was a beautiful creation of heavily carved mahogany. Presently, the green baize was covered not with billiard balls but with currency for a game of hazard. Several gentlemen were gathered around the perimeter placing their bets against the repetitive shakes of the dice box.

Katherine was about to suggest to Evan that she ought to return to the ballroom when Mr. Nutley caught sight of her. He crossed the room and immediately began setting her at ease. "You have come at last, Miss Pamberley! Well done! Now, now, do not let any of these fellows frighten you off. We need a lady here now and then to soften our countenances and ease all this masculine competitiveness."

She relaxed and accepted Mr. Nutley's proffered arm.

Evan released her into Mr. Nutley's care and watched the older gentleman take her on a tour about his personal refuge. He obviously delighted in Katherine's company, a fact which caused Evan to take a long look at her. He had great respect for Mr. Nutley, who was a man of few pretenses, with a well-informed mind and a knowledge of the world far beyond the narrow interests of the *beau monde*. His preference for Katherine's society spoke warmly of her character.

Over the course of the past month, Evan had come to realize that Katherine had changed a great deal since he had first met her during his stay last summer in Berkshire. She had certainly acquired a nice layering of Town Bronze, a circumstance he attributed to her having left her home to take up residence in Brighton. She was gowned quite fashionably, and her hair was dressed in the popular Greek mode. She seemed older somehow, and her interests had expanded widely beyond her love of horses, which, as he recalled, had been her sole occupation when he was last at Lady Brook.

Presently she was shaking hands with Mr. Raikes and Lord Walford. Faith, but she was so very beautiful. Her eyes were an unusual hazel which seemed to change as the day progressed—at times more blue than green, and at night almost a golden brown.

Her countenance was unequaled, which he supposed had much to do with her love of riding. She was an excellent horsewoman and had the finest seat in the south of England. She carried herself with the grace of a queen.

His chest tightened as he watched her. She did not appear to know how beautiful she was, which only made her that much more appealing. She had a warmth, an honesty, and a genuine fascination with everyone she met, which had brought a group of masculine admirers besieging her at every event she attended.

Was it any wonder that he had been but a handful of days in her company in Brighton when he had kissed her for the first time? He had come across her in the mews where her horse was stabled. She was brushing her gelding, Prince, and talking to him as was her habit. He had been caught by the homey portrait she presented. Her bonnet hung on a nail by the stall gate, and a blue smock covered her muslin gown. He had observed her for a long time before making his presence known. He had watched her smile and pet her favorite horse. He had watched the horse respond with nickers and snorts of obvious pleasure.

He had been overcome by a desire to take her in his arms, to feel all that warmth of spirit against his body, to see if she might respond as engagingly to him as she did to her horse.

And she had, so much so that he had never quite shaken the initial shock of having her arms wrap themselves about his neck as he moved his lips over hers. Even now he could conjure up the sensation of that first embrace as though it had happened but a few moments ago. How surprised he had been, even stunned, particularly since he knew her to be a complete innocent.

Still, however charming the experience had been, he had come to regret that kiss, because ever since that time he had developed an almost insatiable hunger for her. He did not understand why he desired her as much as he did. He only knew that he was rarely in her company when he did not search for ways he might be alone with her, that he might kiss her again.

Was this love? he wondered suddenly, the notion clanging in his head like a heavy bell, for he had never considered the matter before.

His soul grew very still. The sounds of the billiard room dimmed to a soft hum. His gaze became fixed upon Katherine. Was he in love with her, this beauty from Berkshire? Was that the cause of his persistent need to take her in his arms?

He gave himself a shake. No, surely that was impossible. He had never been much interested in matters of the heart, and he certainly had no intention of marrying, ever, even if he did enjoy kissing Katherine Pamberley more than any lady he had ever kissed before. His was a bachelor's existence and had been since time out of mind. His soldier's life and ways had extended themselves to England once he sold out. He spent much of his time at his home in Worcestershire, and when not breeding horses, he was hunting in the fall, and avoiding spending too much time in London in the spring. He had little interest in the kind of life that women always brought about in a man's world.

No. He was content and meant to remain so the rest of his days.

Mr. Keymer, playing at hazard at the billiard table, called to him, "Are you feeling lucky this evening, Ramsdell? I fear I have already written my vowels more than once, and it is but a little past midnight."

Am I feeling lucky?

Well, Katherine had made a sort of peace with him this evening, so yes, he rather thought he might be feeling lucky.

"Indeed, I believe I am," he responded, ready to join

in the play since it was obvious Katherine was in excellent hands. He entered into the spirit of the game, grateful for the diversion since the direction of his thoughts had become rather distressing. However, he found he was never so caught up in the game that he forgot entirely about her presence. He had escorted her to the billiard room, and as soon as she was ready to retire, he meant to return her to the ballroom.

An hour later, he had just placed a bet when she drew up beside him.

Lord Walford held the dice box, and because he was situated so near her he asked, "Miss Pamberley, will you do the honors and roll the dice for us?"

"I should be happy to," she responded brightly.

Evan liked that about her. She was game for any lark, including shooting the dice from the box amongst a group of men.

She smiled at Lord Walford and with a flick of the wrist sent the dice flying across the table. As a pair of ones turned up, several groans were heard along with one or two whoops of success.

Lord Walford, having emitted a long groan himself, called out in a playfully strident voice, "I vow I shall have a pair of dispatchers made up if my luck don't change soon!"

The group about the table chortled loudly.

Katherine leaned close to Evan. "What is *a pair of dispatchers?*" she queried.

His breath was on her ear as he spoke, "False dice."

"Oh, dear," she murmured. "Well, I suppose he was merely joking."

"Lord Walford? Of course. He is as honest a man as you will find."

For the next half hour, Katherine remained in possession of the box, though she did not place any bets herself. She congratulated every winner and consoled each loser, which meant she became a quick favorite at the table.

When Mr. Raikes, quite in his cups, began to write his vowels for yet another hundred pounds, Katherine intervened hastily. "Mr. Raikes!" she cried. "Would you be so kind as to fetch me a glass of sherry before the play continues?"

"What?" he responded, blinking heavily upon her and weaving on his feet.

"A glass of sherry. I should very much like a glass of sherry. Would you be so good?"

Several understanding chuckles riddled their way about the score of gentlemen crowding the billiard table.

Mr. Raikes glanced from one countenance to another as though sorely confused. He whispered loudly to Ramsdell, "Does Miss Pamberley wish for a little sherry?"

"Yes, my good man. Will you not oblige the lady and bring her a glass of sherry?"

Mr. Raikes glanced at the table, now littered with dozens of banknotes. "Should be honored," he mumbled at last, pushing away from the table. He turned, the object of everyone's attention, took two steps toward the table of refreshments and promptly collapsed in a heap. A round of laughter greeted his foxed antics.

Evan watched Katherine smile and then resume rattling the dice in the box. "Are we ready, gentlemen?"

A round of assents followed.

When the dice landed on the table, Evan leaned over to her. "Well done," he whispered.

"You mean concerning poor Mr. Raikes?" she queried, glancing over her shoulder where two footmen were deciding how best to remove the young gentleman from the billiard room.

Evan nodded, chuckling.

"Nonsense," she responded. "I made a sensible suggestion, nothing more."

"Do you truly wish for a little sherry?"

She held the dice box to Lord Walford, who dropped the retrieved dice within.

"No, thank you," she said, shaking the box. "I am having a great deal too much fun as it is. Are all the bets placed?"

Receiving a general acknowledgment, once more she let the dice fly.

Evan regarded her wonderingly. Another woman in such a circumstance would never have tricked Mr. Raikes into leaving the table for the purpose of sparing him the loss of another hundred pounds. He found himself suitably impressed.

After ten minutes had passed, he was preparing to offer to return her to the ballroom when Mr. Wooding suddenly appeared. Evan felt Katherine's demeanor change, and her attention was suddenly all for the newcomer. He found himself greatly irritated, for he was in no way content to relinquish her, at least not yet, and certainly not to a man he considered beneath her notice.

However, a moment later she excused herself. "I have promised the next country dance to Mr. Wooding," she explained to the collection of gentlemen about the table. "You will forgive me if I leave you now?"

A series of regretful sighs passed around the table, which served to make Katherine chuckle as she thanked them for allowing her to take part in their play. More than one gentleman suggested she return as soon as the dance was concluded.

To Evan, she held out her hand. He shook it as she said, "You were very kind to escort me here."

"My pleasure," he responded in kind.

He watched her leave, noting that Wooding was not content merely to wrap her arm about his, but he must cover her hand with his own as well, a circumstance Evan had little doubt would continue until the ballroom was reached.

* * *

Katherine could not hear what Mr. Wooding was saying to her, at least not yet. Her mind was whirling with the delight of having assisted the gentlemen in their game of hazard, and with the pleasure of standing beside Evan, and of receiving his compliments. The entire experience was so at odds with her previous encounters with him that she could do little but emit a series of small, silent sighs.

"Do you think you should like that?"

Katherine was snapped from her reverie. "I do beg your pardon, Mr. Wooding. I fear I was distracted for a moment. Should I like what?"

"Riding out tomorrow with me. There is a style to the north known as Caesar's Style. I had thought we might search it out, perhaps enjoy a nuncheon at Hove and return to Brighton I daresay about three?"

"You know how very much I enjoy riding, but I could not go without Miss Alistair."

"The invitation was of course intended for both of you. If you like, I could get up a larger party."

"That would be marvelous."

By that time they had reached the ballroom. He led her onto the floor, which was just forming for the promised country dance. She took up her place opposite him, and smiled. Oh, how much she loved a ball, and a game of hazard now and then!

Four

On the following afternoon, Katherine encouraged Lydia to break into a trot as together they made their way to join Mr. Wooding's riding party which was assembling just north of the Steyne. Lydia agreed somewhat reluctantly, for she was not a great rider, but very soon they drew to a stop near Mr. Wooding. Mr. Horsfield and Mr. Sawyer were present, along with Miss Page. The party wanted only two more arrivals—Mr. Keymer and Captain Ramsdell.

Katherine could not think of Evan without feeling as though a bubbly champagne were swimming in her veins. She felt oddly excited at the mere thought of seeing him again, and strangely nauseous. She could not in the least account for such sensations except that he had been kindness itself last night. He had even approved of something she had done! She chuckled as she thought of poor Mr. Raikes, so completely in his cups. She had little doubt he was presently suffering acutely for his overindulgence.

Her gaze frequently scanned the horizon to the south for any sign of the gentlemen. Every minute that passed seemed to increase the tempo of her pulse, and before long she found herself in the acutest anxiety.

At a moment when she had forced herself to attend to Mr. Sawyer's discourse, Lydia drew abreast. "They are coming," she whispered. "At last." A moment later, she added, "Mr. Keymer certainly sits his horse well, does he not?"

Katherine glanced cursorily at Mr. Keymer in the lead. "Yes, I suppose he does." He was nothing, she thought, to Evan Ramsdell, but then, what man was when the good captain had lived astride a horse for the past decade?

How erratically her heart was beating. Almost, she could not bear it. She looked away from the sight of the men cantering toward the party and let her gaze drift anywhere but in their direction. Mr. Wooding's laughter drew her attention. He was clearly amused by something Miss Page had said to him, in the same way that Evan had been charmed by her society last night.

Miss Page was something of a mystery to Katherine. Earlier that morning, she had been dipped alongside Miss Page and was left somewhat bemused by the young lady. She had hoped to further her acquaintance with her, but Miss Page seemed to lack conversation, at least with her and Lydia, for she had had scarcely two or three anecdotes to share with them.

As she regarded her now, however, Katherine could not help but note that the blond, waifish chit was chattering away like the happiest of birds to Mr. Wooding. He in turn was smiling warmly upon her, a circumstance which caused Katherine to wonder about Miss Page's abilities to be of great entertainment to the gentlemen while having so little to say to the ladies of her acquaintance.

She intended to ask Evan about her, should the day's exercise provide a private moment.

Mr. Sawyer drew near to Miss Page, and Mr. Wooding took the opportunity to encourage his mount to Katherine's side.

"We could not have chosen a better day for a ride," he said.

"I have not seen such an expanse of blue in a long,

long time," Katherine returned. "There is not a single cloud in the sky." She lowered her voice and addressed another matter of curiosity. "Only, I must confess, Mr. Wooding, that I was surprised to learn you had invited Captain Ramsdell to join our party today, for it is well known you are not a friend to him."

Keeping a tight rein on his mettlesome mount, he spoke in a low voice, "I have no objection to Captain Ramsdell or to his friend Mr. Keymer, particularly since I am not well acquainted with either of the gentlemen. And though I should be happy to extend my friendship to the good captain, I have for some time felt he disapproved of me."

"I cannot imagine why," she said.

"You are kind to say so. As for inviting him to ride out with us, I did so because of Miss Page. Desiring to get up a large party, I approached her, only to find she had obligated herself to ride out with Captain Ramsdell, but she asked if I would extend the invitation to him and to Mr. Keymer, who she said has a profound knowledge of the downs. For your sake, and Miss Page's, I could not refuse her sweetly proffered request, nor could I hardly explain to her that Captain Ramsdell had taken a dislike of me."

His smile was crooked. In that moment, Katherine thought him a very fine gentleman, for there was no love lost between the men. Yet, not only had he spoken politely about Evan, he also did not hesitate to invite him to join a pleasure party when the occasion required. She could not imagine how Evan had formed the opinion that Mr. Wooding was anything less than honorable.

The brief tête-à-tête came to a close as Evan and Mr. Keymer drew up to the assembled party.

Katherine's gaze traveled swiftly to Evan. He sat tall in the saddle and wore a blue riding coat with black facings. He did not carry a whip but wore spurs which jingled with each trotting step of his horse. His black horse, Cronus, was magnificent, standing a full hand taller than her chestnut gelding. The proud lines of the animal were a perfect reflection of Evan's strong, athletic countenance. Something warm and exciting flitted within her as she watched man and horse move together, a duet of infinite knowledge and understanding, for the horse had seen battle with the captain. His years as a cavalry officer were quite evident in his upright carriage and his sun-worried visage. Deep lines were etched beside his eyes, giving him the appearance of one who has lived many adventures.

She realized he had done just that, a circumstance which gave her pause. What manner of woman would ever match his level of command and experience? He had been in battle numerous times, and the very thought of it caused her to hear suddenly the roar of cannon. How had he managed to control his men and his mount under such circumstances? Had he lost a horse in battle, as Wellington had? How many times? Had he ever been seriously wounded, or even slightly? How many men had died under his command? How many of his fellow officers never returned from Waterloo, or Salamanca, or Vitoria?

She felt awed but in a proper sense, as one who values the returning soldier who has fought to protect his homeland from invaders.

Mr. Keymer addressed the party first, offering his deeply felt apologies for having kept everyone waiting. "My horse threw a shoe just as we quit the mews," he explained.

At that, a general commiseration passed from lip to lip, for there were few things more frustrating than a thrown shoe or a lamed horse when one was preparing to embark on a pleasure expedition.

With Mr. Wooding in the lead, the party set forth, both Mr. Keymer and Evan taking up the hindmost positions.

Katherine worked her way back to them.

"What a fine day for riding out, is it not, Captain

Ramsdell?" she called to him happily. A cool breeze rolled from the northwest, promising a comfortable excursion.

"A very fine day," he agreed. "You are looking well, although I must say your nose is quite pink."

She could not help but smile. "I forget myself far too often while at the beach. This morning, I was dipped with Lydia and Miss Page and I could not seem to keep from turning my face toward the sun."

"And did you swim very far this morning?" he asked.

She noted the twinkle in his eye and was instantly reminded of his having kissed her three days ago. However, instead of being furious that he had broached the subject, she found herself surprised that their goodwill of the evening before had rendered the subject harmless.

She decided to answer him honestly. "Yes, for I knew you were not bathing. I sent my maid ahead to ascertain your absence, and then I must have passed three machines before turning back. I do love to swim."

He smiled at her speech, but said nothing.

Mr. Keymer reined his horse closer. "I enjoy a hearty swim myself," he said, entering the conversation. "I believe it an excellent sport besides being beneficial to one's health. Charles II was quite fond of it as well."

Evan turned to him. "Indeed, was he? You never cease to amaze me with your curious quantity of information. Is there anything else you wish to tell us?"

He glanced about the grassy downs and pointed to a large daisylike flower in a nearby field. "I have become acquainted with much of the flora since our arrival several weeks ago. Do you see the patch of flowers, there? The inhabitants hereabout call that plant the scentless mayweed, though I have no idea why. And there is a dog violet which I was assured only grew near the Dyke Road or upon Lady Ogle's estate." He seemed a trifle contemptuous as he gestured to another plant. "The geranium, which of course one finds anywhere, although I am told that near Preston there is a pink-flowered geranium called the dove's-foot which is purportedly quite beautiful. However, we shall not discover as much today, for I daresay we are not going as far as Preston."

"Not nearly," Katherine said, "for we mean only to make a broad circuit to the north and then to the west toward Hove and enjoy a little refreshment there before returning to Brighton."

Mr. Keymer seemed slightly distracted as his gaze moved over the remainder of the party in front of them. Though he smiled politely at her comment, he said, "I see that Miss Alistair is bereft of company for the moment. I ought to join her." He set his horse at a trot and quickly moved past them both.

Katherine found herself a little surprised but said nothing.

"Come," Evan said, spurring his horse as well. "We are lagging too far behind."

Katherine did not hesitate to join him and clucked her tongue a trifle, which sent Prince charging forward. He was a competitive animal, and once his nose bounded past Cronus, she could feel in the movement of his muscles that he had no interest at all in returning to a sedate trot. Evan's horse, she could see, was of a similar disposition.

She glanced at Evan and issued a silent challenge with a lift of her brow. His expression altered for the barest moment as he met her glance. A smile ensued, his spurs jingled, and before she knew what he had done, his horse lengthened into a hard gallop.

A side trail appeared and he was off, the downs opening up like an ocean of rolling green. Katherine followed, her heart swelling with a very pure excitement as she first galloped in his wake, then gradually began drawing abreast.

The horses were wonderfully matched in temperament, and the trail was wide enough to accommodate them both. A stream was taken in a joyous bound. The ribbons of her bonnet failed, and before she knew what had happened, her hat had disappeared off her head. Her hair began to stream behind her, though she scarcely noticed. Her thoughts, her desires, were in the boundless movement of the horse beneath her and in the green sward as it swept continually up to her and disappeared under the thunder of hooves.

She had no thought but to let Prince have his head and go as far and as fast as he was wishful of going. She did not think of her bonnet, or of Mr. Wooding's party, or even of Evan's mount pounding beside her. The exhilaration she felt was immense, as grand as the sky, as large as the ocean. She felt as though she could ride forever.

The upcoming path veered around the bend of a hill, and through the joy which had her in its grip, she heard Evan call sharply to her to draw rein. She did not want to stop, but she knew she must, for there was a command in his call which must be obeyed, and then she heard the sound of bleating sheep just as she pulled strongly on the reins.

As she rounded the hill, she discovered that the path was covered with a large flock of sheep trudging slowly toward the southeast, a single dog nipping at an occasional flank.

Katherine burst out laughing, her breath coming in strong gasps. "Good God!" she cried, puffing like mad.

"For a moment, I did not think you would heed me!" Evan cried, bringing his horse about. "As stubborn as you are! I called to you a dozen times before you responded. Why the devil did you refuse to heed me beforetimes?"

She glanced at him, her brow raised. She was surprised. "Why are you so angry? I stopped when I did hear you, and how is it you have called me stubborn? Is that how you see me?"

"Of course. Why else did you not respond until I was fairly shouting at you?"

"Well, if you must know, I was far too caught up in the thrill of riding. I did not hear you until the very last moment."

He stared at her as though deciding whether to believe her or not. "Well, it was very dangerous," he snapped.

"Indeed!" she returned brightly. "Which is why I believe I enjoy riding at a breakneck speed. Besides, what was the worst that might have happened?"

"That you could not have pulled up in time; that you would have been sent head over ears into a passel of sheep; that you would have perished of a broken neck."

"Is that all?" she queried with a laugh.

"What do you mean, *is that all?* Are you deliberately trying to provoke me?" His choler was rising. She could see he was shaken by the experience. "I thought we had come to an understanding last night, or were you merely playing at games?"

"On no account," she responded seriously. "I would not behave so inconstantly. However, I must say I do not understand why you are so overset. Evan, my life is precious to me, but not if I must always take the utmost care in preserving it. Were that much true, I should never have followed you onto what was a completely unknown path."

"You were careless," he stated, scowling.

"I was not," she answered firmly.

"You should have heeded me sooner."

"So you have said, but I did not hear you sooner."

"Well, you should have."

"Nonsense," she retorted with another laugh.

He was silent apace and finally released a sigh. "I did not mean to come the crab."

"Yes, you did. I vow you delight in it, at least where I am concerned."

"Now who is speaking nonsense?"

Well, perhaps it was not entirely true, and she laughed again. "Pray, let us not quarrel. We have been getting on so well. I promise you, I did not hear you until the very last moment, and then I obeyed your warning. But come! Pray forget all that might have happened and turn your horse about instead that you might view the southerly vista. Is there not anything prettier than a flock of sheep heading in the direction of Brighton against the panorama of the sea?"

He craned his neck, then guided his horse to join her. "You are right," he responded, taking in the view. "I am sorry. I was overset, but I do not desire to spoil the day by brangling."

"Nor do I."

After a moment, she guided Prince in the opposite direction, back up the path, that her horse might not become chilled. She let her gaze rove the exquisite sight of Brighton settled on the cliffs above a small bay. The bathing machines were but small dots on the beach, and the strongest landmark was the collection of onion domes of the Marine Pavilion.

He trotted his horse to join her. "Brighthelmstone appears to be sliding into the sea from here."

"Oh, it does!" she cried. "Indeed, it does. I never thought of it in that manner before, but you are quite right. Oh, Evan, I do love it here. I was never happier in my entire existence."

"Not even at Lady Brook?" he asked, obviously surprised. "I vow I thought all the Pamberley ladies were completely devoted to Berkshire."

"There was a time when I would have responded quite unthinkingly that you were correct. However, that was before . . . oh, I do not know . . . before I came to have thoughts of my own."

"Of your own?" he queried. "Whatever do you mean?"

She merely turned to glance at him, smiled, then set her horse at a canter up the path.

"You do not mean to answer me?" he called to her, drawing abreast again.

"I do not know you well enough, Evan Ramsdell, to reveal all of my thoughts. After all, what do I truly know of you except that you are quite used to having your own way, commanding a regiment, or casting judgments faster than even your horse was galloping just now?"

"These are hard words," he complained, but he was smiling.

"Do they apply aptly?" she queried, tossing her head.

He merely grunted in response, which told her he was at least pondering her opinion. "We must find your bonnet," he said, changing the subject entirely.

Retracing the path, Katherine was surprised to find they had covered nearly two miles in the long run, and as rise after rise was crossed, the rest of the party still could not be seen. "They must have gone north, into the hills a trifle," she said. "Ah! There is my bonnet." The black velvet creation, bearing a single white ostrich feather draped across the crown, had become lodged in a shallow dip, beside which a rivulet meandered in the direction of the sea. She drew close and dismounted, gathering up her horse's reins.

Evan also dismounted. "Here, take these," he commanded, thrusting Cronus's reins at her, which she took up in her free hand. "I shall fetch your bonnet. The ground looks a bit soggy." His boots sank past the heels in the low depression in which her bonnet had landed.

He fetched it easily enough, though he smiled at her rather crookedly as he brought the hat to her.

She had a strange feeling as he turned the hat in his hands. He was so close, and she was trapped by her need to keep the horses apart, her arms flung widely akimbo.

He stepped close. "You look a sight," he said.

"I know I must. My hair is completely undone and

tumbled about my shoulders. But it was worth every minute of it. I do love to ride." She sighed happily.

His gaze locked with hers in a familiar manner, and she struggled to take her next breath.

"You certainly do," he murmured.

Evan was again fascinated by her eyes, neither blue nor green and in the strong light of day clearly flecked with gold. Her light brown hair hung in curls all about her face, just as she'd said, clear to her shoulders, but to his eye the effect was wonderfully appealing. The recent exercise had given her entire face a glow as well as a brilliance to her eyes, the whole of which created as charming a countenance as he had ever seen. He was utterly enchanted and could not drag his gaze from hers.

Some part of him wanted to, for he could sense precisely how this particular moment would end, and he did not want to trespass her lips again. He felt in considerable danger of going beyond the pale.

He placed the bonnet over her curls, the dark black velvet enhancing the cream of her complexion and the sparkle of her eyes.

"I think you ought to take the horses," she said, her voice scarcely more than a whisper. "My hair is such a tangle that I daresay you will not be able to arrange the hat properly." She looked up at him in her open manner, her eyes wide, questioning and vitally innocent. Faith, but he was drawn to her, almost wildly so.

Suddenly he plucked the hat off her head and let it slip to the ground. He slid his arms about her waist and drew her tightly against him, still looking deeply into her eyes. He felt as he had the day he found her in the stables, exhilarated that she could not escape him even if she wanted to, for Katherine Pamberley would never let go of the reins.

"I am going to kiss you again," he murmured against her lips. "You were wonderful just now, riding as though nothing else in the entire world mattered."

Not even the faintest protest rose to her lips, which he realized were parted invitingly.

"Evan," she breathed. She said his name just so.

His mouth was on hers quite forcefully. He had no thought except in some wayward manner to express his pleasure in the race. As before, as so many times before, he felt her lips move beneath his, searching and hungry. The sensation of her desire to be kissed by him was overwhelming. The day disappeared and in its place were a thousand memories of everything he valued most, whispering to him, begging him to listen to all that was good and wonderful in life.

Waterloo rose up within him along with a dull ache he could not identify. He had lost so many friends, life had lost some of its beauty and wonder. Kissing Katherine returned some of this to him.

He touched his tongue to her lips, bidding entrance. She parted her lips more fully, tilting her head so that the next moment he was gently probing her mouth. He heard her coo like a dove.

He took the reins of his mount, releasing one of her arms, which became wrapped quite suddenly about his neck. She clung to him fiercely, which encouraged him to hold her more tightly still. He was locked to her in the fervency of the embrace, in the depth of the kiss. He did not want to let her go. Life was calling to him; life and a future and hope as he had never known it before.

Katherine did not understand what was happening, nor why she was permitting him such an intimacy as taking his tongue in her mouth. Nor did she understand why her arm was snaked so fiercely about his neck, nor why she did not release him and remonstrate with him for having assailed her yet again with his lustful embraces.

She knew his intention, for he had spoken it to her. *I have kissed no one but you since my arrival in Brighton and intend on kissing no others, at least not until you have tired of my advances.* It would seem she had not yet tired in the least of his advances.

She could make no sense of it, except that he was very strong and powerful, he rode like the devil, and she loved that he simply took kisses from her as though they already belonged to him.

Yet, she sensed something more, something intense and vital in the shared embrace, as though she already knew something too wonderful to be put into words. All the while, she was confused, bewitched and exhilarated. She felt just as she had a few minutes ago while racing down the path astride Prince and letting the speed of the horses flood her with passion. Yes, that was it! She felt passionate in Evan's arms.

The question again surfaced in her mind: Had she tumbled in love with Evan Ramsdell as Lydia believed? She simply did not know.

When Prince gave a serious tug on her arm, she could not help but draw back from the sweet ferocity of Evan's kiss.

"Prince," she explained, utterly mesmerized. She did not want the kiss to end.

Evan caught the reins of her horse with his free hand so that now he could not hold her, since he still held Cronus. But once she was liberated, she slid her arms about his neck and returned to him the kisses he had just given her. It would seem the experience was far too potent for Evan, at least for him to care any longer about keeping the horses close, for he suddenly let go of both sets of reins and enfolded Katherine fully in his arms. He kissed her wildly, recklessly, until a series of coos warbled in her throat.

"Katherine, this is madness," he breathed against her lips.

"Yes," she murmured softly, kissing him again. "A wonderful madness."

He began releasing her in slow stages as one who

would be injured to do otherwise. He petted her hair, smoothing it away from her face. "You are so beautiful."

"Why do you kiss me?" she asked quietly, looking into his blue eyes in wonderment.

"Because you are so willing," he responded, kissing her again.

After a moment, he released her completely and picked up her bonnet. She began very slowly tidying her hair. Was she dreaming? Her body felt unaccountably lethargic, and her mind would not function.

She had finally settled the bonnet over her rearranged curls when Evan said, "I'm sorry, Katherine. I know I should not be kissing you."

She laughed and tossed up a confused hand. "Of course you should not be kissing me, nor should I be kissing you, for I . . . I do not love you." She still felt desperately muddled as she attempted to explain, "That is, I do not believe I am in love with you, nor do I think I ever could be, for we do not agree on many things."

"Yet you enjoy my kisses," he said, his expression softening. "How do you explain that?"

"Who would not?" she returned earnestly, ignoring the laughter which sparkled suddenly in his eyes. She felt obliged to enlighten him. "You are quite one of the handsomest men I have ever known, your eyes are bluer than the sky, and you have perhaps the finest figure in all of Brighton, particularly on horseback, undoubtedly because you have been a soldier since time out of mind."

"All these compliments passing your lips! I vow you may turn my head if you are not careful."

She was grateful for his teasing smile and for the way he swept a finger softly over her cheek. "Fetch the horses, gudgeon," she said at last.

He did so while she tied the ribbons of her bonnet beneath her chin. As she watched him returning with both horses in hand, she could not help but release a deep sigh. She regretted again that she was so woefully inexperienced in the art of flirtation; otherwise she might have been able to make sense of how easy it was for her to fall into Evan's arms.

He helped her mount while she in turn held both sets of reins. Once she was seated comfortably, he mounted as well.

"We should travel to the west, I think," she said, "since Hove is in that direction. I daresay we shall intercept our party as they descend to the south."

"I would agree."

Katherine fell silent and gave in to a long string of sighs.

"I have not meant to bedevil you all these weeks, Katherine. I shall try . . . that is, in the future, I shall make a valiant effort not to assault you again."

She glanced at him, wanting to determine just how serious he was and whether an amused glint was in his eye, but he would not meet her gaze. She realized with a start that she was not certain she wanted him to restrain himself. This she could not say to him, however.

A few minutes later, as Katherine drew round yet another hillock, she met Mr. Keymer, Mr. Horsman, Mr. Sawyer and Lydia cantering easily in her direction.

"What ho!" Mr. Sawyer called out playfully. "Where is the rest of our poor party? I vow I have not seen a group of riders scatter so quickly before the wind."

Evan called abruptly, "Where is Miss Page?"

Lydia gestured in a northeasterly direction. "Mr. Wooding took her to see a style of some interest, supposedly Caesar's Style, and the rest of us wished to continue. We were to meet here, where the road leads to Hove." The bridle path was indeed separated at this juncture from the lane to Hove by just a few feet.

"Damn and blast," Evan muttered. Katherine guided her horse back to him.

"Whatever is the matter?" she queried in a low voice. "Is something amiss with Cronus?"

"No, my horse is perfectly sound. I simply cannot like Miss Page being separated from the party as she is. I feel a degree of responsbility. I have known her famIly for many years, and today she was given most particularly into my charge."

"I do not believe you have cause to be concerned. I know we disagree on Mr. Wooding's character, but with me he has been perfectly gentlemanly in conduct. I have no doubt he will be attentive to Miss Page, who must be nearly twenty years his junior, but nothing that would be considered improper."

"She is a complete innocent."

At that, Katherine opened her eyes wide. "And I am not?" she murmured.

Since his back was to the rest of the party, he smiled ruefully and whispered. "You do not kiss like one."

She was utterly shocked and oddly enough not in the least offended, though she knew she ought to be. "What a completely disgraceful thing to say," she whispered in return.

He held her gaze forcefully in his. "Accept it as a compliment. One day, you will make a most excellent wife for a very fortunate fellow."

But not for you. The words shot through her mind with painful force. *But not for you.*

What direction her thoughts might have taken at this point were interrupted by Lydia, who called out, "Mr. Keymer, what flower is that? The very small one, like a star."

"Stitchwort."

"And this one, amongst the furze?"

"Wild marjoram."

"These I recognize," she added. "Cowslips and buttercups, but what of—"

Her question was halted by Miss Page's voice calling from a rise to the north. "Hallo!" she cried, waving her arm and appearing like a sunbeam against the blue of the sky. Mr. Wooding traveled some yards behind her as together they descended the hill.

"There, you see?" Katherine murmured in Evan's direction. "She is perfectly sound, and he is following after her just as he ought. He does not seem overly content, however. I do not wonder if he was bored in her company."

"He will not allow himself to be bored in Miss Page's company," Evan said, more to himself than to her. She wondered what he meant by it, but the arrival of the remainder of their party did not allow for further conversation. Was it possible that Evan was in love with her? The very thought of it twisted her heart in the oddest manner.

Five

The following afternoon, Evan mopped his brow with his kerchief and tried not to be so serious. The subject had turned to Katherine. He and Keymer had only just finished a game on The Level at the Prince Regent's Cricket Ground.

"Do you think she suspects why we are here?" Mr. Keymer queried, wiping sweat off his forehead with his handkerchief, which he immediately stuffed into the pocket of his breeches. He was in his shirtsleeves, as was Evan, who also dripped perspiration.

"Hot today!" Evan cried. "Too damned hot to have been playing at cricket. As for Miss Pamberley, she would have no reason to, unless . . . damme, Keymer! Have you told someone?" He paused in mid swipe and glared at his friend.

Mr. Keymer feigned an expression of innocence. "I might have mentioned something about it to Miss Alistair."

"You are no spy, Keymer," Evan said, laughing.

"That I am not."

"You meant to warn me, then?"

"Yes, I suppose so. I did not want you to be shocked if Miss Pamberley asked you about our involvement on the Prince's behalf."

"Ah, well. Much good we are doing, anyway."

"There is hardly more we can do except await events to unfold and inquire after rumors here and there. You and I are hardly inconspicuous characters, after all."

"I suppose you are right. However, in the next few days I intend to see what I might discover at Hove. When we were at the inn earlier, there seemed to be a greater variety of men about than one finds even at The Ship." He wiped his brow once more, then flung a hand toward the Castle Inn. "A tankard would be most desirable right now. What do you think?"

"I am of a mind with you. Should we scandalize the ladies and enter the tavern *en déshabillé?*"

"We will not be the only ones to do so."

Several players were already headed in the direction of the large hotel in Castle Square which was the main posting Inn for the *haut ton.*

"I am willing if you are," Mr. Keymer responded.

Evan nodded, and together the men headed in the direction of the inn.

Evan was grateful to have so excellent a friend as Geoffrey Keymer. He had known him since Oxford days, before buying a pair of colors and joining the officer corps of His Majesty's Army. He trusted no man more than Keymer, who was a year older than himself. He was the third son of a wealthy baronet in Somerset and had served as secretary to the Duke of Relhan for the past eight years.

His Grace was an elderly man who had been a close advisor to George III before the king's final collapse into madness in 1810. The duke now served the present ministry in domestic affairs of the deepest national concern, addressing problems such as effects of the French Revolution, the rise of Jacobin activities in England, bread riots, suspected French spies associated with the smuggling activity along the southern coast of England, and assassination plots against the Crown and other important government officials. Geoffrey Keymer was one of several pairs of eyes frequently sent to various locations in England to observe and take the measure of any troubling events around the countryside. Whenever there had been a bread riot in the past several years, Keymer had been sent to investigate and report.

Presently, the duke had desired him to involve himself in the circles closest to the Prince Regent. Trouble was brewing.

Lord Ramsdell, also involved in national concerns, had sent Evan on the same mission, since there had been several threats against the life of the Regent in the past six months.

"I enjoy Miss Pamberley's company a great deal," Mr. Keymer said, altering the course of the discussion at hand.

Evan glanced sharply up at him, wondering what he was about. "She is much changed since I first met her last summer. Wonderfully so."

Keymer lifted an amused brow. "I suppose you have kissed her."

Evan nodded. He noticed that his friend wore a slightly troubled frown. "You disapprove?" he queried, laughing.

"She is little more than a child."

"Nonsense. She is two and twenty."

"A child in terms of experience. I have been given to understand that all the Pamberley sisters were quite impoverished until your brother crashed his curricle on their property."

"Quite true."

"And did not the second eldest, Miss Marianne, bring the future Earl of Bray up to scratch?"

"Also true."

Keymer whistled long and low. "Stiff-rumped, that one. But she did not wed him?"

"No. She married Sir Jaspar Vernham only a few weeks past. She knew him forever."

"The stable boy!" he cried, the gossip of the past several weeks suddenly fitting within his head.

"The very one. Since became a nabob. A fine fellow, a gentleman. He was the son of a parson in Yorkshire, I think, or some outlandish place. When his father died, he found employment on Mr. Pamberley's estate, then left for India. He was gone quite some time and, after performing a service for Prinny—I believe it had something to do with Princess Caroline and a nasty incident in the Mediterranean—he was knighted."

"There is a story for you, to leave England impoverished, having worked in the stables, now to return a wealthy knight."

"Extraordinary, I would say."

Mr. Keymer eyed him askance. "I have heard of the Pamberley sisters since time out of mind. They have been reputed as a passel of beauties."

Evan chuckled. "One and all."

"Ah, well, so you kissed her. There can be no harm in a little cuddling now and again. I should like to kiss her myself. There is certainly a most pleasing wildness in her eye—"

"Take care how you speak of her," Evan growled. "She is nearly my sister-in-law."

"I was not being in any manner disrespectful. If I thought for a moment she would shift her interest in my direction, I would not hesitate to pursue her with the intention of marrying her."

Evan was stunned. "You admire her that much?"

"And you do not?" he queried. "Good God, you *are* above being pleased."

"She ventured that opinion, I'll wager," Evan stated.

"Yes, and at the time I did not pay much heed, for by then the pair of you were brangling whenever you but laid eyes upon one another. Now, I am not so certain. What fault can you possibly find with Katherine Pamberley, and do you tell me you are not the least bit interested in her as a possible future wife?"

"I do not mean to marry," Evan said. "I do not believe I could ever be happy in the wedded state. Since it has been given to my brother to bear all future Lord Ramsdells, I have felt free to ignore the call of matrimony and have thus far succeeded without the smallest twinge of conscience or interest."

He had not given his predilection for bachelorhood a great deal of thought, at least not until now when Keymer's questions prodded him to the task. Yet he did not know what else he might tell his friend except that he simply could not imagine ever being interested in matrimony. Was Katherine right? Was he above being pleased?

He enjoyed getting up a flirtation, and had Katherine not been the most obvious choice, he probably would have sought out another willing female, someone not averse to his kisses, yet cognizant that he would be gone in a few weeks. The diversion of the female sex could be quite exhilarating.

Keymer intruded into his thoughts. "A confirmed bachelor," he stated. "I suspected as much, though I think it a great irony that a man in possession of a fortune as you are, and a fine property in Worcestershire, fully able to support a wife and children, should be so disinclined to marry when there are so many second, third and fourth sons desperate to find the very rare heiress. You must give me a reason, some reason for your dislike of marriage."

"I think the many years campaigning had an effect on me, something I cannot explain. I am perfectly able to enjoy the company of Ladies of Quality, do the pretty in a drawing room, make polite conversation, etc., but only for a short time. The rampant pettiness of such a life begins to pall severely after a few weeks. Since marriage would thrust me into the heart of such a life, dare I say, I could not bear it."

"I begin to understand. You have had experiences which make this life seem absurd." Keymer gestured with a hand toward the Steyne, along which several score of Brighton's finest personages strolled or rode about on horseback.

"Absurd is precisely the word I was searching for."

"How do you bear the Prince's company, then, for if ever there was a more complete combination of absurdity and pettiness, I have found none."

Evan could not help but smile. A child ran by, hitting a hoop with a stick, and both men stopped to allow him to pass. "Yet in all his ridiculous behavior, I have found him at times more conversant about Waterloo, and any of the other battles of the war, than most generals who were actually there. I know he did not leave England during the war, but his protestations that he saw battle, even at Waterloo, are almost believable because of the scope of his knowledge of the event."

"He has charmed you," Keymer stated simply.

"Perhaps so. It is his most prominent quality, to be charming. He is an attentive listener and never ceases to ask the most pertinent questions about my many experiences. I find his interest in my years on the Iberian Peninsula quite refreshing." The war with France had lasted over twenty years. A generation had been born and raised during that time, and Napoleon's rampaging over the Continent was met with a great deal of ennui in England, particularly after Admiral Nelson vanquished the French fleet during the Battle of Trafalgar so many years ago.

After a moment, Keymer's eye took on a wicked gleam. "If you are not intent on wedding Miss Pamberley, perhaps you would permit me to attempt to engage her. I was restraining myself because I believed you had a particular interest in her."

Evan regarded his friend with some astonishment. "If

you do not mind having your cork drawn, I have no serious objection!" he stated.

Keymer smiled in some satisfaction, which caused Evan to ask, "You were not serious, were you?"

"No. Even a nodcock can see that you have formed a *tendre* for her."

"It is no such thing!" he declared.

"Then how do you explain your conduct? For instance, just how many times have you kissed her since we arrived?"

"Four. No, five including yesterday on the downs."

"You kissed her while we were out riding!" he cried. "What a complete hand you are."

"Her bonnet had come off. In retrieving it, I found I could not resist."

"And you insist you have no serious intentions toward her. I must say, did I not know you as well as I do, I fear I would begin to suspect you of trifling with her."

Evan frowned slightly. He felt certain Keymer was offering a warning, one that he had given himself several times in recent days. The last kiss he had shared with Katherine had been rather intense. He was already resolved not to kiss her again, at least not for a time.

Worse still was Keymer's insistence he had formed a *tendre* for Katherine. That was, of course, ridiculous. In truth, he was a man who loved an excellent flirtation and damme if he wasn't in the middle of the best he had ever known.

Having reached the Castle Inn, he opened the door for Keymer. "I am not trifling with her," he stated as his friend passed through. "You may have no worry on that head. Come. I'll lay out the blunt for our tankards today, if it pleases you."

"It does indeed!" Keymer cried enthusiastically.

* * *

That evening at the Castle Inn, Katherine sat at a table for four playing whist. She held her thirteen cards loosely in hand, a new rubber just commencing. Her partner was Miss Page, whose eyes were still glimmering from her triumph of the last rubber, and who was giving her signals to Katherine in quick succession.

Try as she might, Katherine could not involve herself fully in the game. She misplayed several cards until even Miss Page demanded to know if she had the headache. Rather than attempt to explain that she had little interest in cardplay, she nodded, a circumstance which caused Mrs. Alistair and Lady Chiltingham to offer consoling words.

Mrs. Alistair then signaled to Lydia to replace Katherine, and she was free to roam about the assembly room in which several card games were in progress. Mr. Nutley was involved in a lively game of Casino, Mr. Horsfield and his group were playing at Trade and Barter, a very large table at which Mr. Wooding presided was engaged in a lively game of Silver Loo, and yet another large table was full of shouts and exclamations in a riotous game of Speculation.

The twice-weekly Card-Assemblies at the Castle Inn were some of the liveliest during the summer. A great many persons who had paid their annual subscriptions fees to the rooms were present. She came upon Evan playing Vingt-et-un with five others. She drew a chair forward to observe the play and went unnoticed for quite some time, during which she reflected upon the restlessness which had taken possession of her since earlier that day.

Of course, her thoughts were rarely far from the last kiss she had shared with Evan. The experience had changed her in a way she did not yet comprehend. This kiss had been different from the others in that Evan had actually placed his lips on hers several times. How her heart beat wildly as she recalled the moment when he had released the horses and engulfed her in his strong arms. She could still feel the experience as though it had happened a moment ago.

She touched her finger to her lips, her mind returning to earlier in the summer when Evan had first arrived in Brighton. She had known he was in town, for Mrs. Alistair had informed her of his arrival. Mrs. Alistair always had all the news first. Katherine knew it was but a matter of time before she would meet him. Oddly enough, however, she never expected to do so in the mews where she was brushing out her dear Prince.

"Miss Katherine," he had said softly, emerging from the shadows. How startled she had been. "Whatever are you doing with a brush in hand? Is there no stable boy to whom you will entrust your horse?"

"Captain Ramsdell," she had said, trying to still her startled heart. "I had heard you had arrived in Brighton. How do you go on?"

"Very well, thank you." He glanced about him. "The stables seem to be deserted at this hour."

She remembered pausing in a brush stroke. There was some tenor to his voice that kept her heart beating erratically. She had launched into a speech, for his presence was disturbing her. "I know it must seem odd of me to be here, but Prince has been with me forever and I have been missing the earthy stable life, brushing my horse and talking to him as has been my habit for the past nine years." She became aware of the appearance she made in her smock. Her bonnet was hanging on a nail nearby. Whatever must he think of her?

He drew near, entering the stall and latching it behind him. "You are doing your hair differently," he had remarked.

She glanced at him, feeling puzzled but not knowing precisely why. "I am doing many things differently," she had returned, wondering why he had closed the stall door.

"The curls are becoming, I think."

"Thank you."

He moved closer. She continued brushing, but she could feel that her cheeks were blooming with color.

He stroked Prince's forelock. "I hope to see a great deal of you when I am here. You will not object if I call in West Street?"

He already knew where she lived. "I should be delighted," she responded honestly. She went on brushing but knew he was staring at her.

"I have been told," he said, "that you attend all the balls, all the usual engagements."

"Yes," she responded simply.

She glanced at him and saw a slight frown crease his brow. "I do not recall your having done so in Berkshire. What I recollect was a young lady rather shy of company."

"I suppose I was . . . then. But if you will recall, I was circumstanced quite differently when first we met. Your brother changed everything, not only for Constance, but for the rest of us as well. It is by his generosity that I have been able to make my home here in Brighton."

He moved to stand behind her. Over her shoulder he said, "You are very beautiful, Miss Katherine." His voice was a low, husky sound that sent ripples of gooseflesh down her neck and back. She turned around to face him, to see his face in order to determine what he was about, but she did not realize he was standing so close to her. She nearly bumped into him. As it was, she dropped the brush.

He did not let her retrieve it. Instead, his hand was suddenly upon her waist. She stepped slowly backward, to the side of her horse, moving more deeply into the stall. He followed, smiling quite wickedly, his hand remaining on her waist. "Will you greet an old friend with a kiss?" he had asked.

Her heart was racing. "A kiss?" she had whispered in response. Her knees were trembling. She had imagined several times the moment she would see the captain, but never did it include a kiss.

"Just a small one," he had said. "I was remiss summer last. I should have sought you out more frequently. How I came not to take advantage of such an opportunity, I cannot imagine."

He placed a hand flat upon the wall behind her. Only then did she realize her back was pressed up against the cool brick, and he was so near that she could feel his breath on her forehead.

"Will you grant me a kiss, silent Katherine?"

She was still so stunned by the request she did not immediately respond. Instead, she parted her lips as though in doing so she might summon the proper words with which to answer him.

His smile grew crooked as his gaze fell to her lips. "I have my answer," he had murmured.

The next moment he drew her roughly into his arms. Never had she been so shocked in her life. She could not imagine in what manner she had encouraged him to take advantage of her. She even meant to push him away, but for some reason, his sudden assault had stunned her into acquiescence and then utterly charmed her in a manner she doubted she would ever comprehend.

She was backed against the stable wall. He pressed himself against her, and a sharp, physical desire passed over her like an ocean wave. She felt drenched with a sensation she had never before experienced. He kissed her for a long, long moment. He drew back, staring down at her as though seeing her for the first time. She had a sense he meant to disengage from her even then, but she parted her lips and touched his cheek.

The second kiss was devastating.

After a long moment, he let his forehead touch hers quite gently. "Katherine, I never meant—"

The sounds of a stable boy bringing in a horse had

parted them abruptly. She had turned away from him and, deeply embarrassed, had left the stables abruptly.

How did he have this power over her? she wondered now, utterly bemused. She regarded him in some confusion as he played Vingt-et-un. He won, caught her eye and winked at her. As though of a volition not her own, she rose from her chair and moved on.

In truth, she felt in no small degree of danger where Evan was concerned.

Six

On the following day, Evan attended a musicale at which he knew Katherine to be performing. He arrived late, however, and was concerned he had missed her execution of the Bach Preludes and Fugues he knew her to have been practicing diligently for weeks.

"I must say, you appear positively done in," Mr. Keymer remarked.

Evan sipped his champagne and glanced about the music room of Lady Chiltingham's home on the Steyne. A number of young ladies were to perform at Her Ladyship's musicale as well as Katherine, who he could see was seated near the front of the elegant chamber.

He released a sigh. "You do not know the half of what I endured today," he responded. "I attended the bull-baiting at Hove, imbibed four tankards of ale in the course of the afternoon, ate some very flavorless boiled beef, and achieved nothing for my efforts. I vow I listened to three score of drunken louts from one end of the small village to the other and heard nothing untoward, nothing that might direct our search. I am beginning to believe the whole thing is a hum. I have been in Brighthelmstone over a month now, and not one hint of desperate activities."

"Were you truly expecting to overhear a group of conspirators exposing their plot to whomever might be listening?"

"Of course not. What I was expecting, however, was some drunken fool to say he had overheard several hardened assassins intent on harming the Prince."

Mr. Keymer laughed, then addressed another subject entirely, "How was the baiting?"

Evan shook his head. "Have you not heard? The bull broke his stake and charged into the crowd. Fortunately, no one was injured."

"Fortunate, indeed! So there was no baiting?"

"No. The bull very quickly trotted out of Hove and was not seen again. Ah, here is Miss Page prepared to perform for us. I was used to hear her frequently in Worcestershire. She is quite skilled on the pianoforte. Am I very late? Has Miss Pamberley played her pieces yet?"

"You are only a little after the hour. Miss Page is the first to take the stage."

Evan glanced around the music room and felt some of his vigor renewed by the sight of so many pretty females. His occupations of the day had cast him in an ill humor from which he was not quite recovered. He accepted a second glass of champagne from a passing footman, but instead of taking a seat chose to remain standing beside Keymer at the back of the room.

The windows were open, but there was a stillness to the air, which he realized was a precursor to a storm. He smelled rain in the air. "We shall be wet through before reaching North Street tonight."

"Nonsense. It shan't rain. I will not allow it."

Evan chuckled and sipped more of the bubbling drink. He was beginning to feel a great deal better, moreso when Miss Page struck the first notes of her sonata and entered with considerable verve into the piece.

He let his gaze rove the audience and found a stranger, a man, seated beside Wooding. He leaned toward Keymer and whispered, "Who is the dark-haired fellow beside Wooding? I have not seen him before."

"A cousin. Lunsford. Also from the Midlands. He is just arrived this afternoon. I met him on the Steyne during the Promenade. The ladies generally seem quite taken with him."

"What did you make of him?"

Mr. Keymer shrugged. "Tolerable enough. Shrewd gray eyes, I think. Conversant, not in the least arrogant. I daresay he will be invited everywhere."

Since Mrs. Alistair, who was seated directly in front of Mr. Keymer, turned around and begged him to be quiet, both gentlemen bowed and fell silent. Only when Miss Page had completed the sonata did Evan query softly, "What brings Mr. Lunsford to Brighton?"

"What has brought most of the people here? He desired to do a little sea-bathing before returning to Lincolnshire for the remainder of the summer, or so he informed me."

A perfectly reasonable answer, and Evan once more fell silent as Miss Alistair approached the harp. She and Miss Page performed a beautiful duet of harp and pianoforte which set the chamber wild with applause once concluded.

A brief interlude provided an opportunity for further conversation. Evan gave himself to addressing the several personages about him, Mr. Horsfield, Mrs. Alistair, Lady Chiltingham and Mrs. Nutley. Regardless of his fatigue, he summoned the appropriate drawing room conduct and engaged in the usual discourse. He was always anxious to continue in the good graces of Brighton's most prestigious hostesses.

"Do you mean to attend Prinny's dinner this Saturday?" Mrs. Nutley queried.

"Of course," Evan responded. "I have been anticipating the event since I first received the invitation."

"Nothing will be finer, of that I assure you, Captain

Ramsdell," Lady Chiltingham added, batting her fan over her plump cheeks.

"Indeed," Mrs. Alistair agreed. "Only it is too bad it is not to be a musical evening, for His Royal Highness's musicians are always the most accomplished."

Mr. Horsfield nodded. "I could wish for more strings, however. After a time, so much brass does become hard on the ears."

"You will hear none of us say so," Lady Chiltingham stated dampeningly.

Mr. Horsfield took to staring at his quizzing glass.

Mrs. Alistair turned the conversation in a different direction entirely. "Mr. Keymer, are you a great dancer?"

"I wish that I might say I was," he responded. "Alas, I frequently confuse my right foot with my left. Regardless, I do enjoy the sport prodigiously, and I hope that what I lack in skill is provided for in my enthusiasm so that I do not entirely disgrace my partner on the ballroom floor."

Mrs. Alistair smiled beatifically. "You are quite one of the most modest young men I have ever chanced to encounter. I should like to see you dance with Miss Pamberley at the next Castle assemblies, which will be on Monday. I hope you will allow me the pleasure of seeing the pair of you together."

"If Miss Pamberley will honor me by agreeing to go down two sets, I shall oblige you most happily."

Evan had listened to this exchange with the sure knowledge that Mrs. Alistair had singled out Mr. Keymer as a suitor for Katherine. He would have been amused by it, but having since learned that Mr. Keymer admired her as well, he found himself in the odd circumstance of being rather irritated.

Fortunately, the interlude drew to a close and he did not have to listen to anything further about Mrs. Alistair's hopes concerning Mr. Keymer and Katherine. Miss Framfield performed next, followed by Miss Kelly and

Miss Horsfield. Evan found his interest waning severely until at last Katherine took up her place at the pianoforte.

Much of his fatigue quickly dissipated. He listened with some interest, for he had not heard her play but once since his arrival in Brighton. However, on that occasion, noise from an adjoining card room had quite ruined his ability to attend to her. He could not recall her playing at The Priory last summer, yet she must certainly have done so, for all the Pamberley ladies played.

How odd that he had only the vaguest recollections of her from a year ago. Had she altered so much in a mere twelve months that though he could scarcely recall her from last summer, he was now utterly intent on everything that pertained to her?

Except for the sound of the music, the chamber had fallen silent. Many leaned forward in their seats attending to each rippling of Katherine's fingers over the keys. She played with great expression, and her face was fairly enrapt as she gave herself entirely to the music, apparently forgetting about her audience completely.

When at last she played the final note of the final Bach fugue, a burst of applause rose from Lady Chiltingham's guests. Several gentlemen were quick to leave their seats and surround her. Compliments fairly filled the air, which prompted Mrs. Alistair to turn and smile encouragingly upon Mr. Keymer as though to add substance to her obvious desire to see him as a serious contender for Katherine's hand.

The annoyance Evan had been feeling previously transformed into a stronger sensation he could ill define. He felt trapped suddenly. He detested Mrs. Alistair's knowing nods and smiles.

He felt himself scowling, and his earlier ill temper seemed to return in force. He felt the weight of society's pressure at the back of his neck, but he would be damned before he would submit to the machinations of the *beau monde*. He wished his brother had chosen anyone else to have performed this service in Brighton. He was ill suited to going about in the *beau monde* for an extended time, and what was worse was that he could not seem to keep from kissing Katherine, which he could now see was giving rise to all manner of complications in his otherwise simple, orderly existence.

After conversing for a few minutes more with Lady Chiltingham and Mrs. Alistair, he made his excuses and quit the fine seaside house.

Geoffrey Keymer watched his friend's retreating back and could not resist a smile, for he thought he understood the source of his obvious aggravation. He doubted, however, that Evan comprehended as much.

When Mrs. Alistair moved away quite hastily, heading in the direction of Lord Gravestock, a spotted youth attempting to engage Miss Alistair in conversation, Mr. Keymer was left to converse with Lady Chiltingham.

"Whatever is the matter with Captain Ramsdell?" Lady Chiltingham queried, peering up at Mr. Keymer. "He did not seem at all content just now. A gentleman, of course, but not at all happy."

"He was at Hove today when the bull broke loose. I daresay he has the headache from all the excitement."

"Ah, yes, of course," she returned, wide-eyed. "I have heard it was a terrifying sight when the old bull snapped his tether and charged at all those children and several elderly people. I have since learned that three residents of Hove perished in the onslaught."

He responded appropriately from years of training and habit and he clucked his tongue. "I *hope* it was not as bad as all that."

"As do I," she responded with a sincere nod of her head. "There is Mrs. Nutley waving at me. Pray excuse me, Mr. Keymer. She is of a very flighty temperament and I must tend to her at once or she will fly into the boughs."

"Of course," he returned, bowing politely. Lady Chiltingham moved swiftly away. He had little doubt she meant to share her knowledge of the events at Hove with her friend.

Left for a few moments to his own devices, Keymer sipped his champagne and pondered Evan's predicament. The day before, after the cricket game, a certain suspicion had entered his mind concerning Evan. His conduct just now upon hearing Mrs. Alistair encourage not good Captain Ramsdell, but rather himself, to court Miss Pamberley tended to confirm these suspicions.

For all of Evan Ramsdell's protestations of detesting the married state, there was just such a look in his eye when he gazed upon Miss Pamberley that caused him to think Evan was not as indifferent to her as he proclaimed. Only why did he not see, or even suspect, that Katherine Pamberley was in a fair way to winning his heart?

He smiled to himself. It would seem Cupid had been busily employed in the last month, pricking *two* gentlemen quite solidly with his golden-tipped arrows. His own dilemma was quite different from Evan's, however, for the lady he had in mind had made it clear that her mother was expecting her to marry into the peerage.

He sighed deeply and tossed off the remainder of his champagne as his gaze fell upon Lydia Alistair. His heart seemed to expand in his chest as he watched her mother encouraging young Lord Gravestock to converse with her. This was a terrible impediment to his hopes and desires—the ambitions of a well-established matchmaking mama.

He might have fallen into a brown study, but Miss Page suddenly came up to him bursting with news. "Have you heard of the bull-baiting at Hove?" she queried, her large brown eyes blinking rapidly with excitement.

"Why, yes, as a—"

"Is it not the most horrifying occurrence?" she continued unchecked. "I have heard that the bull gored at least seven people, two of them children! Five persons have died already, and the remainder are not expected to last the night."

"Truly horrifying," was all that Mr. Keymer thought to say. It would seem the tale of the bull pulling his stake at Hove was undergoing the usual drawing room changes and exaggerations.

Katherine approached him afterward. "Have you heard of the bull-baiting?" she queried.

"At Hove? Yes." He wondered what she would tell him. He had conversed many times with her and knew her not to be given to any form of hysteria.

"I cannot believe half of what I have heard this evening, of people dying! I would tend to think that one good man on horseback could have had the beast under control before the animal contrived to injure anyone seriously."

He leaned toward her in a conspiratorial manner. "I would recommend you hold your tongue. Unfortunately, such a sensible response will give no pleasure in Lady Chiltingham's music room."

Katherine could only laugh. "You are being quite non-sensical."

"Admit it is true."

"That much I will not allow. I am acquainted with far too many people of sense to believe your opinion to have the least merit."

"Look about you, then. Tell me someone who is of a different opinion."

Katherine cast her gaze about the crowded chamber. "Mr. Wooding. I am convinced he would not be so ridiculous as to believe such errant gossip."

"Let us determine the matter at once." He offered his arm to her.

She took it, and together they ambled in the direction of Mr. Wooding.

Katherine enjoyed the company of Mr. Keymer prodigiously. She understood quite well why Evan obviously preferred his society to many others. Mr. Keymer was a knowledgeable gentleman who always chose sense over absurdity, and who treated his acquaintance with an abundance of respect. He was not in the least given to gabblemongering or embellishment.

Mr. Wooding greeted Katherine by extending both his hands to her. She released Mr. Keymer's arm and took Mr. Wooding's hands.

"You played brilliantly this evening," he said, smiling.

"You are very kind to say so. But to play two preludes and two fugues by Bach, which I have practiced since I was very young, is perhaps not to say a great deal. I do enjoy the music very much, however, which must account for your expressions of admiration."

"Regardless of how you came to your mastery of these pieces," he responded kindly, "I am grateful for your wonderful performance tonight."

The gentleman next to him cleared his throat by way of offering a hint.

"Ah, pray allow me to present my cousin, Mr. Lunsford."

"How do you do, Mr. Lunsford," she said, offering her hand to him.

"Very well, thank you, Miss Pamberley," he said, taking her hand in a firm clasp. "And may I add my own appreciation of your performance this evening. Truly delightful."

Katherine saw very little resemblance between the men. Mr. Wooding was a tall man with graying brown hair and round brown eyes. Mr. Lunsford was of average height, had narrow gray eyes, and hair nearly as black as Evan's. He bowed over her hand.

"You are very kind as well, Mr. Lunsford. May I present Mr. Keymer?"

"We have already met. How do you go on, Mr.

Keymer?" Mr. Lunsford queried graciously, bowing slightly from the waist.

"Because I am in Miss Pamberley's company, I must say I am doing exceedingly well."

Katherine laughed. "Now, that was a great deal too gallant of you, Mr. Keymer. No more of that, if you please, or I shall cease to call you friend."

"Are you as lacking in sensibilities as Captain Ramsdell?" he queried, regarding her from laughing eyes.

"As to that, I cannot say. I am not sufficiently acquainted with the captain to have formed such an opinion. Perhaps you must be the sole judge on that score. But more to the point," and here she turned to Mr. Wooding, "Mr. Keymer and I were arguing another matter entirely and wished to know what you perceive must have happened earlier today at Hove with regard to the bull."

At that, Mr. Wooding chuckled. "I have heard so many reports as to have concluded that none of them must be correct except the one which detailed the entire occurrence as rather insignificant with not even one injury of merit."

Katherine inclined her head to Mr. Keymer and smiled broadly. "There, you see? I told you he was a man of some sense."

"I did not doubt it for a second," he responded easily. "But here is Miss Page."

Mr. Wooding immediately turned in the direction of Mr. Keymer's gaze and drew Miss Page into their circle. Katherine could see that Mr. Wooding meant to open his mouth undoubtedly to praise her superior performance on the pianoforte, but Miss Page was before him. "Mr. Wooding, have you heard of the truly wretched events at Hove this afternoon? I know Miss Pamberley and Mr. Keymer have, for I informed them of it but a few minutes past. Only I must say I was mistaken and the whole of the incident was far worse than I was originally told.

Only consider, Mr. Wooding and Mr. Lunsford, that at least twelve persons were killed outright by two stampeding bulls!"

When her audience erupted into a spontaneous burst of laughter, she could only eye everyone with wide-eyed innocence followed by a reproving glance. "I must say, you are not showing a great deal of compassion for those families who have lost loved ones today."

"No, we are not," Katherine interjected hastily. "However, before I allow my heart to be wrung completely, I should desire to know more of what happened at Hove. Only then, when for instance I have read an account in the *Brighton Herald,* will I be assured of the day's true events. Though I have every confidence you are not given to exaggeration, Miss Page, I believe it an unfortunate circumstance that there are those among us who enjoy aggrandizing even the misfortunes of others should it prove an opportunity to draw attention to themselves."

"I believe you to be quite mistaken, Miss Pamberley," Miss Page said most sincerely, "for I heard this most recent account from Lady Chiltingham, herself."

Both Mr. Lunsford and Mr. Wooding cleared their throats, and Mr. Keymer began admiring the ornate stucco work on the ceiling. Katherine regarded Miss Page's open-eyed innocence and wondered if she was truly as naive as she appeared.

Since she did not know what to say to Miss Page, she was grateful that Lydia arrived with news of an entirely different nature.

"I have just heard from my mother that there are to be several rather quaint contests tomorrow morning, around ten o'clock, on the Steyne."

Katherine's heart took a leap. "Is there to be a horse race I might enter?" she queried excitedly.

"No, I fear not. The contests are much simpler in nature. For instance, one of Lady Chiltingham's servants is to race one of Mrs. Nutley's, on foot. In addition, there are to be several sack races, a donkey race, and several impoverished young girls from the workhouse are to race for a new smock and a new hat. What do you think of that!"

"How charming," Mr. Keymer said.

Lydia met his gaze and immediately blushed. "I thought you might think so, Mr. Keymer, for you were telling me only the other day of your village's quaint customs."

"I should be happy to escort you tomorrow, both you and Miss Pamberley, if you wish for it?" he said.

"I should be delighted," Lydia responded happily.

"And I, as well," Katherine added.

Since at that moment a hard pounding of rain was heard on the roof, the small group groaned together. *What a nuisance,* Katherine thought, *for we shall all be wet through.*

She glanced toward the window. It had not escaped her notice that Evan had departed the townhouse earlier, before he could greet her or express even a mild appreciation for her performance this evening. She had hoped to speak with him, but since he left, she had begun to wonder if he was actually avoiding her. She had not seen him once the entire day in the usual places—at the beach, Fisher's, the piazzas on the Steyne. She felt much depressed of a sudden.

Mr. Keymer said, "And I should like to invite Captain Ramsdell, if that would be agreeable to you, Miss Alistair. He was at the bull-baiting today and I believe had the headache as a result of the tumultuous events there. I daresay he should profit from a little diversion tomorrow morning."

"Then you must invite him," Lydia responded.

Katherine turned to look at Mr. Keymer and saw the oddest light in his eye as he met her gaze, one of understanding, even compassion. She understood then that Mr. Keymer had invited Evan quite purposefully.

She felt her cheeks warm with the sure knowledge that Mr. Keymer suspected that she and Evan were somehow more than mere acquaintances, which of course they were. But how much more?

Acquaintances who enjoyed kissing one another? How absurd! Yet how else could she describe her tumultuous relationship with Constance's brother-in-law?

One thought, however, rose above all the rest: Unless Evan was truly wishful of avoiding her company, she would see him tomorrow at ten o'clock. Somehow, of the moment, nothing else mattered.

On the following morning, Katherine was walking beside Evan on the Steyne where a great crowd of spectators had gathered. Mr. Keymer had discreetly guided Lydia in the opposite direction, for which Katherine was grateful, for she wished to know why Evan had quit Lady Chiltingham's musicale so early last night. She kept the stronger question from leaving the tip of her tongue: *Were you avoiding me?* Instead, she queried, "So you did not have the headache last night, as Mr. Keymer believed?"

Evan shook his head. "No, I was merely fatigued from having spent the day in Hove."

"Why were you at Hove all day?" She saw his countenance darken a trifle and immediately added, "Forgive me, Evan. The question was impertinent."

He glanced at her and huffed a sigh. "I suppose it makes little difference were you to know the truth. Besides, I strongly suspect Miss Alistair has already hinted to you that Mr. Keymer and I are not kicking our heels in Brighton solely for our own amusement."

"Oh, I see. Well, yes, she did mention that you were in the service of the Prince, though she did not know in what way."

"Then Mr. Keymer showed some discretion after all, though I wish he had not confided in her at all."

Katherine followed the line of Evan's gaze and saw that he had turned to look at Lydia and Mr. Keymer.

He clucked his tongue. "Is this a love match forming? He will never do for her. Mrs. Alistair means to see her daughter married to a duke if she can."

Katherine sighed. "Unfortunately, you are right on that score. Mrs. Alistair is desperately ambitious for her daughter. But do you truly think this is a love match?" She saw nothing in Lydia's aspect to warrant so strong a description.

"Look how she smiles at him," Evan stated.

Katherine shrugged. "Lydia is always smiling in that manner, like an angel, which I often think she is. Sweetness of temper defines her completely. During all these months of residing in her home, I have never heard a cross word pass her lips."

"She is very different from you," he observed.

She snapped her attention back to his face and gasped. She was stunned that he would say anything so unhandsome to her, particularly when they were getting along so well. However, the warm, laughing light in his blue eyes softened her temper instantly. "How unkind of you," she cried, "to remind me of one of my faults, particularly when I have begun to think you an agreeable sort of fellow of late."

Evan laughed and offered his arm. "Take this as an olive branch. I should not have teased you so."

She took his arm. "Very well."

A round of applause could be heard in the distance near the starting line.

"Come," Evan said. "I believe the contests are about to commence and I would like to see the donkeys before the first race begins."

The activities were typically summerish for Brighthelmstone—sack, donkey and foot races. Katherine found the donkeys highly amusing as they brayed their discontent. The brown, unhappy beasts would race first, followed by the contest in which the five young girls from the workhouse would run the distance of seventy-five yards and the winner would be awarded a new gown and bonnet.

"I wish the turf was not so damp from last night's rain," she said. "My half-boots are wet through, and by the time the donkeys have forged their way across the sward, half the Steyne will be muddied."

"Did I miss anything of significance after your performance at Lady Chiltingham's?" he asked.

"No, merely Miss Page's relating the gossip about the bull-baiting not once but thrice so that by the time Mrs. Alistair requested we leave, there were at least a score of children either dead or maimed because of the bull—no, because of two bulls."

"Two bulls!" he cried, chuckling. "It is always the way."

"What did happen yesterday? You were there, were you not?"

"Indeed I was, though I fear boring you by a truthful recounting of the day's activities."

"Well, the gossip last night did provide a considerable measure of entertainment, but I would still prefer to hear exactly what happened."

"Very well. The bull pulled from his stake and broke through the crowd causing a few bruises, but nothing more. I believe the animal was far too happy to be rid of Hove to spend even the smallest time trying to injure or kill anyone. Last seen, he was racing across the downs in the direction of Preston. I was told this morning he was caught just off the Lewes Road where he was found contentedly eating his breakfast in a nearby field."

Katherine chuckled. "I daresay Miss Page will be sorely disppointed when she learns the truth. Ah, here she is now."

The young lady, on the arm of Mr. Wooding, greeted them first, then immediately launched into how badly she was taken in by the gabblemongering of last night. "Imagine, the old steer was found near the king's highway. I was never more stunned, for I had heard such stories last night and believed every one of them. Is Brighton always so full of gammon?"

Captain Ramsdell laughed outright. "What town is not?" he queried. "You are far too trusting, Miss Page."

"I suppose I am," she returned mournfully.

"You could never be *too* trusting," Mr. Wooding interjected swiftly, patting her hand which was wrapped snugly about his arm. "For I do not believe a lady can possess a finer quality than to have such a belief in the goodness and rightness of others."

Miss Page smiled warmly up into his face. "How kind of you to turn what I clearly see as a dreadful shortcoming into a virtue. However, I mean never to be so gullible again, and at the very least I intend to begin by not believing what Lady Chiltingham might choose to say to me."

Since no one argued the point with her, she seemed satisfied in her decision.

"Oh, do but look," Katherine said. "There are the five young ladies now. My, but how thin they are." The girls were lined up a few yards behind the donkeys.

Captain Ramsdell grunted. "The workhouse is not kind to its inmates, I fear."

"If I had sufficient largess," Katherine said, "I should purchase each of them a new gown."

"I would advise against it, Miss Pamberley," Mr. Wooding stated somberly. "You would give them a hope that is as false as it is meant to be kind."

She was silent apace. "You may be right," she responded. "However, I believe I know something that may be done without inflicting harm."

Evan regarded her with a frown between his brows. "What?" he queried.

"I mean to visit Hannington's in North Steet, the linen drapers, this very afternoon. I was going to purchase all manner of frippery for my sisters, but I know their dispositions well, that they would want me to make this gesture on their behalf, and so I shall."

"To have dresses made up for them?" Miss Page queried, startled. "All of them?"

"No, not in the least, for I do have some experience of the poor in Berkshire. Our household was always very much involved in helping where we could. Those who suffer the misfortunes of life desire above all things to make their own way, I promise you. Besides, fabric is not nearly so dear as a made-up dress. A pattern card or two, a few needles, scissors and thread, and in the process a skill is acquired which might help one or two of these young girls escape the workhouse. A town this size must always be in want of capable needlewomen."

"Do you mean to instruct them yourself?" Mr. Wooding asked.

"If I must," she said. "Do you disapprove?" For he seemed startled by her idea.

"No, not in the least. It is just that I have never heard of such generosity before."

"I could never do as much for the poor," Miss Page announced. "I am far too selfish a creature, besides desiring never to cross the threshold of a poorhouse if I can help it. There is too much lice about. One hears of it forever."

"From Lady Chiltingham?" Katherine asked sardonically.

Evan was quick to interject, "Come! The donkey race is about to begin."

Seven

Just as the donkeys had been brought into a semblance of order by their riders, a commotion on the opposite side of the Steyne forced the festivities to a sudden halt.

The Prince Regent had arrived, much to the astonishment of everyone assembled.

"How very like him to take part in all our fun," Katherine whispered to Evan as she joined in the applause. "Whatever he might be, he is certainly one for every manner of amusement."

"I believe you are right," he responded.

The Prince, quite high in the flesh, waved congenially to the crowds thronging the edge of the racing field. Even from across the distance of the field, his chubby, aging face was flushed, for the day was hot and His Royal Highness was dressed fashionably in a dark blue coat, striped silk waistcoat, elegantly tied neckcloth, shiny beaver hat, buff pantaloons and glossy Hessian boots. Aware that his arrival had stopped the games, he soon gestured for the race to begin.

The donkeys and riders took their places. Of the latter now struggling to bring their mounts to the starting line, Katherine was acquainted only with Mr. Sawyer. Each man called out loudly to his donkey, and when it seemed that the riders were holding them steadily enough, the starter fired his pistol into the air. Four of the donkeys flew in the general direction of the finish line, but the remaining hapless beast jerked his rider in circles near the starting line, whirling him around and around until the nearby crowd was howling with laughter.

In the other direction, the race was on. The long legs of the riders hung over the bellies of the donkeys, spurred boots nearly touching the sward below. The brown animals kicked up buckets of mud from their hooves, and the debris most unfortuitously flew into the crowds. A great many ladies began to squeal and cry out with considerable dismay, but this tumult was soon lost in the nature of the race, for the nearer the four donkeys drew to the finish line, the greater the whoops and cries filled the air. More than one spectator, lady or gentleman, had staked a wager upon a favorite donkey and rider, and the air was rent with voices urging this or that beast to beat his fellows all to flinders.

In the end, a Mr. Crispin won the race, with Mr. Sawyer coming in a close second. Unfortunately for Mr. Crispin, he unwisely threw both his hands in the air upon winning and, after letting out a wild cry of exultation, found himself flung heavenward by an exasperated donkey. His partner was clearly not so satisfied with the outcome of the race as his rider had been. Poor Mr. Crispin rose up limping and rubbing his backside, sending ripples of laughter up and down the ropes along either side of the makeshift racecourse.

Katherine laughed until her sides ached.

The young ladies were to race next, a sense of excitement and hope evident on each face. Katherine watched them, her heart swelling with pleasure at the sure knowledge that, regardless of who was to win today's gown and bonnet, each of the girls would soon receive the fabric which she was determined now more than ever to bestow upon them.

The oldest could not have been more than ten or eleven and the youngest appeared to be about eight. As a pistol shot again ripped the air, the girls took off as fast as their young legs could carry them. Each made a valiant effort in running the racecourse, though few things could be more difficult than racing in a gown which caught time and again between one's knees. The winner, however, somewhat scandalized the crowd by drawing up her skirts well above her ankles and letting her legs quickly outdistance her competitors and crossing the finish line with an exultant squeal.

Katherine rather thought she would have done the same and said so in an undertone to Evan. He merely laughed and then asked if she had laid a wager on any of the races.

"No," she confessed. "I rarely gamble, for I cannot bear to lose. I believe it comes from Constance's rigorous economies at Lady Brook Cottage. She was forever reminding us of the costs in managing even a small estate like hers, and I daresay her strictness in such matters will be with me always. A farthing may not seem like a great deal of money to most everyone here, but when you have had to choose between beef or sugar in any given year, I vow the thought of foolishly wasting a shilling or two in gaming is beyond what I can bear."

"Was that why you were not playing at cards on Wednesday evening? I remember thinking it odd at the time."

"Our stakes were a mere tuppence a point, so I did not mind in the least. I simply could not fix my attention on the game in the manner desired by Miss Page. I was her partner, and she had quickly become exasperated with how stupidly I continued to lay down my cards. I am no whist-player."

"Nor I," he confessed. "Though I am partial to Vingt-et-un. Ah. Here comes the next set of contestants. The tall black man on the left is Lady Chiltingham's groom, the one everyone speaks of. He is also fond of boxing, if I do not mistake the matter."

"He is exceedingly well muscled!" Katherine exclaimed.

Evan turned to her and, upon meeting her gaze, could not restrain a bark of laughter. "You ought not to say so in company. You will undoubtedly set the tabbies to gossiping."

Katherine smiled in return but bit her lip in some perturbation. "I believe my candor in such matters must come from having lived in the stables. I was always used to speak of horses in such a fashion. I do not think it so large a stride to appraise an athlete in a similar manner, do you?"

He held her gaze for a long moment, his expression thoughtful. "You are an unusual female," he stated at last.

She sighed. "Only in your company, for now that I think on it, I do not believe I would have been comfortable giving my opinion of Lady Chiltingham's servant had I been with either Mr. Wooding or Mr. Keymer."

"I will take that as a supreme compliment."

"I suppose it is. Oh, look at Mrs. Nutley's man!" She wisely lowered his voice. "He is well muscled also, but much slighter in build and a bit short of bone. If I were to wager, I should wager on him!"

"Indeed?" Captain Ramsdell queried, his brow puckering. "He hasn't nearly the strength of Lady Chiltingham's man."

"But he does not need so much strength to win a race, as speed."

Captain Ramsdell grunted. "We shall see," he muttered.

"Oh, dear!" she cried. "I see what it is. You wagered on Lady Chiltingham's servant, did you not?"

"Yes," he muttered.

"And already you know I am right."

"I know no such thing," he countered readily.

Katherine was bumped slightly from behind and

turned to find that a man selling slingshots and other toys to children had been so surrounded by his patrons that he had accidentally collided with her.

"Beg yer pardon, miss," he said, tipping his hat.

Katherine could only smile at the urchins clamoring for his wares. "You are making them very happy," she said kindly as the man bowed to her and moved away, his crowd of children following him eagerly, each demanding to be shown the handmade toys which he carried suspended on the front of his long black coat.

Evan called her attention to the Steyne. "The race is ready to begin," he said.

Katherine turned just in time to watch the starter lift his arm in the air and fire his pistol. The race would require a few minutes' time, since the length had been tripled. The men would run to the finish line, back to the starting line and once more to the finish line, a total of 225 yards.

By the time the men returned to the starting line, Mrs. Nutley's servant had the lead by several yards. The air was full of riotous shouting. Katherine leaned over and into Evan's ear cried, "You should have consulted with me before placing your bet. I recommend you do so next time!"

He merely scowled playfully upon her and watched with some interest as the men ran the remainder of the course. The black runner gained ground toward the end, which caused Evan to shout his own encouragement into the already noise-laden air. In the end, however, Mrs. Nutley's man won, but only by little more than two yards.

Evan groaned his disappointment as did many others. He took his loss with reasonably good grace and only complained of it a half-dozen times. Katherine remained silent on the subject, though he did glare at her, undoubtedly because she had assumed her most triumphant expression.

After a time, as a number of boys were lining up at

the starting line, their legs planted in heavy burlap sacks, Evan suggested they remove to another location in order to view the absurdity of the sack races nearer to the finish line.

Katherine agreed readily. However, she had not advanced very far when the loud cacophony of lit firecrackers struck the air, quite near to her. She cried out as did many others and hastily moved away from the sound for fear that her gown might catch fire. She was not the only one with such a thought and felt herself shoved and struck as others began pushing in her direction.

The firecrackers had been lit so close to her that her ears began to ring. The screams and shouts which came to her were oddly muffled.

Evan caught her arm. "Are you all right? Are you injured?"

"I am perfectly well," she returned, nodding, "except for my ears and perhaps a little bruising."

"Something has happened, Katherine. I detest leaving you at this moment, but I must." By this time, Mr. Keymer was beside him, urging him away.

Another round of lit firecrackers exploded some twenty yards to the south.

"Where is Lydia?" Katherine cried.

Keymer shouted above the noise, "I left her some minutes ago with her mother."

Evan gripped her arm. "Are you certain you are all right?"

Again she nodded. Though she felt far from well, she could see that the men were desperate to be going. "Perfectly. I shall look for Lydia. Go. Everything will be all right."

"Very well." He seemed wholly reluctant to go, but she knew he must and gave him a tremulous, encouraging smile.

A moment later, he slipped beneath the ropes and

dashed across the sward in the direction of the Prince Regent. She turned in a circle as the ropes broke and people began to pour onto the field. She looked across the Steyne and saw that there was an equal degree of chaos surrounding the Prince, who no longer wore his hat.

She was not certain just what she should do. She felt greatly distressed. People were running and shouting in every possible direction, and she could see a group of boys escaping at a hard run toward Castle Square. The crowd still pressed close to her. A man bumped her, striking her thigh so hard that she exclaimed at the sharpness of the impact. She met his gaze briefly and recognized the toy seller. He begged pardon quite hastily, then moved away, limping. He, too, must have been hurt, but she wished he had not collided with her, for she would surely have a bad bruise on her thigh. Others around her were complaining of having been hurt. Nearby, she noted that Mr. Wooding was clasping Miss Page to his chest, his expression one of deep concern.

Katherine began moving slowly in their direction. She was afraid of getting hit again, her thigh hurt, and she was still not hearing very well at all.

Miss Page was weeping. Mr. Lunsford was on his knees, and blood was pouring from a cut on his head. Katherine felt ill. Her head hurt. She knew she had to get back to West Street. She watched Mr. Wooding release Miss Page and assist his cousin to rise to his feet. She felt she should help him somehow and withdrew a kerchief from her reticule. She felt queasy.

Miss Page espied her, blinked and cried out. "Your nose. It is bleeding!"

Katherine touched her nose with her kerchief and indeed found blood on the white cambric. She carefully pressed the kerchief to her nose. "What happened?" she queried. "Can you see Captain Ramsdell?"

"Yes, he is with the Prince," Mr. Wooding said. "Did he desert you?"

"Not until he ascertained I was well."

"But you are not well," he stated severely. "He should not have left your side."

Katherine could scarcely think clearly. "He was under some manner of obligation," she responded. Not wishing to argue further with Mr. Wooding, she addressed Mr. Lunsford. "Are you all right?"

"Yes, tolerably." He had his own kerchief pressed to his head. "I was knocked down in all the confusion. I must have hit my head on a stone or something equally as sharp. I feel a lump forming, I fear."

"Come," Mr. Wooding commanded all of them. "My coach is nearby. I shall escort each of you home."

Katherine hesitated. "I only wish I knew what happened to Lydia and Mrs. Alistair."

"I see them both!" Miss Page cried. "They are standing near the Regent's party, as are Mr. Keymer and Captain Ramsdell. Do but look! His Royal Highness's servants are helping the Prince into his sedan chair. I wonder if he was wounded in all the excitement."

Katherine watched the group gathered about the Regent, her thoughts settling on the absence of his hat. *He must have been fired upon,* came to her abruptly. A chill went through her, as though she had known it was true all along. She thought back to the exact moment the firecrackers exploded. She could now recall that in the midst of the noise there had been a shot fired, and so very near her!

She glanced at the departing crowds, realizing she had stood very near the one who had fired a pistol. However, the knowledge of what had happened occurred too late for her to attempt to identify those who were close to her at the time.

Her head began to pound suddenly, though her nose had at last stopped bleeding.

"Come, Miss Pamberley," Mr. Wooding said gently, taking up her arm. "I must—and I will—get you home."

"Thank you," she murmured, holding his arm gratefully.

After making certain Miss Page was properly attached to his other arm, he slowly escorted the small party to his waiting coach.

Katherine spent the remainder of the day and the evening resting in her bedchamber, suffering from a severe headache. Mrs. Alistair's physician had examined her and pronounced her to be suffering the ill effects of having had a loud noise discharged so close to her. She asked after the Regent and learned that it was true, someone had tried to shoot him, for there was a hole in his fine hat, pierced straight through.

Both Mrs. Alistair and Lydia, equally shaken by the horrid nature of the event, had remained quietly at home as well.

By the following morning, Katherine was much improved, though a certain anxiety had taken hold of her. Brighton no longer seemed so safe and comfortable as it had been. She longed to speak with Evan, hoping that he might be able to assuage her concerns, and looked forward to the evening when she knew she would be seeing him at the Pavilion for dinner.

Because she was feeling a great deal better, Katherine began her morning by taking part in her most favorite activity—sea-bathing. She was certain the salt-laden air, the sea mist, the shock of the water and the tug of the tides would be precisely what she needed to be fully restored to her usual buoyance. She even indulged in a little swimming while her maid sat on the top step of the wagon and chatted contentedly with the dipper. Lydia, decidedly overset by the entire episode, remained in West Street.

The waves were negligible, and she swam just past the breakers that she might float on her back, the yellow flannel ballooning up about her in a series of air pockets that made her look like an upside-down turtle. The sun was still off to the east and not yet powerful enough to singe her vision so that she could let her gaze drift into the deep blue sky. Seagulls streaked the wide expanse, vying for the largess of the sea, swooping and dipping with great wheeling cries.

After several minutes of drifting rather aimlessly in the calm swells of the sea, she heard the dipper call to her. She wondered with a start if she had perhaps drifted too far out, but upon taking her bearings she could see she was not. She chanced to glance down at her stomach, however, and rose up in the water with a sudden disgust as she kept herself afloat with gentle kicks of her legs and strokes of her arms.

A fine layer of coal dust was covering the yellow flannel of her bathing gown as well as all parts of her exposed skin. Her hands were dotted with black flecks. She glanced about and saw that several coal brigs had arrived and were discharging their cargoes. How it came about that the place generally set apart for the ladies to bathe, below the cliffs between West Street and Middle Street, was also the same location for the unloading of coal, she could not imagine.

She began swimming toward her machine and found her dipper smiling but apologetic. "I do be that sorry, miss. Ye seemed quite content, and I thought to warn ye a trifle too late."

"It does not signify, Mrs. Berry. Do not trouble yourself. If I recall, the last time the brigs were present, there was hardly a mite of coal in the water."

"Aye, there was not. Will ye be needing the machine on Monday? The coal should be gone by then."

Katherine nodded. Mrs. Berry knew her habits—that she would attend church tomorrow morning and leave off sea-bathing until Monday. Once in the machine, she did her best to remove what coal flakes she could, but to little avail. She realized she would have to bathe completely when she returned to West Street, including the washing of her hair. She groaned, for that meant, besides missing all the pleasures of the day, she would also have to postpone her trip to Hannington's at which time she meant to order the fabric for the young girls from the workhouse. She would be dining at the Pavilion, and the meal was served promptly at six o'clock.

When she reached her bedchamber, she found two billets awaiting her, one from Mr. Keymer and one from Evan. She opened the latter first and read in the scant few lines his apologies, again, for having deserted her on the Steyne, but he had seen at once that the Prince was in some danger.

And not from firecrackers, she thought.

Katherine felt quite ill suddenly. The memory of the firecrackers erupting near her returned in full force, and through the images which struck her, she could hear the sharp retort of the pistol again, quite near her head.

The assassin, she now realized, had been standing somewhere behind her!

Katherine had never before felt so close to fainting. Fortunately, the bed was within reach, and she sat down on the edge. Her temples were pounding. She took several deep breaths and was not at first able to respond to a scratching on the door.

Lydia peeked her head in, smiling at first, then opened her eyes in horror. "Whatever is the matter!" she cried. "You look quite ill! I shall fetch the doctor—"

"No!" Katherine cried out. "I am merely feeling a little faint. Would you bring me a small glass of sherry? And pray, Lydia, say nothing to your mother nor to the servants, I beg you."

"Shall I send for your maid?"

She shook her head. "It is not necessary, for she will

be here any moment. She is at present preparing my bath."

"I will not be gone but a minute or two," Lydia said.

Katherine moved to the window and opened it wide, for she was in desperate need of fresh air. Very soon, the entire chamber was flooded with a soothing breeze, and the sensation of swooning disappeared quickly.

Lydia returned and handed her a glass of sherry which was full to the brim, a circumstance which made Katherine laugh.

"You *must* have been worried about me!" she cried.

Lydia smiled and settled herself on the edge of the bed opposite her. "Very," she said.

Katherine seated herself on the chaise longue and sipped the sherry. She then explained to Lydia about the pistol and her belief that it had been fired very near to her. "In the midst of the explosion of fireworks undoubtedly to mask the sound, which must account for why I had the headache so severely yesterday. I can now recall hearing the shot from just behind me when it was fired."

"You could have been killed!" Lydia cried, her eyes wide.

"I might at that," she said. Katherine again sipped the sherry.

"I cannot believe someone attempted to harm Prinny!" Lydia cried.

"It is truly horrible," Katherine responded.

Lydia nodded several times in agreement and afterward scanned Katherine's face carefully. "I know this is perhaps not the time to mention it, but do you know you are covered in very small black dots?"

Katherine began to laugh and could not stop. After a time, she said, "The coal brigs arrived while I was seabathing and my dipper did not warn me in time. I do not blame her, for the last time the brigs came, there was hardly a speck of coal in the water."

"Who are your letters from?" Lydia queried, gesturing to the two missives lying on the bed beside her.

"The one I have opened is from Captain Ramsdell. He apologized for having left my side yesterday. The other is from Mr. Keymer."

"Mr. Keymer?" Lydia asked, her complexion paling.

"Yes," she said, "though I cannot imagine why he felt compelled to send me a billet, but if you will hand it to me, then we both might discover why he has done so."

"Of course," Lydia murmured, handing her the missive.

Katherine read the contents with surprise, for Mr. Keymer was requesting two dances for Monday night, the first set, at the weekly Castle Inn Assemblies. She thought it odd and said so.

"I am not surprised," Lydia said, frowning slightly. "You see, Mama told me she had asked him to request the dances of you."

"Whatever for?" Katherine asked.

Lydia sighed. "Mama means for you to wed Mr. Keymer."

"What!" she exclaimed, laughing. "But I do not love Mr. Keymer. When . . . how did she come by such a notion?"

"I do not know precisely. But she has seen you together and somehow concluded you would suit very well. She said he has an excellent portion as a third son of a wealthy baronet, and of course his connections to the Duke of Relhan as his secretary give him the *entrée* into the first circles. She does not think you could do better than to marry a man of his position."

Katherine was a little surprised that Lydia seemed so sad as she related her mother's hopes. She wondered if it was possible her friend had indeed tumbled into love.

Whatever the case, she could at least relieve Lydia on one score. "Mr. Keymer is a fine man and I do enjoy conversing with him, but I could never love him in a truly romantical sense, and I certainly have no intention of marrying him. In fact, I do not know that I mean to marry anyone. Now that I think on it, I realize I am quite content as I am."

"Are you certain?" Lydia asked, her brow puckered. "He would make you a most amiable husband."

At that Katherine laughed. "I do not want an amiable husband. I do not want a husband at all. I am even considering taking a house of my own in the next few months."

"Here in Brighton?" she asked, shocked.

"Why not?" she asked.

"Because it is not done!" Lydia cried. "You are not married!"

"I could hire a companion," she said. "Someone of estimable reputation to lend me the proper countenance."

Lydia stared at her for a long moment. "What of Captain Ramsdell? I think you should marry him."

"Why do you say that?" she asked, stunned.

"Because, no matter what you say, I believe you are in love with him."

"Nonsense. We . . . we are very different people, too different to be entirely comfortable together. Besides, I suspect he has no intention of marrying . . . ever."

Lydia nodded. "That is what Mr. Keymer said of him."

"Indeed. And he told you as much?"

"Yes," Lydia answered simply.

Katherine found herself surprised at the level of intimacy Mr. Keymer and Lydia presently enjoyed. She felt a terrible unease about it. If Lydia was indeed falling in love with Mr. Keymer, Katherine knew she would not find the support she needed from her mother. Mrs. Alistair had made her wishes known to her daughter since time out of mind: She was to wed a peer and nothing less!

Since two of the undermaids arrived carrying buckets of hot water, and the footman followed with a large tub for bathing, Lydia let the subject rest. She left the chamber with a profession of hope that Katherine's hair would be dry enough to curl sufficiently for the evening at the Marine Pavilion.

A half hour before six o'clock, Katherine stood beside Mr. Nutley in the long corridor of the Marine Pavilion, wafting her fan over her features. Her hair had indeed dried properly and her curls were coiffed to perfection.

Mr. Nutley tugged at his right shirt point. "This place is always dreadfully hot. Can scarcely abide being here. And what was Prinny thinking to have concocted such a design for the hall? I am perfectly mystified."

Katherine felt she had something of an answer and so took his arm. "Mr. Nutley, if you will escort me down the length of the corridor, I shall tell you a story."

Mr. Nutley offered his arm most willingly. "I should be obliged to you," he said, "for then I might forget this heat for a moment."

Katherine viewed the sheen of perspiration on his brow and pitied him. She did not hesitate, therefore, to launch into her story in order that she might offer him some diversion from his obvious suffering. "Many, many years ago there was a young gentleman of excellent family, fortune and breeding. He was an extremely affable young man with a fine mind given to imagining a long trip about the world in which he might captain a ship. Unfortunately for him, he was the eldest son, one of many sons, and had responsibilities exclusively to his father's estate, for he was heir and would one day command the whole of it. His father, if you must know, was a hard man. A good man, but a hard man.

"Day after day the young man repined his lot, wishing that he could be aboard his ship, that he could be anywhere but under the yoke of his demanding parent. He begged his father several times to permit him to make at least one trip around the world that he might see for himself the tobacco fields of Virginia, the vast sugar plantations of the West Indies, the verdant coasts of Africa, the elephants and tigers of India, the spices of the East Indies and most especially the far-off palaces of the Chinese emperors.

"His father forbade the desired trip and, what was worse, fell under the exigencies of a long and debilitating illness, so that even if he had been allowed to go, now it was an impossiblity.

"The young man could have fallen into a decline, so disheartened was he that his life would never be what he wished it to be, but the day he came of age and found that he could run up any number of tradesmen's bills without the least repercussion, he built a temple in a corner of his father's estate, much resembling the palaces of India. In this temple, he did not limit his imagination in the least, but selected his decor based on all the hindered dreams of his youth, even going so far as to transform much of the inside of the temple into a complete reflection of China. He began to collect furniture of bamboo, much like this chest here." She gestured to an imitation bamboo cabinet. "And he adorned the walls of this temple with a fine linen upon which was painted a ground of delicate peach blossoms, decorated in a lovely pale shade of blue with trees, rocks, birds and shrubs all in the manner of the Oriental, just as these walls are decorated in the very same fashion." She gestured in a wide sweep of her arms to the walls running the entire length of the corridor.

"He collected several Chinese figures similar to the ones in the various niches we have passed, and he pretended he had come to know the people they represent in the course of his journeys.

"He retired to his temple every summer, after his duties had been fulfilled over the course of the year, where he was fully restored to his agreeable temper so that he could go on being his father's son."

Mr. Nutley patted her arm. "I know what you are about, m'dear, and I begin to have some compassion."

Katherine was silent apace as she walked sedately beside Mr. Nutley. The Chinese Gallery was over one hundred feet long. "And what is it you wished you could have always done in your life?"

He chuckled and leaned close to her. "I should have enjoyed being Mr. White and opening up a club in London and one here in Brighthelmstone, just as Mr. White has."

"But, Mr. Nutley, you did open your own club," Katherine exclaimed. "For I have seen it myself and even assisted the gentlemen in playing at hazard a few nights past."

He laughed outright. "So you did," he said. "And so did I." He paused before a fireplace which had the appearance of being made of bamboo. He approached it with a heavy scowl on his face. "Damme, but if this don't look like the real thing!" He rapped on the chimneypiece, which resounded oddly. "What do you know!" he cried, turning to stare round-eyed at her. "I vow it is made of iron or brass or some such thing, yet it looks just like bamboo."

From behind her, Katherine heard a strong voice say, "It is excellent workmanship, is it not, Mr. Nutley?"

Katherine whirled around and found herself staring into the face of the Prince Regent himself. She glanced down the length of the hall and could tell by the expressions of the Prince's other guests that she and Mr. Nutley had been followed by His Royal Highness for some time.

"Oh, Your Royal Highness!" she cried. "I hope I have said nothing untoward which has caused you to be offended. If I have, I am deeply apologetic. I . . . I was merely attempting to entertain Mr. Nutley." Oh, dear! She felt her cheeks grow quite warm.

He offered his arm to her with a warm smile but addressed her companion. "Mr. Nutley, you will forgive me if I detach Miss Pamberley from your side."

Mr. Nutley offered his best bow.

Katherine took the Prince's arm. "Pray tell me I have not offended you."

"On the contrary," he responded in his agreeable manner, but continued to address both her and Mr. Nutley. "You have explained me exactly, but however did you manage to discover it, I wonder, particularly being such a *young* lady as you are?"

She was deeply embarrassed but summoned courage to give him a reasonable answer. "I looked about me and was reminded of my life in the stables at Lady Brook Cottage. I created my own world when the one I had been brought into was shattered by the death of my father. I believe I recognized, reflected in your home, the same deep desire to be anywhere other than where I was. I truly adore your Pavilion for that reason, since it reminds me of how I spent my youth and survived so many unhappy days."

"You honor me with your confidences," he said. "Not many do, you know." He turned to Mr. Nutley. "Do you indeed wish to be as Mr. White? You would make an excellent proprietor of a gentlemen's club. Should you ever take the notion into your head, I shall be your first member."

Mr. Nutley smiled broadly and once again bowed quite low. "I am indebted," he responded in his simple, direct manner.

"And now, I hope you will not take it amiss that I escort Miss Pamberley the length of the corridor, for I am longing to hear more of her story about this intriguing young gentleman."

She had not traversed many steps when she met Evan's gaze. She had conversed with him but briefly upon arriving at the Pavilion. Though she had desired to speak to him of the events of the day before, she had recognized in Mr. Nutley a soul in need of some relief and had excused herself to attend to the older gentleman, whose wife had been deep in gossip with Lady Chiltingham and Mrs. Framfield.

What she saw in Evan's expression now surprised her, for he was regarding her from eyes filled with something akin to admiration, certainly approval. The experience was so novel that she might have spent the next ten minutes considering precisely what he meant by it, had not her attention been entirely grasped by the Regent. He led her to the central division of the long gallery, which was surrounded by a Chinese canopy in trelliswork of imitation bamboo. The ceiling was an enormous panel of stained glass to which he directed her attention. The dimensions appeared to Katherine to be about twenty feet in length by ten or eleven in width.

"There, you see the figure above?"

"Yes, quite magnificent. Whoever is he?"

"Lin-Shin, the God of Thunder. Do you see his drums, and there in his right hand is a mace which he uses to strike the drums and bring the thunder down from heaven."

"Not unlike our Zeus," Katherine said.

"Precisely. Every culture must have some explanation for the roll of thunder."

"I love that it rests here, in the center of the corridor, as though the very heart of your house is filled with thunder if only one could hear it."

"I daresay you hear it."

She met his gaze with something close to awe. "I do hear it in the same way that when I am dashing across the downs the thunder of my horse's hooves fill my heart with exhilaration."

"We are kindred spirits," he announced suddenly.

"I would not know about that. However, I do appreciate your home so very much. When I am here, I feel as though all the bad parts of my life have been laid to rest and the future is opened up wide to me."

"What do you see in your future?"

She shook her head. "Only that were I to dream the largest dream I could, that it would come true—at least, that is how I feel when I am in your Pavilion. Now, when I awaken in my bed in the morning after having been enchanted by your home, my dreams do not seem either very large or very real, but I am always happy."

"I shall have dreams tonight, Miss Pamberley, of ocean voyages, I think. I used to have such dreams when I was young."

Eight

The Regent soon left her side in order to pay his courtesies to the other guests present. Katherine watched him go, marveling at his ability to make even an insignificant young lady from Berkshire feel as important as the sun. She did not have a great deal of time to reflect on her conversation with him, however, for she was quickly descended upon by several ladies desiring to know what she had said to Mr. Nutley that had caused the Regent to follow them down the *entire length* of the hallway. She only laughed and said she would answer no questions tonight, but might be prevailed upon to do so after church on the morrow.

However, when Evan partnered her in the procession entering the banqueting hall, she could not help revealing something of what was said. "The whole of it was ridiculous, indeed it was," she whispered. "I was telling Mr. Nutley a fable, as it were, the story of a man who wished he could go on a voyage about the world but whose father insisted he remain on his estate that he might learn to care for his inheritance."

"You were speaking of the Prince, then?"

"I was."

"I will tell you this much, Katherine. He did not appear in the least offended. On the contrary, he gave every indication of being vastly amused and more than once nodded to the rest of his guests as if in complete agreement with what you were saying."

"He is a very kind man, much more tolerant than one might be led to believe. If he has given himself to creating a unique world of his own, I do not believe one could find fault with his purposes."

"Yet his tastes are excessive. You must admit as much."

"I will not argue with you on that score," she said, keeping her voice low. "I was only attempting to explain his extravagance, not to justify it."

She glanced at Evan and saw that he was regarding her as he had done earlier, as though trying to make her out, yet all the while there seemed to be a gleam of admiration in his eyes. She found herself curious. "What are you thinking?" she asked.

"That you have surprised me," he said, smiling, "more than once since my arrival in Brighton. I wish you to know that you are a very noble and gentle woman, Katherine Pamberley, and I am happy to call you my friend."

"Captain Ramsdell," she returned, addressing him formally but with a smile, "I vow that is by far the loveliest compliment I have ever received, and I proclaim even now that if you continue in this mode I might even begin to like you."

At that he burst out laughing, which set several pairs of eyes turning back to frown upon them as one by one each guest was seated at the Prince's table.

Katherine had dined at the Marine Pavilion before, but she doubted she would ever become accustomed to the enormous dragon and equally large lustre which was suspended over the table. The clawed, winged beast was colored a magnificent glimmering green and silver, its feet supporting a ring which held what she understood to be an entire ton of metal and glass. The lustre was a full thirty feet in height, twelve feet in width, and appeared to be covered with pearls, rubies and diamonds.

Dragons were represented everywhere in the chamber. Flying dragons supported the gold and crimson draperies on the east windows; a number of tall candelabra, several feet in height, sported dragons descending the columnar portion of the base, each candelabrum topped by a lotus flower whose stems were entwined with golden dragons. Nearer to the ceiling, in small, arched sections of stained glass, various dragons, also golden in color, were displayed. Each of the four doorways to the banqueting room was flanked with columns that supported two finely carved dragons. Katherine had heard on her first visit several weeks past that these last dragons were made of solid gold!

She found herself overwhelmed by the sheer opulence of the chamber. She wondered in some amusement what her own fantasies might have become had she sought them with unlimited funds as the Regent had done. Perhaps she might have had a horse stable erected of even greater magnificence than the Prince's nearby Rotunda, which was nearly as large a structure as the Pavilion proper.

She smiled at her thoughts and only left them when she became aware that Mr. Nutley, seated opposite her, desired to take a glass of wine with her. She lifted her glass to him, the rich claret swirling in her goblet as she inclined her head to him and took the remainder of the glass, which was the custom. Afterward, she gave herself to the enjoyment of the meal, as well as lifting and draining her glass of wine, with three others during the course of the dinner.

In the end, she left the table feeling drowsy, replete and a trifle giddy.

Later, while the assemblage was gathered in the Red Saloon, Katherine strolled about the large chamber on Evan's arm. She was happy for the opportunity to speak with him about the events of the day before. In particular, she told him that she could recall the sound just behind her of a pistol being fired at the same moment the fire-crackers were exploding.

"Is this indeed true?" he asked, his expression sober-ing.

"Yes. I am certain I heard a pistol shot." Her words, even to her own ears, sounded if not slurred then a little lazy.

"Did you see anyone who might have been the cul-prit?"

She shook her head. "Everything happened so quickly. The crowds began screaming and pushing. I was shoved past counting, and my head began to ring alarmingly. I truly cannot say that anyone nearby struck me as villain-ous."

He led her to a quiet place near the doorway and looked down at her with a rather content smile.

"Why are you smiling?"

"I believe you had some wine this evening."

At that, she giggled. "I lifted my glass far too many times. Am I half foxed?"

"No, just rather relaxed."

"Yes. It is a pleasant sensation." She glanced about the chamber and noticed the Prince speaking with Lady Chiltingham. Her thoughts were drawn back to the events of the day before. "Do you believe, then, that it was a plot of some sort, against the Regent I mean, and that the boys who lit the firecrackers were involved?"

Evan's gaze drifted to His Royal Highness as well. "Not necessarily involved. It would seem the boys had been merely engaged in a little devilry. Though I was not privy to the questioning of them, I have since been informed that the eldest was given the firecrackers by a man he could only describe in the most innocuous of terms—his height average, his hair black, his features plain."

"There must be a thousand men of such a description

in Brighton, not to mention strangers traveling through on the road to Lewes."

"Precisely."

"And the firecrackers were given to the boys on the very day of the races?" she queried.

"Yes."

"So it would seem that someone calculated the likelihood that such a group of daring fellows would take delight in setting them off in a crowd, and the man who provided the firecrackers simply followed them, believing his opportunity would soon follow."

"I believe the scheme worked to perfection, and had the assassin been a better shot, we should not be sitting here tonight discussing the matter and drinking to the health of our future sovereign."

"All of Brighton would be in mourning, I daresay, not just for the present, but for years to come. I believe that had the Regent not made Brighton his summer and fall residence, this town would still be a rather small, insignificant fishing village."

"Undoubtedly you are right. However, there is nothing more to be done about these hapless events. Would you care to take a turn about the Chinese Gallery with me, or do you reserve that particular amusement for Mr. Nutley alone?"

Katherine chuckled and once more took his proffered arm. Upon entering the corridor, she noted that only Mr. Wooding was present, standing by the staircase. He informed them both that he was awaiting Miss Page, who had yet to return from the ladies' retiring room upstairs.

Katherine felt Captain Ramsdell stiffen slightly and wondered yet again why he had taken such a dislike of Mr. Wooding. Katherine addressed the very subject she and the captain had been discussing a few minutes past. "What do you think of the near-assassination of our Prince?" she asked quietly.

"I was never more horrified," he said, appearing perfectly sincere. "The sudden eruption of the firecrackers was bad enough, but to have since learned that someone had fired a pistol at His Royal Highness at the very same moment was beyond bearing. I have thought of little else since."

"I have experienced something very similar, but I would like to thank you for helping all of us on Friday. You were most kind."

"You are not suffering overly much now, are you?" he queried. His glance slid to Evan and contained a rather hard, critical stare. Katherine thought she understood why.

"No, not a bit. I went sea-bathing this morning, though I must confess I was rather covered in coal dust by the time I emerged from the waves."

Mr. Wooding chuckled. "It is an extremely unfortunate circumstance that the ladies must bathe where the coal is discharged."

"I could not agree more. Only, tell me, how does your cousin Mr. Lunsford fare? His cut did not seem too severe. I trust that much was true?"

"I took him to North Street, to the Brighton and Hove Dispensary which is become part of the Sussex General Infirmary. Do you know it? It is located at the corner of Salmon Court, opposite Ship Street."

Katherine nodded, for Mrs. Alistair had pointed it out to her during an excursion on one of her first days in Brighthelmstone.

Mr. Wooding continued, "The good doctor applied a sticking plaster and suggested Mr. Lunsford drink a healthy draught of brandy and lie upon his bed for a day or two. I can assure you that though the brandy did not sound half onerous to him, the notion of having to kick his heels for even two days together, lying upon his bed, did not suit my cousin by half. He would rather be occupied than lying abed, regardless the reason."

"I comprehend him perfectly," Katherine said with a smile.

At that moment, Miss Page descended the stairs, drawing Katherine's eye to the banister, which had been created in a stunning mock bamboo of welded wrought iron.

"Miss Pamberley!" she called out. "What excitement you gave us this evening when His Royal Highness actually attended so intently to your conversation with Mr. Nutley."

"Do not remind me. I was greatly mortified."

"I wish that he might pay such an attention to me. Alas, I am generally bereft of anything interesting to say."

"Nonsense!" Mr. Wooding cried, taking up her defense immediately. "I am never bored in your company."

"Now you are being wholly chivalrous, and I will thank you, Mr. Wooding."

Captain Ramsdell addressed Miss Page. "You would do well to follow Miss Pamberley's lead," he said, "and begin reading the newspapers every morning at Fisher's that you might become better informed. Then you would have no reason to doubt your ability to please in public."

Katherine was a little astonished, and wondered how Miss Page would manage what Katherine felt to be an officious suggestion on Evan's part.

The young lady, however, merely trilled her laughter. "I am far too stupid, Captain, to make any sense of the newspapers, as you very well know. Besides, I had much rather hear Mr. Wooding's account of what he has read. He is a great reader, you know. However, I must tell you that I cannot delay returning to the Red Saloon a moment longer, for I have been given to understand that Lady Chiltingham wishes to hear me play the Mozart again and so I mean to oblige her. The servants are just now moving the pianoforte into the room."

"Why is not everyone adjourning to the Music Room?" Evan asked.

"The ladies requested of the Prince to keep the atmosphere a little more intimate, the Music Room being so very grand. Besides, I am completely undone by the thought of my poor fingers trying to execute the music to such an extent that it actually reaches the dome of that ceiling! No, no! I much prefer the saloon."

Evan bowed to her and permitted Mr. Wooding to escort her to Lady Chiltingham. Katherine moved as if to follow, but Evan stayed her with a light touch on her arm.

When the couple had disappeared into the saloon, he was still watching the doorway through which Miss Page had disappeared. "I have tried to discourage her from accepting his advances, but she seems intent on keeping his company a great deal more assiduously than I should like."

"You are not her father," Katherine countered forcefully, the wine emboldening her. "Mr. Page is residing in Brighton. He ought to tend to her concerns, not have you scowling down upon her every word or upon every friend she chances to make."

"Mr. Wooding is no true friend to Miss Page."

Katherine felt irritated all over again. "You do him an injustice. Besides, he was not particularly enamored of your conduct yesterday. He had much to say on the subject."

"I am all agog to know in what way he disapproves of me," he said facetiously. At the same time, he drew her more deeply down the corridor, away from the saloon. Night had fallen so that the hall was no longer illuminated through the dragonesque skylight.

Katherine felt compelled to continue, "If you must know, Mr. Wooding was horrified that you had quit my side when I was obviously unwell."

At that, Evan patted her arm. "I detested leaving you as I did, so in this I must agree with your friend."

Katherine turned to look up at him. "You did?" she asked, her voice softening.

"Of course I did," he stated, meeting her gaze with a frown. "I abandoned you in the middle of a crowd. Had the situation not involved the Prince, nothing could have separated me from you at that moment."

Katherine felt very strange all the way to her toes, as though the wine had begun to affect her after all.

Evan led her just past the central division, where a narrow band of iron trelliswork divided the chamber. He turned toward her rather suddenly, and Katherine found that her back was nearly touching the wall. This section of the long corridor was quite dark, since the sun had so recently set and only the central lustre had been lit. The band of trelliswork partially obscured her view of the saloon doors.

"Will you forgive me, Katherine," he murmured, his blue eyes glittering in the dusky light of the hall.

There was just such a timbre in his voice which gave Katherine pause. "Of course," she whispered. Why was she whispering? If only her head were a little clearer, for a small warning resounded deep in her mind. Evan leaned very close to her. "You smell of heaven, Katherine."

Another warning sounded, but she found she could not move.

He slipped his arm about her waist, and finally she understood. She pressed her hands against his chest. "On no account," she said softly, "may you kiss me again. I have become fond of you, and I do not wish the easy discourse between us to be disturbed by something so fleeting as a kiss."

"But you enjoy my kisses," he whispered against her cheek, still not releasing her. He gentled his arm another inch about her waist. "What harm could there be in one kiss?"

His hand was warm on her waist. Her gloved palms

felt equally so against his chest. "You said you were not going to kiss me again." She sounded very reasonable, but already her hands were sliding up his chest and one of her fingers was actually stroking the angle of his jaw.

"I meant I would not kiss you again unless we were at the Pavilion together," he said in the most wonderfully nonsensical manner. "Katherine, I have been longing to kiss you so. I vow, every time we are in company together, I am tempted." He caught up her hand with his own and kissed her fingers, then very gently began removing her glove. "Tonight I have stolen a moment alone, in the dimmest place of the corridor, in hopes of a little flirtation."

Perhaps Evan had had too much wine at dinner, for he was not making a great deal of sense! Yet he seemed perfectly capable of slipping off her glove one finger at a time.

And she seemed perfectly incapable of refusing him!

It was all the fault of the practice of taking wine in which one was expected to raise a glass and then drink the contents in one gulp.

The glove slipped off her hand entirely.

Katherine tried in vain to force herself to rail at him and complain of his ungentlemanly conduct, but of the moment he had begun nibbling on one of her fingers. "You are a very absurd man," she murmured inattentively.

"I am," he agreed, his lips sliding down the side of her finger.

She knew for a certainty she should insist he cease tormenting her, but not a single word rose to her lips in protest. How very odd! It must be the wine, or maybe it was just Evan and how much she loved his touch, his embraces, his kisses.

He drew closer still, his arm now encircling her waist fully. He quit her finger and began kissing the palm of her hand. Her eyes closed of their own volition as the delight of his assault began to edge away all thoughts of refusal. His tongue made a very wicked circle on the palm of her hand. The sensation, so soft and warm, caused a fire to ignite in her veins. He kissed her wrist, lightly and gently, then proceeded down her arm, again most wickedly, until he reached the very tender crook of her elbow. Such an ugly word, *elbow;* such a daring and teasing sensation to feel his tongue wedged in a place as practical as it was vulnerable.

She did not want him to stop. Ever. And why was she permitting him *such* a liberty?

She could hardly breathe. Her breath came in little gasps. Finally he stopped kissing this most tender part of her arm. He let her arm slide downward through the gentle grasp of his hand and slid his fingers between hers, clasping them firmly. Only then did he capture her lips with his own.

He dragged her hard against him. She felt the length of his muscular legs through the silk of her gown. Her heart beat furiously in her chest. His tongue sought entrance, and she opened her mouth as though begging for him to take possession of her—again!

The entire act—the clasping of her fingers, the tight hold he had on her waist, his demanding tongue—put her in mind of the full act of love. Her mind wandered down uncharted paths. She had never before considered what it would be like to be married, to share her husband's bed. However, there was something about the manner in which Evan surrounded her with desire that brought her to an imaginary place of lying naked against cool bed linens, her hair brushed out about her shoulders, and her body willing to oblige him.

She felt utterly lost as he kissed her more deeply still. She was no longer in the Marine Pavilion, she was in his bed, sinking further and further into a soft feather mattress. He was covering her.

"Katherine," he whispered hoarsely. "I cannot go on kissing you."

She did not want the visions to stop. She had succumbed to his flirtations. She was unwilling to leave this place of beauty and passion.

"Katherine!" he snapped.

She opened her eyes abruptly. Both of his arms were about her and he was supporting her completely. She would have collapsed onto the floor otherwise, in an unladylike heap. She giggled at the very thought of it.

"For a moment I thought you had fainted," he said, his expression worried. "Oh, my dear—you have had too much wine."

It is not the wine, Evan, but you, she thought.

"N-no," she responded slowly. "I was never in danger of that. Evan, for a moment I felt as though we were married and you were . . ."

She broke off as she met his startled gaze. "No, you do not understand. My mind became full of . . . oh, dear. I cannot say these things to you, can I, for they are quite wicked." She felt a blush completely suffuse her cheeks. "What an accomplished flirt you must be to make me even think such things."

"Can you stand?" he asked quietly.

"Of course I can stand," she responded, piqued. He tried to release her, but her knees buckled again. "Perhaps you should lead me to a chair. No, not in that direction. Away from the saloon, for I hear Miss Page playing her Mozart. There is a chair behind you. Yes, that will do nicely."

He lowered her onto the chair but did not choose to take up the seat beside her.

"Here is your glove," he said softly, handing it to her. He walked several feet away from her. In the distance, Katherine could hear a lovely faint melody coming from the Red Saloon. She began carefully to draw on her glove.

She looked at the pale blue birds on the pink walls, feeling disconnected from herself but in the nicest way. She knew that Evan was distressed, but she did not care. She understood now how it came about that so many young ladies succumbed to the caresses of a gentleman without the benefit of matrimony; why Miss Framfield's governess had been turned off without a reference because Miss Framfield's older brother had seduced her and she was with child by him; why Constance, who had so loved Lady Brook, would easily set her home aside to share Lord Ramsdell's home as his wife.

She felt she had been initiated into a world meant only for women. She did not look at Evan, nor did she even wonder at his actions; she could only marvel at how she felt, how awakened she felt to life and to the possibilities of having a home of her own and of sharing her life with a man. She had never contemplated such things before. Now, she wondered with a laugh whether she would ever be able to think of anything else.

"Katherine, I must apologize," he said, interrupting her thoughts. "I can see that I have overset you and certainly gone beyond the pale—"

She lifted a hand and cut him off. "Pray, say nothing more," she said, her voice oddly faint.

He moved toward her and began again. "No, I must tell you that I am deeply apologetic—"

"No, you are not!" she cried, rising to her feet with renewed strength. "You are merely feeling quite guilty, just as you ought, but I tell you it is not necessary for you to say anything. You cannot undo what you have just done, and I do not know if I wish it undone, for you have shown me something about myself and about the world which I was hitherto completely ignorant of, even though you have kissed me before."

He seemed rather dumbfounded. Though he opened his mouth to speak, she stayed him yet again. "No, please, say nothing more. Perhaps we can discuss this tomorrow, if you like, but not tonight. Will you please escort me back to the saloon?"

"Of course," he responded politely.

Evan walked beside Katherine, feeling uncertain for the first time in his existence. She had done this to him, bewitched him in some inexplicable manner, and now he could not rid himself of the feeling that he had just overturned his life, and not in a way that made him the least content.

He had been intent on kissing her tonight from the moment she had begun to stroll down the corridor with Mr. Nutley. She was so beautiful this evening, her hair pulled up into a knot of curls and wound throughout with a narrow scarlet satin ribbon. Her gown was an unusual dark blue silk covered in tulle so that she appeared to be walking in a cloud. She wore pearls and in every respect was a lovely, elegant creature. But it was her kindness to Mr. Nutley, who was clearly suffering because of the pervasive heat of the Pavilion, which he now believed had fixed his desire to possess her mouth again.

He was always one to enjoy a flirtation, even with an innocent. He knew where the bounds were, so why he had kissed her hand and run his tongue over her palm and then assaulted her arm as he had he would never know, except that she had fallen so quickly under his spell. He knew, *he knew,* that had he not been a man of conscience, he could have had his way with her. He could feel that she was utterly given to him, and for a moment he could see himself sharing her bed, naked, covering her and loving her as a *husband.*

That was when he had awakened from the deeply felt kiss, to the reality that he had gone beyond the pale, that he must draw her back from such wretchedly inappropriate conduct, that he must at least attempt to apologize to her. Would he ever forget, though, the passion-drenched expression on her face as he drew back and looked at her? She was so limp, it was humorous that she could not find her feet. It was also extremely seductive. For an instant, he knew the most powerful desire to forget entirely about the severe consequences of such an action, and to make her his wife, if not in fact, then in deed.

That she should marry was a given—the sooner, the better!

But to what man? The very thought of her gathered up in someone else's arms—in Wooding's arms, for instance!—was enough to set his blood to boiling.

Now she walked beside him, her head high, her manner utterly sedate, as though she commanded the world. He could not comprehend what her thoughts might be, particularly since he had expected her to fly into the boughs. He could have managed her then, but this! This command she had was fully incomprehensible to him.

Well, perhaps on the morrow he would call on her and they could discuss the matter rationally.

However, just as he led Katherine across the threshold into the Red Saloon, he heard her murmur rather absently, "I must find me a husband. Indeed, I must."

Nine

On the following morning, Katherine awoke to the sound of a gull's cry. She blinked and shifted her head on the pillow that her gaze might find the window. In the distance, through the white muslin curtains gently shading the windows, a red dawn teased the day. She could hear the surf faintly from her room. Oh, how she loved Brighton!

Her dreams had been so wondrous. She had been transported to a world of great possibilities and extraordinary beauty.

She was changed, deeply so.

She was awakened, to life and all its wonder, in ways beyond comprehension.

She turned on her side and breathed deeply. She took in life with every rise of her chest. She released every tiresome worry as her chest fell. She thought back on Evan's kiss of the night before, and a lethargy stole over her body in successive waves, like the surf rolling in from the deep.

She was caught in the tumble of the surf as she let her mind and heart roll around playfully. She could feel the kiss as though it were happening to her again, the sensation of his lips against her finger and his tongue on her palm, the kisses he sent along her arm, the gentle touch of his tongue in the well of her elbow.

How lost she had become with such tender assaults. She had wished the moment would go on forever.

She felt herself pause in the midst of the memories at the very moment when she began to feel herself in his bed. This was the precise moment which had changed her. She had never before comprehended young ladies who hinted wantonly at such pleasures. Now she did; now she understood why Constance had stolen into the woods with Lord Ramsdell, long before the day of their marriage, when the hour was past midnight and she was certain no one was looking.

Katherine remembered being shocked and utterly bemused. How could Constance, usually so staid and impervious to flirtation of any kind, have actually agreed to so many assignations with Ramsdell?

Now, however, she had begun to comprehend Constance's inability to refuse the man who ultimately conquered her heart.

Would she be able to refuse Evan were he to entice her into a darkened corner again?

She covered her lips with her fingers.

A new fear rose to assert itself, something that spoke of preserving herself, her heart, her soul. If he could command such a kiss from her, he could command other things as well. He could command her to his bed!

She sat up abruptly. To his bed!

On no account would she ever follow a man to his bed without benefit of a ceremony involving a great deal of orange blossoms!

Oh, what horror was this, the knowlege that Evan could ruin her, forever!

She fairly jumped from her bed, the planked floor cool against her bare feet. A chill was in the air, but she had far more difficult matters to contemplate than the gooseflesh which suddenly assailed her arms.

She began to pace. She must think, she must plan. Of primary importance was the fact that she must never be in Evan's company alone again; that much was for certain.

What horror! Oh, what a beast of a man who could engage her in a meaningless flirtation only to fairly seduce her! Yet she had never thought of Evan Ramsdell as a beast. What was he, then? A man who loved a flirtation but who she suspected never intended to marry.

She would refuse to dance with him, particularly the waltz or any country dance that by its nature would bring a couple together holding hands and touching a great deal more than would be at all wise. The quadrille! Yes, she would agree to the quadrille with him, for everyone was so busy minding their steps and keeping to the pattern that not even so accomplished a flirt as Evan Ramsdell could harm her during the quadrille!

What else?

She would never permit him to engage her in private conversation, for that was when she was most vulnerable, when she invariably found herself opening her heart to him, revealing her deepest thoughts. A kiss always seemed but a breath away in such moments!

What else might she do?

She would refuse to stroll with him during the Promenade, for the hour was just prior to evening, and at dusk one could do things that others might not detect—he could squeeze her hand, or run his fingers down the length of her back, or accidentally brush up against her.

Such thoughts were not at all useful, she realized, for she soon began to feel lethargic once more. She flopped down on the bed, clasping her hands across her stomach and staring up at the canopy of blue watered silk. Oh, what a wretched state she was in, for the more she began to contemplate not seeing Evan Ramsdell again, the more she felt weak all over and desirous of nothing else!

A tear suddenly escaped her eye and rolled down the side of her face and into her hair. She pressed the dampness, her fingertips wet. Why was she now weeping? she wondered as a tear escaped her other eye. Oh, dear, why had life suddenly become so wretchedly complicated?

"She has the headache?" Evan queried, watching Miss Alistair's face carefully. "But she appeared well enough in church this morning. Indeed, there was a lovely bloom on her cheeks."

"Yes, I know," Miss Alistair responded, frowning slightly. "The, er, headache came on quite suddenly once we returned. She is laid down upon her bed even now."

"But I heard her giggling only a few moments ago, just before I knocked on your door, and then a flurry of movements as someone running."

A faint color appeared on Miss Alistair's cheeks. "I do not know how that was possible," she said, "when Katherine is laid down upon her bed. Perhaps you heard one of the undermaids." When he continued staring at her, she shifted uneasily on her feet, then added, "She . . . she is burning a pastille even as we speak."

"Katherine Pamberley, burning pastilles?" What nonsense was this?

"Y-yes, of course, and also she has just taken a dose of laudanum, the pain is so severe."

"Laudanum. I see. Then you must convey my condolences as well as my hopes she will recover quickly from her illness."

"I will be happy to give her your message."

He quit West Street uncertain whether Katherine was ill or not. He suspected Miss Alistair had been bamboozling him, yet to what purpose he could not imagine. Why should she desire to prevent him from seeing Katherine, and why would Katherine feign an illness?

Did she truly not wish to see him?

That was the rub. He had behaved so badly the night before that it was only logical she would close her door to him.

He found himself severely disappointed, for he desired above all things to make his apologies to her yet again for his unconscionable conduct at the Pavilion. He still could not credit that he had assaulted her as he had, and she so innocent, yet so wretchedly responsive. He could not remember a time in his life when he had felt so much warmth and yielding in a woman. He had been utterly astonished and had remained so since.

The following evening, he decided to attend the assemblies at the Castle Inn, knowing Katherine never missed an opportunity to dance if she could help it. He was not particularly fond of the weekly balls, but tonight he was unable to restrain himself. Two days had passed since he had kissed Katherine and he had still not received from her the forgiveness he sought. He would not be able to rest until she had exonerated him completely.

When he arrived, he saw her surrounded by nearly a dozen men, a sight which had never met his eyes before. She had always had several admirers, but never a throng as now. Each gentleman seemed to be hanging on her every word, and what was there in her expression and in her eyes that seemed to be a sparkling invitation, intimate and beckoning? He was stunned and something more, something which seemed to be quite possessive. He did not like seeing so many men gathered about her.

I must find me a husband. Indeed, I must.

She had spoken those words at the Pavilion. Was she, then, seeking a husband in earnest?

When Miss Alistair chanced by, he drew up before her and offered a bow. "Well met, Miss Alistair. How do you go on?"

"Oh! Captain Ramsdell! Exceedingly well, thank you." She dipped a nervous curtsy and cast a frightened glance in the direction of Katherine.

He narrowed his eyes. So that was the game. "I see that Miss Pamberley has recovered from the headache."

"Yes, indeed she has."

"Then we must both be grateful that no dire illness followed her recent malady."

"Very grateful," she responded hastily. "Now if you will excuse me, I am promised for the next set to Mr. Keymer."

He prevented her from leaving. "Ah, yes, of course, but I beg you will stay a moment." Here he smiled. "I was hoping you would grant me a waltz this evening, or are all your dances commandeered tonight?"

"Captain," she began with a frown between her brows. "I do not think . . . that is, am not certain . . ." She paused, biting her lip nervously. He wondered if she meant to confess something, for she was appearing rather guilty. "I suppose it would not signify in the least were *I* to dance with you. That is, I have heard you are an exceptional partner and I would be greatly honored were you to waltz with me."

"The honor is mine," he responded with a second bow.

She smiled shyly up at him, then hurried away. He followed her with his gaze for a long moment, wondering what precisely was amiss. Clearly, Miss Alistair had entered into some covenant or other with Katherine, an agreement which involved *him,* but to what purpose?

His gaze drifted to the ballroom floor where he watched Katherine leave her court as Mr. Crispin, who won the donkey race on Friday, led her onto the floor. He was smiling as one besotted. She, in turn, was smiling up into his face as one who had just learned she was the sun and was now shining most happily upon the earth. Evan could not tear his gaze from her.

She wore an azure blue gown, the color of the sea in the bright light of day. Her light brown hair was caught up in waves of curls which cascaded from gold bands in an elegant flow down the back of her head and onto her shoulders. She was all Grecian elegance, and in the movements of the country dance, she performed each sweep of her arms and feet as one who had been destined to dance. Was this truly the creature he had conversed with several times last summer and whose only apparent interest had been her horses? Was this truly the creature with whom he had previously danced, for he had never seen her perform so gracefully before, or had the kiss he had shared with her somehow bewitched his eyes and now he was seeing her anew?

He no longer believed she had had the headache on Sunday. Instinctively, he understood she had been avoiding him. He recalled how distant she had been with him at the Pavilion after he had kissed her, how differently she had behaved toward him the rest of the evening. He had expected her to be nervous or at the very least angry over his conduct. Instead, she had appeared not in the least overset, but rather very much in command.

He watched her now as one mesmerized. He could not drink in enough of the sight of her. He felt odd vibrations in his chest as he watched her. Brighton had changed her somehow. Was Brighton changing him as well?

He had work to do here on his brother's behalf. With a start, he realized he had not made one inquiry to that effect in the past forty-eight hours, even though the Prince had nearly lost his life on Friday. His thoughts had been consumed by Katherine Pamberley. Tomorrow, he would change that.

On the other hand, there was tonight.

The dance ended, and his feet moved as if of their own will. He crossed the room in a straight line toward her. He did not circumnavigate the ballroom floor as would have been proper. His object was clear—he must speak with her, command a dance if he could. However, he was not alone, apparently, in his hopes, for he was but one of several gentlemen who converged on her at the same moment.

She was fanning herself. He could see her profile. She was smiling beatifically upon her court. Her cheeks were rosy from the heat of exertion. A lingering, heady fragrance greeted his nostrils, of roses in a well-tended garden. Why had he not noticed before that she wore oil of roses?

She turned toward him as one in a dream, or perhaps he was dreaming. The noise of the ballroom, all the chatter and the distant tuning of the orchestra's instruments, blended into a strangely pleasant hum. Her lips parted, her smile dimmed a trifle. Something rose in her eyes, not of fear precisely, but a wary quality he had not seen before. He watched her lips form the greeting, "How do you do, Captain?" but the sound of her voice was lost to him. She extended her hand to him and he took it, lifting her fingers to his lips. He felt her resistance and could only kiss the air above her glove. She quickly withdrew her hand.

She turned away from him. "To whom am I promised next?" left her lips so cheerfully he did not at first recognize her voice. She sounded different to him. He had never known her before. Mr. Clarke offered his arm, and suddenly her back was to him, the pleats and gathers of her blue Empire silk gown all that remained to him of the brief encounter.

"I had not noticed her beauty before," Mr. Sawyer stated. "How is that possible?"

Mr. Horsfield grunted. "A fine beauty. Exquisite lines. Only see how she holds her head."

Mr. Kelly joined the ranks. "I heard the Prince is enamored of her. Walked the length of his Chinese Corridor supporting her arm. Who would not tumble in love with such a creature?"

Mr. Crispin, who was mopping his brow, said, "She dances like an angel. I mean to offer for her before the night is out."

"Not before I do," Mr. Horsfield stated suddenly.

Two other gentlemen, unknown to Evan, chimed in with similar intents. There was no mention of dowry or any of the usual discussion in which men engaged while considering the marriageable merits of a lady. Here was a frenzy only to be the man to wed Katherine Pamberley.

Evan moved away from Katherine's court feeling numbed by the encounter. She had seemed indifferent to him, determined to keep him at bay while her court was not merely in pursuit of her attentions and favors but of her hand in marriage as well.

She would undoubtedly marry soon, probably before the end of the summer, just as she now clearly intended.

He turned back momentarily and surveyed her suitors. Which of the men present was worthy of her? he wondered. Who could love her well and care for her? Who did he desire to see lead her to the altar?

He could not say. None of them, by his quick summation. Mr. Horsfield hadn't the bottom to take such a spirited filly to wife. Mr. Sawyer had too many spots. Mr. Crispin rode donkeys, and Mr. Clarke, though wealthy, was already an acknowledged gamester. The rest—oh, what the devil did he care for the rest of these puppies who had collected themselves about Katherine? Not one whit. Let her marry where she would. He had no interest in the matter at all!

He glanced in her direction and felt angry that she had somehow transformed herself into the sort of young lady whose sole intention was to win for herself as many beaux as she could garner in one season, whether spring in London or summer and fall in Brighton. And why the devil had she suddenly become so intent on marrying?

She met his gaze at that moment, as though divining his thoughts. She seemed stunned and then hurt, probably by the severity of his expression. He turned away, chagrined. She had done nothing wrong, nothing to earn his displeasure. He was . . . damme, he was jealous that she had nothing but the air above her fingers for him and that she was all smiles for Mr. Crispin, Mr. Horsfield, Mr. Clarke and the rest of them.

He quit the ballroom in something of a temper. He

was sorry he had requested a waltz of Miss Alistair, for of the moment he desired nothing more than to leave the Castle Inn. For the present, perhaps he would join a card game until Miss Alistair called for him.

Later that evening, Katherine was grateful when the last notes of the quadrille were struck. She dropped into her final curtsy to Mr. Clarke and took up his arm that he might escort her from the ballroom floor. Once again, she was swiftly surrounded by her throng of admirers, yet she found she was not nearly so content as she had been earlier. Evan had approached her, a circumstance which had set her heart to beating so strongly that she had felt close to swooning. She had turned from him as swiftly as possible that he might not know how much his mere presence was affecting her.

She was for a brief time happy that he had left the ballroom, particularly because she could see he disapproved of her conduct in some manner. However, not even fifteen minutes had passed before her gaze returned again and again and again to the entrance to the grand chamber in hopes of catching a glimpse of him. She had tried to curb such a ridiculous impulse, but with only nominal success.

The presence of so many admirers was strange to her and not entirely comfortable. She begged Mr. Horsfield to escort her to the windows overlooking the Pavilion gardens, for she was feeling quite heated from having danced the quadrille. Mr. Horsfield took up the duty as one who had been assigned the rarest treat in all of England. His chest appeared to puff up like a balloon, and further swelled when a round of jealous groans accompanied his victorious smiles.

She fanned herself and let him talk. He was a garrulous man, which was why she had chosen him above the others. She wanted a chance to think and to ponder all that had happened in so short a time while he held forth on whatever topic appealed to him. When she reached the top of the ballroom, she begged Mr. Horsfield to pause for just a moment. "I wish to view the entire length of the chamber. It truly is magnificent, is it not?"

Mr. Horsfield did not follow the line of her gaze but kept his attention pinned to her face. "Quite magnificent," he murmured, his voice hushed, even solemn.

She realized he was speaking about her, but she chose to ignore him for the present. She lifted her gaze instead to the splendid arched ceiling which had been painted to portray the rising sun. Her mind drifted back quite suddenly to Sunday morning when she had awakened at dawn and the sky had been blooming like a red rose. Her thoughts had been entirely of Evan Ramsdell.

But she would not think of him now. She would discipline her mind not to dwell on his most recent kisses and embraces. She would view the decor of the ballroom without thinking of Evan.

She lifted her chin in a determined manner and cast her gaze about. The windows to one side of the chamber overlooked the Steyne, and those on the opposite side, the beautiful gardens of the Marine Pavilion. The walls of the room were hung with extraordinary paintings, some reflecting the story of Psyche and Cupid, others displaying nymphs in the ancient style. Innumerable lustres, along with side-lights and three chandeliers, lit the chamber in a glittering glow. She felt as though she were seeing the room—indeed, all of life—through eyes made entirely new.

"I am so happy," she murmured.

"Indeed, is this so?" Mr. Horsfield cried impatiently, gripping her arm very hard. "Tell me you are happy, that my declaration is the source of such happiness, and I shall in turn be the happiest of men."

Oh, dear.

Katherine turned to look into eyes that were wild with emotion. "I beg your pardon?" she queried. "Oh, Mr.

Horsfield. Do forgive me, but I fear I was not attending to you. I was looking at the ballroom. I was speaking of the beautiful chandeliers, the paintings, the vista of the gardens and the Steyne when I said I was so happy."

The expression which entered his eye was shot through with agony. "Then . . . then my proposals did not fill you with the happiness of which you just spoke?"

She had never before been placed in such a predicament as this, to have received an offer of marriage in a ballroom by a man completely besotted. "You asked for my hand in marriage?" she queried, unable to believe that Mr. Horsfield had actually been speaking his heart to her just now.

"Indeed, I did," he gushed. "I love you quite desperately. I have for some time and I thought—"

She cut him off abruptly. "Mr. Horsfield," she began in a quiet voice. "I do not know how to answer you. I had not expected . . . that is, heretofore you have exhibited a decided preference for Miss Framfield. I am utterly astonished."

"As am I, but you seem so different tonight, or perhaps it is I who am changed. I see you for who you are now, an exquisite woman, a diamond of the first stare, who I desire more than anything to be the mother of my children."

The thought of bearing Mr. Horsfield's children was going a deal too far. She cleared her throat. "Mr. Horsfield, pray say no more, I beg you. This is hardly the place to discuss such things—"

"You are so very right," he interjected, trying to seize both her hands in his.

"Mr. Horsfield!" she cried, twisting her hands out of his grasp. "Please take command of yourself." She glanced about her, certain she was being observed by a score of people, and she was not mistaken. Abruptly she flipped open her fan and began to walk about the perimeter of the floor. He followed her.

"I do beg your pardon," he said in a hushed voice, "but you have driven me to distraction with your excellent character, your beauty and your utter perfection."

"You are speaking nonsensically," she responded, hoping to dampen his ardor even a trifle.

"I know what I see," he murmured, leaning close to her ear.

She drew back and glared at him in a meaningful manner. He merely smiled. "I will call upon Mrs. Alistair in the morning to discuss the marriage contracts."

She paused abruptly and turned to face him squarely. She understood now that her subtle hints were useless. "There will be no marriage contracts, no wedding," she stated. "I cannot marry you, Mr. Horsfield, and though I was previously reluctant to broach the subject in so public a place, your demeanor requires that I speak. I am grateful for your offer, but I cannot, I will not, accept of your hand in marriage. Do you understand me?"

He nodded, his expression rather anxious. "May I at least hope that in time you might consider my proposal?"

Katherine looked into eyes which held an acute anguish and for that reason gave him an obscure answer. "Mr. Horsfield, I have no intention at present of marrying anyone."

He did not seem to know what to say. "Then I may hope," he stated at last.

"You must do what seems best to you." She sought about for an avenue of escape and found one. "Oh, there is Miss Framfield and she is quite without a partner. I beg you will go to her and relieve her of her present embarrassment." When he hesitated, she added, "I would consider such an action a very great favor to me personally."

"Then I shall most certainly oblige you, for I would do anything for you, my dear Miss Pamberley."

With that, he bowed very low and quit her side with a great rush of determination. A moment later, a grateful smile slid over the woebegone features of Miss Framfield.

"That was well done."

Katherine heard Evan's voice behind her. She whirled around and found herself staring into deep blue eyes. How horrible to have been caught completely off guard by him—again, just as she had been earlier. Her heart trembled in her breast.

"I—I was not acting in kindness alone, though I did comprehend Miss Framfield's mortification." Her voice was little more than a whisper and possessed a hoarse quality which surprised her. She could not seem to tear her gaze from his face. She felt as though she were drinking at a deep pool, her throat parched.

"Will you complete your turn about the room with me?" he queried, offering his arm to her.

She knew she should not, that she should make some excuse to him, but none rose to her lips. She took his arm. "Thank you. It is always an awkward thing to be left alone in a ballroom."

"You would not have been left alone for long. I was watching and waiting for an opportunity. I could see Mr. Horsfield had in some manner distressed you, and I suspected it would be but a brief matter of time before you got rid of him. I was not mistaken; only what did he say to you to cause you to send him away?"

"You did not hear everything, then?" she queried.

"No, only your wish that he might be of service to Miss Framfield."

"He offered for me."

"In a ballroom?" Evan cried, disgusted. "What a coxcomb."

"He is no such thing. We were both admiring the beauty of the chamber, and I daresay he was merely overcome with feeling and made his declaration."

"Now you are speaking humbug. He is completely besotted, as are a dozen other halflings present. You have cut a dash, Miss Pamberley. Indeed, you have."

One circuit of the ballroom only, she told herself sternly. Even the feel of his arm beneath her own set her heart to racing and her mind to wandering down forbidden paths.

He was speaking, but as with Mr. Horsfield, she was having difficulty hearing him, only this time it was not the chamber which had distracted her so completely. She was acutely aware of his physical presence beside her.

"So what will you say to me? Will you not give me the answer for which I am hoping?"

The words burst through her thoughts. *Oh, dear.* What had he been saying? Had he proposed to her as well? No, that was impossible.

"I do beg your pardon, Evan, but I am not certain to what you are referring. What question have you posed?"

"Were you not attending?"

She shook her head. "I am having a great deal of trouble in that regard tonight. Something has changed within me. I see everything as with eyes made new." His gaze caught hers and held mightily.

She felt close to swooning all over again!

This was the very thing she had meant to avoid. She would not be able to tear her gaze away from his now. His flirtation had captivated her, his kisses had changed her, he had but to look at her and she was completely lost. How grateful she was that she was in a crowded ballroom, for he could not touch her here. He covered her arm with his hand. His gaze dropped to her lips. His voice was a whisper. "Faith, I would kiss you again if we were not surrounded by so many people—and that is not at all what I meant to say to you! Have you bewitched me, Katherine?"

She swallowed hard. "As to that, I believe you are being ridiculous. But, Evan, you must not kiss me again.

Promise me, You must promise me. I . . . I do not love you, I could never marry you—"

"Miss Pamberley, this is our dance!" a cheerful voice called out.

The spell broke, and Katherine dropped Evan's arm abruptly. Mr. Kelly had come to claim her hand. "So it is," she returned, forcing a smile to her lips. Never in her life had she been so grateful that a set was forming.

"Good evening, Captain," she said formally, taking up Mr. Kelly's arm.

Evan watched her go, frowning deeply, all the way to his soul. Whatever had she meant by saying she could never love him, never marry him? He did not wish her to love him and he had no intention of marrying, yet her words rankled. Why the devil couldn't she love him? Whatever had she meant by saying anything so ridiculous, especially when she so easily fell into his arms?

Not that he desired her to love him. He desired no such thing. No such thing at all!

Ten

On the following day, Tuesday, Evan ignored the powerful need he felt to set his boots in direct and purposeful pursuit of Katherine Pamberley. She had intrigued him terribly last night at the Castle Inn, regarding him in that way of hers as though her soul might come walking out for a stroll were he but to ask. He would have kissed her again, truly he would have, all the while he was apologizing for having kissed her at the Pavilion on Saturday night. How the deuce she had succeeded in bewitching him, he would never know.

However, he had no intention of letting what he knew to be a completely transient sensation dominate his existence, or even his day. For three days now, he had delayed making the inquiries which he knew he must, even though the Prince's men had already thoroughly combed the entire city of Brighton. Keymer had told him last night, after the Castle Inn assemblies, that a single, consistent rumor had surfaced to the effect that whoever had attempted to harm the Prince had acted alone. Those radical groups usually suspect claimed no part in the event.

Evan was in no way certain just how reliable this information was. Regardless, he was intent on avoiding West Street—in particular, inquiring whether Katherine would care to tumble into his arms once more—and instead headed in the direction of Hove, hoping that the smaller village, so near to Brighton, might prove more fruitful.

He rode the short distance to the hamlet on his black horse and stopped at The Ship Inn for a tankard of ale and a long listen. He settled himself into a corner and slowly sipped his ale. He scrutinized every person who entered the establishment, flirted a little with the maid who brought him a plate of cold chicken, asparagus, potatoes and a fine plum cake. Later, he traded his ale for a claret and found that on this occasion he would be able to boast of having enjoyed a fine nuncheon in Hove.

Three hours after his arrival, he had heard little of interest save numerous predictions concerning the forthcoming corn harvest and when the next bull-baiting might take place. He decided, after some consideration, to approach the landlord. He broached the subject with care, posing the question, "Did you hear of the odd circumstance during the races on Friday?"

"Aye," he responded, "I did that. I were shocked. Someone shooting at the Prince when he's all but made Brighton a place of prosperity. Hove prospers as well because of him."

Evan nodded. "Any speculation among your customers as to what might have prompted such an action?"

"Nay, save that the man must be nicked in the nob. He couldn't be any what live here, for what inhabitant is not grateful His Royal Highness made his summer and winter home here?"

Evan felt he could learn little else and offered his card to the cheerful publican, requesting that should he hear anything untoward, he direct his communication to him at his address in North Street.

"I should be happy to oblige you, Captain."

Evan might have at that moment quit the establishment, but the good man was desirous of engaging him in some conversation about his involvement at Waterloo. After passing a good half hour happily recounting his adventures in Belgium, he bade good-bye to the worthy man and headed back to Brighton.

As he approached the town, he once more ignored the urge of his spurs to encourage his horse toward West Street and instead headed to the Steyne. The hour was nearly two o'clock, and he felt certain he would find any number of persons about with whom he might converse at his leisure. In particular, he hoped to find Keymer, who he knew had been attending to his duties with far greater assiduity than himself.

Stabling his horse at the Castle Inn, he headed in the direction of the long row of buff and blue houses. He had not taken but a few steps when he saw Keymer who was just taking his leave of Miss Alistair and Katherine. They were grouped at the southern region of the common closest to the ocean. When he reached them, both Miss Alistair and Katherine bade him a polite good day, then hurried their feet in the direction of Fisher's where purportedly Mrs. Alistair was awaiting them in her carriage.

Mr. Keymer regarded him with a crooked smile. "What grievous sin have you committed," he queried, "that must send the ladies flying from the Steyne? The moment they saw you, they began taking their leave of me. I was never more disconsolate, since I enjoy the company of both ladies exceedingly."

Evan gripped his hands behind his back. "I kissed her, damme!" he confessed. "Again. I should never have done so, and now she will not speak to me."

Mr. Keymer glanced about him and, seeing that Mr. Clarke and Miss Framfield were close enough to overhear their conversation, guided Evan away from the crowd in the direction of the sea. "But you have kissed her before. Why should she suddenly take a pet over this kiss?"

How could Evan explain? "This last one was a bit more than just a kiss."

Keymer raised his brows. "You begin to frighten me," he stated somewhat jokingly. "Have you taken to seducing innocents?"

"No, no, it is nothing so bad as that," he countered, feeling very cross of a sudden. "Merely, the experience was oddly wonderful. I know I came away a trifle bemused."

"Wonderful, you say? If it was so wonderful, then why does she run away as though you've the plague?"

"I believe it frightened her."

"Hard to believe Miss Pamberley frightened of anything. Something else, perchance?"

"Dashed if I know, but it is just as well she does avoid my company. I do not mean to marry her, and a kiss like that . . . well, with any other chit, she would have been expecting me to offer for her."

"Ah, I see. But are you truly disinclined to offer for her? The whole of it seems most promising!"

Evan stopped walking and turned to glare at Keymer for his complete stupidity. "You know deuced well I have no such intention or desire! I have told you times out of mind my feelings on that score. No, the property in Worcestershire will go to one of Ramsdell's younger brats once his nursery begins to fill up."

"Which will be quite soon, if I do not miss the mark."

"November," Evan said with a shrug. He had reached the cliffs and glanced at the dwelling nearest the beach. "Good God! Cumberland's house looks as though it means to drop off into the sea at the very next storm."

"I do not think so," Keymer countered. "The groynes are solid enough. It will hold. I do so like the location. What a view! Even the Regent's Pavilion does not command such a fine aspect."

"Cumberland has been coming to Brighthelmstone forever."

"So I have heard." Keymer breathed deeply, "Is there anything finer than the sea air?"

At that, Evan glanced at his friend and was finally drawn out of his brown study. He realized Keymer was appearing rather contented of late, having lost much of the pinched look he habitually wore. As secretary to the Duke of Relhan, he was kept much occupied. Brighton was appearing to have a happy effect upon his friend.

His temper softened. "I did not seek you out to discuss Cumberland's house or even Miss Pamberley's dislike of me, but rather to tell you that I just returned from Hove, having spent the last several hours there in hopes of chancing upon a bit of information."

"And did you hear anything?"

Evan shook his head. "Though I did encourage the landlord to send word if he learned anything of significance. However, the asparagus and chicken were excellent, as was the plum cake."

Mr. Keymer laughed. "You and I are not especially skilled at this particular occupation."

"I will not speak for you. For myself, I am far more comfortable aiming a company at the enemy and shouting the command 'Fire when ready' than skirting about the town and trying to see assassins where only reasonable-looking people appear." He turned in the direction of the Steyne. "Who, among everyone you see, would be capable of devising a plot to kill a future king?"

Keymer turned as well. "None of them," he responded. "I am convinced. Come. Let us repair to the Castle. Perhaps we'll have a turn of luck and hear something of use. Besides, you may have dined, but I have not."

Evan had no objection to the scheme. Indeed, after riding back from Hove and letting the sea air beat against his face, he was ready for another tankard.

Crossing the Steyne and the innyard, he was about to reach for the door handle when the door suddenly swung open. Mr. Wooding's cousin appeared before him. "Oh, I say! How do you do, Ramsdell, Keymer?" he said, his expression a little stunned. "I nearly rammed into the pair of you."

"So you did," Evan said. "Are you always in a hurry?"

"Nearly so. Good day to you."

Evan nodded as he passed by in his quick manner, as did Keymer, but he bethought himself. "How is your head?" he inquired.

"Much better, thank you," Mr. Lunsford said over his shoulder. "The wound is nearly healed, and I suffered the headache only the first night. Thank you for your inquiry." He had not stopped, even while answering Evan's question, and continued briskly on his way.

Evan watched him for a moment.

"He seems like a man who can accomplish things," Keymer said, moving inside. He lowered his voice, "I think we ought to give him our assignment and be done with it."

Evan laughed and made his way into the taproom.

"You cannot keep avoiding his company as you did today," Lydia said firmly. She was propped on the end of Katherine's bed, her knees tucked beneath her, as she played with a feathered quill.

"You are right," Katherine responded. "I know you are." Her maid was busily arranging her hair in a lovely knot of curls atop her head. Tonight the ladies were to attend a soiree at Lady Beavan's home on the Steyne, a gathering in which cards, conversation and an occasional unrehearsed performance on the pianoforte or harp would be the order of the evening. "I felt utterly ridiculous when we took our leave of Mr. Keymer, as though I had been running from a bear."

"Captain Ramsdell does not resemble a bear in the least."

Katherine sighed. "No, he does not."

"Have you tumbled into love with him at long last?" Lydia queried.

Katherine looked into the mirror and met Lydia's curious, smiling gaze in the reflection. "Will you never cease tormenting me with that particular question? Besides, when does a lady's desire to be absent from a certain gentleman's company reflect the wound of Cupid's arrow?"

Lydia chuckled. "When the lady is you," she responded pointedly.

"You are being absurd."

"Then you still refuse to admit to any of the tenderer emotions where Captain Ramsdell is concerned?"

At that, Katherine fell silent. How could she express what it was she felt for Evan? She could never admit to the truth, that what she felt was a strong, almost uncontrollable desire to be swept into his arms and to remain there forever. She could not say this to Lydia, or to anyone, nor did she believe for one moment that such a desire was the same thing as being in love with a man. At least, she did not think it was the same thing. The truth was, she did not know what she thought anymore, about love, about Evan, about any of it!

"Why do you remain silent?" Lydia asked.

"Because I am quite confused, something I did not expect to be in Captain Ramsdell's company."

"A certain sign of love, if you ask me."

"Why? Are you confused in Mr. Keymer's presence?"

At that, Lydia blushed quite deeply and twirled the feather briskly between her forefinger and thumb. "Not in the least!" she responded. "Besides, it is not the same thing at all!"

"Not hardly," Katherine said facetiously.

Lydia's blush deepened.

Katherine could see that her teasing had caused some discomfiture to her friend, so she chose to change the subject entirely. "Did I tell you that when Miss Kelly rode her horse toward us, near the railing, she challenged me to a race? My gelding against hers, on the Steyne tomorrow."

At that, Lydia dropped the feather, which floated to the floor. "A race?" she cried, frowning. "On the Steyne? Oh, but you cannot! Mama would be apoplectic were you to do so."

"She would not," Katherine countered confidently, even though a wiggling of doubt assailed her. "I do not believe it would be in the least improper."

"But on the Steyne, with so many fashionable people about and many of them such high-sticklers. I daresay you would receive the cut direct were you to engage in anything so outrageous!"

Katherine's maid quietly bade her to examine her hair, for she had completed her creation. "It is as lovely as always, Marie. I vow you have made me a princess since summer last. Is this not the finest of them all, Lydia?"

Lydia's face resembled a prune. "What will it matter if your hair was as fine as a queen's, if you mean to race? Even an elegant coiffure will not keep you from becoming the brunt of every mean-spirited tabby in Brighthelmstone."

Katherine turned away from the mirror and met Lydia's gaze squarely. "You are quite adamant on this point."

"I am," Lydia stated with a brisk nod of her head.

Katherine considered the dilemma for a moment. "Undoubtedly you are right, then, for you have been going about society far longer than myself. However, what if we were to race to Hove? We could pretend to be riding about and suddenly break into a hard gallop and see which horse has the better strides?"

At that Lydia relaxed visibly. "I think it an excellent notion. Mama could not possibly object, and Miss Kelly will undoubtedly be present tonight so that you may suggest the idea to her. I would be happy to tell her myself, if you wish for it, since I was the one who objected so strongly."

Katherine shook her head. "I may not have a great fondness for Miss Kelly, but I believe her to be a reasonable female. I shall speak with her myself."

Later that evening, Katherine strolled through the principal receiving rooms of Lady Beavan's elegant blue and buff house, very much at ease, for she had already settled the racing dilemma with Miss Kelly but a few minutes earlier. Miss Kelly, just as she had thought, had agreed readily to the slight alteration in their scheme. They would choose a place a half mile from Hove and simply race to the village.

With the details now arranged to a nicety, Katherine was able to enjoy Lady Beavan's soiree. She chatted with friends here and there as she moved from chamber to chamber, admiring the subdued aspect of the decor, which did not exhibit nearly the flagrant use of gilt which characterized Mrs. Nutley's home.

Finally, she reached a small anteroom in which a painting by John Constable was displayed. She was struck at once by the beauty of his composition and use of color. She felt deeply moved and meant to applaud Lady Beavan's choice as soon as she was able.

She had not been observing the painting above five minutes when Mr. Nutley joined her. "I believe he uses a dash too much white," he commented as he came to stand beside her. He squinted at the landscape. "All these little flecks here and there—quite distracting."

"I think it makes the light appear to glitter, like sunshine on water."

Mr. Nutley tilted his head and squinted his eyes a little more. "By Jove, I believe you've the right of it. Hmph. Got a nice, easy style, as does Lady Beavan." He glanced about the small antechamber. He whispered, "Not a jot of gilt in this room."

Katherine smiled. She would have asked tactfully after

his wife, but at that moment he slipped behind her. "Spied m'anchor!" he cried on a whisper. "I'm in search of Lord Beavan, who, I'm told, means to get up a game of whist in his study. Don't breathe a word, Miss Pamberley!" With that, he was gone.

Katherine, who could hear Mrs. Nutley's shrill voice in the adjoining chamber, set to studying the painting once more.

"Miss Pamberley! Miss Pamberley! Have you seen Mr. Nutley? I have been searching for him everywhere."

"Er, no, I am sorry. I have been enjoying this painting and have scarcely seen anyone about."

Mrs. Nutley drew close and peered at the painting as well. "Constable!" she cried, wrinkling her nose in disgust. "Oh, no, he will not do at all! I told Lady Beavan not to waste her blunt on the man's ridiculous work. It will be worth nothing in a generation or two, mark my words. Oh, by the way, I have wagered ten pounds on your winning your race with Miss Kelly on the morrow!"

"Mrs. Nutley!" Katherine breathed, shocked. "I . . . I do not know to what you are referring!"

"Miss Alistair told me all about it. There can be no harm in a friendly competition, quite separate from any of the public places, during a jaunt to Hove. None whatsoever. Miss Alistair told me of your concern that you might kick up a scandal, but I wish you to know that both you and Miss Kelly have gone about it properly. A little race is precisely what is needed to keep the spark in our small society here in Brighton." She giggled as a young girl might. "Well, I am determined to find my dear husband. I do so wish for him to hear Miss Page play the Mozart again. Yes, she has arrived at last. Good Mr. Wooding escorted her and her father, and she has promised to play the Mozart for us all, dear thing. Now, where is Mr. Nutley?"

She disappeared into the hallway. Katherine sincerely

hoped Mr. Nutley had found a place to hide, for his wife would soon discover his whereabouts otherwise.

Here she was wrong, however, for from the adjoining chamber Mr. Nutley's face suddenly appeared. "Is she gone?" he called to her.

Katherine smiled broadly and nodded. "Into the hallway, though I greatly fear you will not be rid of her for long. She is quite determined you are to hear Miss Page play the Mozart."

"Bah!" he cried. "Can't bear that fellow's music!"

"Mozart?" Katherine queried.

"Do not look so surprised. I infinitely prefer a good ballad to all those notes, and not one rhyme or two to make the whole thing palatable." He started to advance into the room, apparently interested in continuing the discussion, but at that moment Mrs. Nutley captured him from behind.

"There you are, Horace! Ah, I see you found our dear Miss Pamberley. But you may not remain and converse with her, for Miss Page is to play. Come! You may speak with Miss Pamberley later, for I know she is a great favorite of yours. For now, you are expected in the music room."

Mr. Nutley's shoulders fell as though large boulders had been lowered onto each of them. He rolled his eyes and turned to follow his wife. He poked his head forward and pouted. Poor Mr. Nutley, ever under the burden of his marriage.

Katherine decided to follow after them, for she did enjoy Miss Page's performances, the last of which she had missed because she had been in the Chinese Corridor of the Pavilion with Evan. *Oh, dear.* What a hapless recollection, for she was soon full of thoughts of him and how wickedly and wondrously he had kissed her.

However, as though these reflections conjured him up, he was suddenly before her.

"Hallo," he said with a smile. "Mr. Nutley said you

were within, admiring Constable's painting, I believe. I had the good fortune to see his work displayed at the museum in London."

Katherine stared at him, her heart setting off at a terrible pace. Her cheeks grew quite warm and her legs began to tremble. If only she had quit the antechamber sooner!

"I . . . I should have liked to see his work assembled," she said breathlessly, stumbling over her words. "I . . . I was just going to hear Miss Page play."

"Show me the Constable," he said, ignoring her last remark. "I have not been to Lady Beavan's house before, but I have been told I must make certain to see this most recent acquisition."

Katherine withheld a sigh. To do anything other than to oblige Evan would have been uncivil. He was intent on viewing the painting, and she could hardly tell him that she could not attend him because she was intent on avoiding him. Instead, she took his arm and allowed him to return her to the painting.

"Exquisite," he murmured, taking in every aspect of the landscape. "These rural aspects can be so pleasing. I feel as though I am in the country."

"I was thinking the very same thing earlier. One can almost feel the sunshine."

"And smell the grass."

"I feel like dozing already," she said, chuckling.

He smiled, turning to meet her gaze. "You can be quite charming when you are not running away from me."

"Evan," she began, searching about in her mind for the right words to say. "I do not know what to say. I . . . it is merely that—"

"You need not explain. I behaved abominably on Saturday night, I made you wretchedly uncomfortable, and you have taken to punishing me."

"No, not to punish you!" she cried. "I would never be so mean-spirited. Indeed, I would not!"

"I was only teasing you a little. Do not look so downcast. You have done nothing that I did not deserve."

He took her hand, clasping it gently. "I have come to value your friendship, Katherine. I was heartily sorry for my conduct because I feared you would no longer count me a friend."

"You will always be such," she responded softly, meeting his gaze and feeling woefully excited by his presence, by the faint smell of his shaving soap, by the touch of his hand over hers.

Silence fell into her mind. She could think of nothing to say. She was far too enchanted by being so close to him to speak even of the weather. Besides, he was regarding her so strangely, so intently.

Oh, dear. Did he intend to kiss her again?

After what must have been a full minute, he gave his head a faint shake and said, "May I escort you to the Steyne tomorrow after your sea-bathing? I know you enjoy reading the papers at Fisher's and I should like to join you."

"Yes, that would be . . . oh, I nearly forgot. I am engaged to ride out with Miss Kelly tomorrow."

"Miss Kelly?" he queried, a frown settling between his brows. "I did not know you preferred her company. Indeed, I seem to recall a time when you expressed a measure of disdain for her, or am I mistaken?"

Katherine smiled, thinking Evan would find tomorrow's escapade a great lark. "Well, you are not mistaken. We are not precisely bosom bows. However, we do share one pleasure in common—our love of horses. She is greatly fond of riding and possesses a very fine gelding who she insists can outrun my dear Prince any day of the week."

His frown deepened a little more. "You mean to race her," he cried. "Oh, Katherine, you cannot. This is madness and would only serve to set up the tabbies."

"I realized as much, or at least I did when Lydia made

me aware of how the race would be perceived by some of the stricter ladies, but it was suggested to me that were Miss Kelly and I to ride out as if on an expedition of pleasure in the direction of Hove, and then chance to put our horses through their paces, say a half mile from the hamlet, who would dare to call it a race?"

"Good God," he murmured. "I was at Nutley's earlier today and there was some betting on a pair of Brighton fillies. I thought it would be a contest on the racecourse. Now I am come to believe it is this race."

"I cannot say if that is the case," she said, frowning slightly, "though I suppose you must be right, for Mrs. Nutley said she had wagered ten pounds on my winning."

"I do not approve in the least," he stated, removing his hand from hers. "What would Constance say?"

"I cannot begin to imagine," she responded, a little piqued. "But it would not matter. I am mistress of my own course, Evan, whether you or Constance approve or not, and I simply cannot find fault with a little racing to Hove."

"I suppose it is not entirely beyond the pale, but mark my words, you will endure some criticism for engaging in such an activity."

Katherine merely smiled, and realized of a sudden how grateful she was that Evan had taken to brangling with her about the race, for now she was not in the least afraid that he might assault her again. "I hear Miss Page has begun her sonata. Will you take me to the music room?"

He frowned at her once more. "As you wish," he said.

Eleven

Wednesday morning, a tidy layer of clouds rolled in from the sea, obscuring the sun and providing what was for Katherine perfect riding weather. She gentled her gelding near the makeshift starting line a half mile from the small hamlet of Hove. Her horse seemed to comprehend full well his purpose even though the race was quite unofficial. He tossed his head gallantly about as if in strong belief that the large number of persons assembled to watch the race, which was not a race, had gathered for the strict purpose of admiring his sleek, powerful lines.

Evan was present on horseback, expressing his disapproval of the event by gesturing in a long, sardonic sweep of his arm to the two rows of persons lining the lane for at least a third of a mile. For herself, she had been rather shocked to find that a great number of the *beau monde* had, indeed, arisen at a sufficiently early hour to witness her contest with Miss Kelly. Yet to her eye, they were not nearly so disapproving—if at all!—as Evan wished her to believe.

Miss Kelly was just now arriving, her head held at a rather proud, arrogant angle, her horse stamping his feet. Katherine had never been partial to her, and certainly her arrogant conduct as she approached the starting line in no way released her from Katherine's original impression that the young lady was rather spoilt and enjoyed an opinion of herself far above that held by her peers.

However, she had no intention of letting her dislike of Miss Kelly affect either her sportsmanship or her enjoyment of the race. From this moment, she saw Miss Kelly only as a competitor and as such turned her attention exclusively to keeping Prince in such a state of readiness that when the race began, he would make a clean and perfect start. Even the presence of the crowd, which continued to swell by the minute, diminished steadily within her scope of awareness to a mere hum in her ears. She concentrated on settling herself well into her saddle, gathering the reins just so, and securing the loop of her whip about her fingers.

Miss Kelly took up her place beside her, acknowledging her only once with a dip of her chin.

Katherine returned the gesture with a quick nod, then set her gaze upon the road to Hove. From the corner of her eye, she was able to see Mr. Sawyer, who had begged for the privilege of starting the race.

There would be no firing of a pistol to distress the horses; rather, Mr. Sawyer would release a handkerchief.

"Are the ladies ready?" he asked in a commanding voice.

Katherine inclined her head, as did Miss Kelly.

He raised his hand aloft, waited a scant few seconds and threw the embroidered square of cambric down.

Katherine's heart was already racing as she leaned forward, kicked her horse's sides and called out, "Ho, Prince!"

Miss Kelly must have done the same, for the crowd suddenly sent up an excited roar, which did not daunt either of their superior horses in the least.

The race was on.

Katherine kept her head low and only glanced in Miss Kelly's direction once. She saw in that fraction of a second the same competitive spirit which possessed her own heart. She could not help but smile, for this would be a race, indeed.

She took long, deep breaths, the rhythmic pounding of her horse on the road, the rising and extending of his powerful sides as he moved his hooves forward, her only interest. She heard her horse snort as he pulled abreast of Miss Kelly's mount. Nose to nose, the horses extended themselves as though forgetting about their riders completely. Katherine knew she no longer existed to Prince; only the sweating beast beside him held any interest for a horse who loved to race.

A quarter mile to go and scarcely a breath of difference between the horses. People cheered all along the way as the race progressed. Katherine only faintly noticed.

Unexpectedly, a child darted into her path. Though he was jerked safely back by his mother, Prince stumbled slightly, losing ground before regaining his stride. Katherine slapped him lightly with her whip, which she doubted he felt in the least, for he had already begun straining toward Miss Kelly's horse.

An eighth of a mile to go and Prince was still half a horse behind Miss Kelly's steed. She felt him strain beneath her with all his might. She leaned forward and praised him warmly, for he was making a valiant effort to recover his position. Length by length, he pulled forward as Miss Kelly's horse showed clear signs of wearying.

The finish line before The Ship Inn loomed before her. "Just a bit more," she urged her horse. He gave of his heart and in the next moment was nose to nose with Miss Kelly's mount once more.

A second flashed, the finish line flew by, and the race was over.

Carefully, she drew her horse in and turned him back in the direction of the finish line. She had no idea who had won. She glanced at Miss Kelly, whose expression had not changed in the least. She would not meet Katherine's eye as she too turned her horse and headed back to the crowd.

Once they arrived, the judges on either side of the finish line proclaimed that by scarcely an inch Miss Kelly's horse was the winner.

Katherine knew a sudden sinking in her heart, a familiar sensation to anyone who ever engaged in a competition. Ah, well. She repressed the tears which always accompanied such a sensation and instead offered her congratulations to Miss Kelly by extending her hand over the pommel of her saddle. Miss Kelly accepted the gesture with little grace, giving one sharp jerk of her fingers by way of acceptance.

"It was an excellent match," Katherine said grandly.

Miss Kelly merely lifted a brow. "I told you Ivanhoe could beat your horse and I have been proven right."

Katherine thought of the child who had darted in the path of her horse and caused Prince to stumble. Surely, Miss Kelly had noted the mishap. It seemed to Katherine that on a more proper racecourse, Prince would have won handily. She was therefore stunned speechless. She could think of nothing to say which seemed suited to her rival's haughty demeanor.

Miss Kelly tossed her head and began walking her horse in a wide circle in front of the cheering crowd. Katherine chose not to accompany her as she had intended, but instead guided Prince in the direction of the seashore. She was so piqued by Miss Kelly's arrogant manner that she found her temper mounting ominously.

She had not been riding long when Evan joined her, his own horse fairly well lathered.

"You must be disappointed," he said, calling to her.

She smiled over her shoulder, waiting for him to draw up next to her. "Only in Miss Kelly. She seemed determined to gloat even though I most happily offered her my congratulations."

"But then you never were fond of her."

"Precisely. I suppose I expected her character to have altered a little during a horserace, the event being more civilized than even dancing in a ballroom."

At that he laughed. "Whatever do you mean?" he queried. "More civilized than dancing?"

She smiled. "I know it must seem odd in me to think so, but after all, horses have been around forever, while ballrooms and dancing are certainly a more recent invention. Besides, in the company of true horse-loving riders, I have always found a sympathy and enthusiasm wholly lacking in many social settings. Admit it is so."

He laughed. "You may be right. As a cavalry officer, I observed a larger camaraderie among the regiment than in the foot regiments. I can only suppose it was because of the numerous horses involved and our dependence upon them."

"Then you may comprehend my disappointment that Miss Kelly's only comment concerning her win was how she had known all along that her horse could beat mine."

"She said as much?" he queried.

Katherine nodded. "And I was prepared to revel with her over the fine contest we had just shared. I only hope that I might have a second opportunity to test Prince's mettle."

"He is a fine horse," he said, casting his gaze over Prince in a warm, appreciative sweep of his eyes.

"Thank you," she said, leaning down and patting him several times on his long, glossy neck. She then glanced behind her and saw that she had put a fair distance between herself and the village of Hove. Any number of the crowd which had cheered the contestants throughout the race were congratulating the winner. "I suppose I must go back, for I do not wish to appear soured by my loss."

"I would have to agree."

She turned her horse and he followed suit, though she

continued walking her mount in order to allow Prince to cool after the rigorous ride. She fell silent, taking pleasure in the prickling of her skin, a fine sensation which usually followed a brisk dash on horseback. She breathed in the sea air and sighed deeply.

"You truly are not overset that you lost the race," he stated at last.

"No. Why should I be? The effort was honest on both parts, and I cannot expect always to win. Last summer, Prince won six races out of seven. Losing today still places him far above the ordinary horse."

Evan regarded her solemnly for a long moment. He had been opposed to the race from the first, but now he was happy to witness Katherine's present conduct. She was a true sportswoman, eager to enter a contest but not so foolish as to believe she would always win, and certainly not begrudging that someone else should be victorious.

He realized with a start that there was much he approved of in Katherine Pamberley. Even now, she sat like a queen astride her horse, appearing radiant in her sky-blue velvet habit and matching hat. A sheen of perspiration graced her brow but did not in the least detract from his admiration of her.

Though it was unlikely he would ever be inclined to marry, he could not help but think she would make him an excellent wife. Her temper was even, her intelligence was equal to his own, she shared a number of his values, and she had a true appreciation of horseflesh, not to mention that she fell into his arms as readily as the waves washed upon the shore.

These were useless thoughts, however, for he had no desire to take a wife.

"You have grown very quiet," she offered gently.

"Have I?" he murmured, still lost in thought.

She said nothing more, which prompted him to look at her again. He chuckled to himself. She even possessed that rarest of qualities of leaving a man to his own thoughts if he wished for it.

"Now, why do you look at me in that odd manner?" she asked, a crooked smile upon her lips. "You are forever doing so, you know."

"Odd, you say?"

"Yes, as though I have suddenly grown a wart you find yourself desirous of removing."

He laughed aloud. "You have no warts," he stated, "which is perhaps why I seem to be looking at you queerly."

"Then why do you insist on speaking in riddles?"

"Am I?"

"There, you see! Another riddle. If I were not so happy to have been able to race my horse just now, I vow I should be vexed with you."

"I shall tell you," he said, not looking at her. "I was thinking of husbands and wives and what qualities make for a good spouse. You, for instance. What do you desire in a husband?"

Katherine lifted her brows, guiding her horse away from a part of the path that had been washed away in a recent rain. "What do I desire in a husband?" she repeated.

"Yes. When you look at all the gentlemen who tend to gather about you—a group which in recent days has grown considerably in number—how do you set about choosing among them?"

"My first consideration is always the same. I ask myself whether the man vexes me or not; that is, whether once begun, he continues to speak in riddles until I am in the boughs. Such a man I eliminate immediately, for I could never stare across the breakfast table at such a one day after day and preserve even a portion of my equanimity. In short, I should become a fishwife."

He laughed once more. "You are teasing me."

"I am."

"Yet I have posed the question in perfect sincerity, meaning to attach no riddle to it. I have become curious as to what it is you are seeking in a husband. Will you not tell me?"

She regarded him beneath a wrinkled brow for a long moment, as though to ascertain whether he was indeed serious or not. After a moment, she said, "In truth, I have not examined the matter before. Until this summer, I have been much engaged in the business of Lady Brook Cottage."

"In the stables, you mean."

"In the stables, yes, but also in the surrounding villages. Although we were a poor family by the reckoning of our peers, both Constance and Mama felt it would be shameful not to share what we had with others, particularly since much of a person's true wealth comes from one's deeds as much as from one's income. The Applegate children were particular favorites of mine, as well as the two ladies—widows and the very best of friends— who lived above the candle shop. I took them apricot tarts and a parcel of tea every week, which they enjoyed during the afternoons. One of them, before she became infirmed, loved to ride nearly as much as me, so you may imagine how we never lacked for topics of discussion. The other lady had fallen in love with a French soldier who had been wounded in Spain and brought to Berkshire as a prisoner until the end of the war. Alas, he returned to his wife in 1814, after Bonaparte surrendered. She never heard from him again, and I often wondered if he perished at Waterloo."

"A great many soldiers did, both French and British. Prussian as well, of course."

"Yes," she murmured solemnly, glancing askance at him. "Do you regret having sold out?"

He shot a glance at her. "Why do you ask?"

"I do not know, precisely," she said, "only I have often thought you did not seem completely content, at least not here in Brighton and certainly not at Sir Jaspar's home. More than once in the past several weeks, I have seen you staring out the window as though lost. I have frequently wondered why."

He frowned at her, wondering how he had ever given her such an impression. "I cannot remember having done so and particularly not at The Priory. Perhaps you saw me admiring Sir Jaspar's grounds, for his improvements, even while we were there, were quite impressive."

"Then you have an odd way of admiring anything," she responded archly, "for you frequently appear just as you are now, with a hard line between your brows as though you were very angry with something or someone."

"Nonsense," he responded, a little overset.

She shifted her gaze back in the direction of Hove, which was now only a little ways ahead. Mr. Keymer and Miss Alistair saw them and, turning their horses, cantered in their direction. "Ah, there is Lydia! Her mother did not approve of our little race at all."

Evan only vaguely heard her remark, for he had just espied Miss Page. "What the devil is she doing descending Mr. Wooding's carriage? By God, he keeps her company a great deal more than he ought."

Katherine drew her horse to a sudden stop. "Then why do you not call him out?" she cried. "For I vow you have been aching to do so since you first arrived in Brighthelmstone. Admit it is so!"

"It is no such thing," he retorted hotly. "Now what is amiss? For I vow, I do not know why you would say such a thing and with such sudden venom."

To his surprise, Katherine rolled her eyes and spurred her horse forward to greet her friend warmly.

Evan walked his horse, his gaze fixed to the sight of Miss Page at the edge of the crowd, staring up into Mr. Wooding's eyes as one caught in a dream. "Hell and damnation," he muttered beneath his breath. "She has no sense, none at all."

"What?" Mr. Keymer cried, coming up to him. "Who? Miss Pamberley? I must take issue with you. I believe she handled the entire race quite tactfully. Even Mrs. Nutley was not offended by it."

"I was not referring to Miss Pamberley, but rather to Miss Page. She is in Wooding's company a great deal more than is at all advisable. Even from this distance, she appears besotted. As for Mrs. Nutley, she has just lost a ten-pound wager. We shall see if she proves as charitable toward Miss Pamberley after the race as before. Besides, Katherine just told me that Mrs. Alistair had disapproved completely of the event. She was foolish to have gone against her hostess's wishes."

"I see nothing wrong in the whole of it. Besides, she has conducted herself to perfection throughout. Only see how she congratulates Miss Kelly. Bah! I wish Miss Kelly had not won the race. She is behaving ridiculously, preening about as though she had won at Newmarket. What a foolish chit! I daresay any given day of the week, Katherine would beat her all to flinders. A child darted forward, and her horse lost his stride to avoid killing the poor thing."

"Many will remark on it, I am sure."

Mr. Keymer eyed him seriously. "I suppose you discouraged Katherine from the first."

At that, Evan glanced sharply at him. "Do you tell me I am at fault for Miss Pamberley's loss?"

"Do you tell me you encouraged her while she was holding her horse in check at the starting line?" Mr. Keymer asked, his expression knowing.

"If you are asking me whether I felt she should race, of course I did not. All of this is quite beyond the pale."

"My dear Ramsdell, when did you become such a dull dog?"

Since Mr. Keymer turned his horse and trotted in the

wake of Katherine and Miss Alistair, Evan could not give him a proper answer. But as he rode sedately to Hove, he realized he had no answer, nor did he comprehend in the least why he had become so censorious, particularly of Katherine's conduct.

He might have given the subject more consideration but at that moment he caught sight of Mr. Lunsford on horseback, glaring at two men who walked very near his horse. Both of them were dressed in the brown stuff of men of trade. The two men disappeared around the corner of the street, but Mr. Lunsford continued riding toward the crowd in front of The Ship Inn, obviously still in a temper.

Evan supposed that one or the other of the men had said something inappropriate, and he would not have given the matter a great deal of thought had Mr. Wooding not left Miss Page's side and sought his cousin out at the same moment. Since he was a few hundred yards from the crowd, and because he suspected Mr. Wooding of injurious conduct toward Miss Page, he watched the two men carefully.

Au argument ensued. He had never seen Mr. Wooding so red-faced before. Mr. Lunsford said nothing, though he, too, seemed out-of-reason cross. Finally, Mr. Wooding returned to Miss Page. Mr. Lunsford circuited the crowds and headed in the direction of Brighton.

Evan wished he knew more of both men. Of Mr. Wooding he was in possession of some information, but of Mr. Lunsford he knew nothing. He felt certain that Miss Page was in danger, and because of his association with her father for so many years, he felt it incumbent upon him to protect her if he could. His father had asked him to support Miss Page while she was in Brighton, and he meant to keep his promise to them both.

* * *

An hour later, Katherine rode back to Brighthelmstone in the company of Lydia, Mr. Keymer, Mr. Horsfield, Miss Framfield, Evan and Mr. Kelly, the latter of whom had grown all out of patience with his sister, who he said was putting on a remarkably unattractive air of superiority because of the race. Katherine, though keeping her sentiments to herself, was quite in agreement with him.

As for Evan, she ignored him entirely, for she found herself irritated by his disapproval of Miss Page's interest in Mr. Wooding.

Fortunately, with so many gentlemen present, each eager to assure her she had ridden the race with exceptional grace and ability, she was entertained quite happily the entire distance to West Street. Once there, she bade adieu to the party, promising a stroll with each of the gentlemen, save Evan, of course, during the evening Promenade.

"What did you quarrel about this time?" Lydia asked as the ladies mounted the stairs to their respective bedchambers on the second floor of the house.

Katherine hooked Lydia's arm. "You refer to Captain Ramsdell?"

"Of course."

Katherine sighed. "I do not know why I became so piqued, precisely, except that we were conversing on an unusual topic, one *he* had introduced about the sort of husband I should prefer, when suddenly he saw Mr. Wooding and Miss Page together and he was immediately critical and disapproving. He put me forcibly in mind of an old man with gout, besides having failed completely to engage me in the subject he brought forth."

"What you desired in a husband?" Lydia queried, ignoring her last remarks completely.

"Yes. What lady does not wish to answer such a question?"

"Particularly when one has a special interest in the gentleman asking the question."

At that, Katherine clicked her tongue. "I have told you repeatedly, I am not in love with Evan Ramsdell."

"Oh," Lydia responded, giggling. "And I was not referring to you and Captain Ramsdell. I was . . ."

She broke off, apparently unable to complete her thought. Katherine glanced at her and saw at once that her friend was blushing—again. She guessed the nature of her thoughts and suggested, "You were thinking of Mr. Keymer." Since Lydia's blush turned nearly a scarlet in hue, Katherine bit her lip, opened her eyes wide, then leaned very close to her. "Lydia," she breathed, "it is you who have tumbled in love, or am I much mistaken?"

Katherine had reached the landing and still held Lydia's arm tightly. "No, no, I shan't let you go," she whispered, smiling broadly when Lydia tried to disengage her arm. "You must come to my bedchamber. You must! And tell me everything, just as best friends ought!"

Lydia's shoulders collapsed as her face took on the expression of an angel. "Oh, Katherine," she murmured.

"No! Tell me nothing in the hallway!" she commanded on a whisper. "For the servants are likely to hear, and then we shall be in the basket!"

Lydia allowed herself to be drawn into Katherine's bedchamber. Once the door was closed, she sank down upon the bed. Katherine joined her.

"I . . . I have never felt this way before," Lydia said, a hand pressed to her bosom. "I feel as though I could fly. The moment I see him, my heart races with excitement. I can hardly wait to steal a moment alone with him, even to exchange but a few words as we did at Hove, in the midst of a crowd." She closed her eyes as she continued, "He told me I looked exquisite today in my yellow embroidered muslin. I shall always keep this gown. I vow I shall." She opened her eyes, and much to Katherine's surprise, tears brimmed on her lashes.

"When he looks at me, it seems as though my feet completely disappear and I am at any moment in danger of falling. At Fisher's yesterday morning, he seemed to comprehend as much, for he took my arm and would not let go. He said I did not seem quite steady on my feet, but he looked at me in such a way!"

"Whatever did you say to him?" Katherine queried, hanging upon her friend's every word.

"I do not recall saying anything. I remember looking up at him and smiling. He smiled back. He said nothing more either. He just kept looking at me. I . . . oh, Katherine, it is very wicked of me, but I wanted him to kiss me! Is that not very shocking?"

"Has he kissed you before?" she asked.

Lydia shook her head. "No, but I know he shall, very soon, if I am not much mistaken."

Katherine blinked at her friend. She was not surprised by her confidences in the least, for Lydia had been showing a marked preference for Mr. Keymer's company in the past few days. However, hearing the words pass her lips made the blooming attachment wonderfully real. "If he were to offer for you, would you accept him?"

Lydia's mouth fell open. "Why, yes, I would!" she cried, as though the very question had caused as much astonishment to her own ears as it had to Katherine's. "I had just not considered it before, but now that you have asked—yes, I would indeed!"

"Then you must be in love with him!" Katherine returned, stunned. "Only what would your mama say?"

This must have been the first time Lydia pondered this notion too, for an expression of horror crossed her features. "Oh, Katherine!" she cried, obviously dismayed. "Mama wanted *you* to wed Mr. Keymer. She said your portion would not command a gentleman of greater rank and that you would be very wise to set your cap at him if you could. But, oh, dear! She would not wish me to marry him, not when her heart has been set on procuring a peer for me these many years and more!"

"But Mr. Keymer is secretary to the Duke of Relhan, he commands great respect in London, for Captain Ramsdell has told me as much often and often, and he has as fine a property as many of the lesser nobility."

Lydia's face crumpled. "Mama wished me to become a peeress. She has said so ever since she first brought me out when I was eighteen."

Since Lydia began to weep, Katherine gathered her in her arms. She thought suddenly of Mr. Wooding's preference for Miss Page's company, and Miss Page's growing affection for Mr. Wooding. Was this why Evan disliked the match so much? Did he believe Miss Page ought to make a brilliant match if she could?

"There, there," she murmured. "Your mother will accustom herself to the match. Besides, Mr. Keymer has not yet offered for you, has he?"

Upon these words, Lydia drew back and wiped her eyes. "I am being such a goose, am I not? Indeed, I have already walked down the aisle in my mind, while Mr. Keymer has barely begun courting me."

"There, that is much better," Katherine said. "We have gone far beyond the mark here. We had much better attend to what gown you should wear tonight, and whether there is sufficient time to have a new gown made up for Lady Walford's ball on Saturday."

"I should like to have a new ballgown," Lydia said, her eyes growing wide again. "Oh, yes, a new gown above anything, for I believe Mr. Keymer has seen all of my best gowns and though I had planned on wearing the gold silk, I have never thought the color suited me precisely. Katherine, I must apply to Mama on the instant, for if we were to visit the linen drapers this very afternoon, I believe the task could be accomplished."

"I shall go with you," Katherine stated, "for then I

can purchase the fabric for the young girls in the workhouse."

Since Lydia's mind had been set on a happier path, Katherine let her friend quit her bedchamber considerably at ease. After all, it was possible Mr. Keymer did not share Lydia's *tendre,* and were that so, then there would be no question about Mrs. Alistair's approval of the match since there would be no match.

Twelve

On Saturday, Katherine stepped down from Mrs. Alistair's town coach in something of a quandary on two fronts. Ever since the race to Hove, neither Evan nor Miss Kelly had conducted themselves as Katherine believed they ought. Evan appeared to be keeping himself at a considerable distance and Miss Kelly not far enough away.

Evan's conduct she could explain simply enough—she had angered him with her cross words about calling out Mr. Wooding, and so he desired to leave her to her own devices.

Miss Kelly, on the other hand, had become a complete enigma. She had won the race at Hove, if not handily then at least without the smallest doubt that her horse's nose had crossed the finish line first. Katherine had even congratulated Miss Kelly, quite warmly, on her win, which must have firmly established Miss Kelly as the victor. Yet somehow there had arisen among the *beau monde* a belief either that the race had not been conclusive of a winner or that some mischief had occurred which caused Miss Kelly to ascend as the winner.

Whatever the cause, which Katherine made certain to dispel at every opportunity, rumors had begun to circulate to the effect that Katherine was the true winner of the match and Miss Kelly was on her high ropes because of it.

The gossip was ridiculous, of course, a veritable storm in a teacup, but apparently not to Miss Kelly, who had begun to treat Katherine with a great deal of contempt. Only that morning at Fisher's Library, Miss Kelly had stared at her with a frosty gaze, her lips set primly in the stark lines of her face.

"What is it?" Katherine had cried, rising from her seat to face her squarely. "Whatever is the matter? What has happened, for I can see that you are decidedly overset?"

Miss Kelly had smiled in an infuriating manner, then sneered, "How innocent you sound, Miss Pamberley. You would appear to be as fine an actress as you are a prevaricator."

"What?" Katherine had cried, stunned.

But Miss Kelly had not been of a mind to continue the conversation. She lifted her chin, straightened her spine and entered the circulating library as one carrying a heavy cross upon her back.

Katherine was nearly out of patience, for this was not the first of Miss Kelly's cloaked condemnations. She would have followed after her to demand an explanation, but at that moment Mrs. Alistair had commanded her presence in her carriage, for it was the agreed-upon hour to return to West Street.

Later, in Lydia's bedchamber, she had asked her friend if she knew what Miss Kelly might have been referring to, but dear Lydia was only vaguely attending to her, for she was removing her new ballgown from the confines of a veritable flutter of silver paper and had only scarcely heard her recounting of her confrontation with Miss Kelly.

"She is probably jealous," Lydia had said distractedly, lifting the gown to her shoulders and sighing deeply. "For she cannot have failed to notice how last night your card table was surrounded by nearly a dozen gentlemen, all ostensibly to watch you play. Oh, do but feel this silk. Is there nothing quite so wonderful as silk?"

Katherine could see in the way Lydia closed her eyes, pressing the gown against her and swaying to the music of an imagined orchestra, that she did not precisely have ears to hear anything but the beat of her own heart at present. "No, Lydia, there is nothing lovelier than silk, and you shall appear absolutely beautiful tonight. Does Mr. Keymer know you mean to wear a new gown this evening?"

Lydia opened her eyes at that and smiled shyly. "Indeed he does, for he called on Wednesday afternoon, the day of your race, but if you will remember we had already left for the linen drapers, so he guessed at my purpose. Thursday night, when we were at Lady Beavan's, I spoke with him and told him I was sorry I had missed him but that I was having a new gown made up."

Katherine forgot her troubles for a moment and queried, "Did he respond with an appropriate degree of interest and excitement?"

"Oh, yes," she breathed. "He could not have been kinder, for he said that were I to wear my oldest and ugliest gown I would still be prettier than the most beautiful lady present, which of course would be you. He did not say *you*, precisely, but I could not help but laugh, for who else could he be referring to except Katherine Pamberley?"

Katherine had told her she was being a perfect ninnyhammer to even think such a thing, which had set Lydia to trilling her laughter. She had left her friend to the enjoyment of her new ballgown as well as her thoughts of Mr. Keymer, and had retired to her bedchamber to ponder if there was some manner in which she could effect a peace with Miss Kelly. She simply did not understand what had caused Miss Kelly to say such harsh things to her that morning.

As Katherine crossed the threshold of Lady Walford's home, however, she still did not have a means by which she could lay to rest the rumors concerning the winner of the race to Hove. Instead, she hoped Miss Kelly might be present that she could lay the difficulty before the offended young woman and see if some reconciliation might be made.

Entering the house alongside Lydia and Mrs. Alistair, Katherine was diverted instantly by a number of potpourris which had been placed about the entrance hall. The strong, heady smell of cloves greeted her senses and made her smile.

Lady Walford received them in excellent good humor. Her gray eyes twinkled with delight. "Mrs. Alistair, Miss Alistair—my, what a lovely gown!—and Miss Pamberley. Are we not enjoying fine weather?"

"Indeed we are, Winifred," Mrs. Alistair said. "And may I say that you are the picture of health and good fortune."

"How kind of you to say as much," she responded, "I admit I could not be happier. I hope you will all enjoy our ball this evening." She waved her hand gracefully toward the staircase beneath which was a tall arched doorway. "You will find the ballroom a veritable crush of our ablest dancers. I hired the same orchestra which pleased us so much at Mrs. Nutley's house last week. I expect the young ladies will wish to dance every set."

With that, their small group moved away from their hostess and on toward the music that seemed to be drawing them ever forward.

"I can scarcely breathe," Lydia murmured. "My heart is beating so erratically. Do you see him yet?"

Katherine's thoughts had drifted entirely in the direction of Evan Ramsdell, wondering whether he meant to grace the ball tonight and whether in his anger he would ask her to dance. Forcing herself to attend to her friend's concerns, she responded, "No, I do not—that is, I do not yet see Mr. Keymer. Oh, yes I do! There he is, beside Mr. Horsfield."

Lydia quickly hooked Katherine's arm very hard. "Do not let go of me," she begged, "or I shall certainly fall to the floor in a heap."

Katherine could only laugh, and suddenly her own troubles seemed paltry in light of her friend's exhilaration. She glanced at Lydia's blond curls and the apple green ribbons wound through her hair. How wonderful to be in love!

She wondered anew whether she would ever know such heady sensations; whether she would ever come to comprehend what it was to be in love.

Her thoughts turned to Evan abruptly. He was the only man she had ever felt any degree of affection for, yet she did not love him. She conversed with him as good friends do, she brangled with him frequently, and occasionally kissed him quite wantonly to excess.

She was under no illusion that these were the hallmarks of love. What they were precisely, she could not say, but they did not suggest *love*. Certainly, she felt none of the enchantment Lydia was experiencing.

Mrs. Alistair found a friend in the long antechamber preceding the ballroom and bade the girls to enjoy the ball. Once left behind, Lydia whispered, "Had she stayed, I do not know how I should have kept my countenance once Mr. Keymer approached me."

"I believe you would have swooned," Katherine said teasingly.

"I believe you are right!" Lydia exclaimed, trilling her laughter.

An elegant *contredanse* was in progress, the music rather slow and staid, which gave ample opportunity for the dancers to express themselves at appropriate moments and gain reputations for elegance and charm. The ballroom was quite large, making it possible for nearly two dozen couples to grace the floor at one time. The orchestra was situated at the end of the chamber in a raised alcove so that the music fairly mesmerized anyone just arriving at the threshold of the ballroom. Who could resist dancing?

"He is coming to me," Lydia whispered, entirely caught up in the agony of her attachment to Mr. Keymer.

Katherine smiled in his direction, but even at that distance she could see that his eyes were all for Lydia.

She felt her friend begin to tremble anew. "He is a very handsome man," Katherine said.

"Oh, yes, he is, is he not?" A deep sigh poured from her lips.

"He seems quite eager to come to you."

"Oh, he does. He does! Katherine, tell me I am not mistaken in believing Mr. Keymer has become attached to me."

"He gives every evidence of it," she responded truthfully.

Suddenly Mr. Sawyer was standing in front of Lydia. "Will you go down the next set with me, Miss Alistair?"

"Oh," Lydia cried, her complexion paling ominously, for Mr. Keymer was still some fifteen feet away and could not effectively intervene.

Katherine heard her friend's dismay and was quick to offer her assistance. "Mr. Sawyer, you are too late, for Miss Alistair's first two sets have already been claimed, but I would be honored if you would stand up with me."

Lydia squeezed her arm appreciatively.

Mr. Sawyer swallowed hard. "I would be most honored, indeed," he said, his face lighting up. "I was going to ask for the quadrille, but I should be most happy to *waltz* with you, instead."

Katherine forced herself to smile. *Oh, dear, the waltz with Mr. Sawyer.* Lydia would be required to perform a very great favor for her in exchange for this one she was now bestowing on her friend. When Mr. Sawyer offered his arm to her, she took it at the very moment Mr.

Keymer made his bow to Lydia. She was afraid Mr. Sawyer might hear Mr. Keymer beg for a dance, but her good friend was up to every rig and row and just as he opened his mouth to speak, Lydia said, "You have come to claim this dance, have you not, Mr. Keymer? You must not think I have forgotten that I promised the waltz to you last Thursday night."

Mr. Keymer paused but a half second. "On no account would I have forgotten such a thing," he said. "I only feared you might have."

Lydia was beaming up into Mr. Keymer's face as Mr. Sawyer led Katherine away from the happy couple.

All is as good as settled, Katherine thought as she waited with Mr. Sawyer at the perimeter of the floor for the *contredanse* to finish. Every now and then, her gaze would move to survey the interesting pair. They had not moved from their original place, but stood very close to one another, conversing with great rapidity and enthusiasm. He laughed frequently; she smiled and smiled. Yes, everything was as good as settled.

Only as she moved onto the floor did she finally notice that Evan was standing several feet behind Mr. Keymer and Lydia, his gaze fixed not on either of them but on herself. He did not smile when he met her gaze, and once more he seemed, if not condemning, then utterly perplexed as though he were attempting to solve a difficult conundrum. Was that what she was to him? A riddle? A puzzle? Something to figure out? She was not certain why, but these thoughts had the severe tendency to make her blue-deviled. She decided, therefore, that she must continue to ignore him else she felt certain her evening's amusement would be ruined.

She succeeded until past midnight, when he came up to her quite unexpectedly and begged for a dance. "I cannot oblige you," she said quietly. "They are all promised."

"I see the cotillion has begun, yet you do not dance."

"Mr. Horsfield was undoubtedly detained."

At that, Evan laughed. "Indeed, for he is become completely foxed. I found him in the library, snoring loudly beneath the window. I did not ask permission to take his place, for he could not have aroused himself to give it to me. However, I do not think he will be able to perform the steps even were he to arrive in the next minute or so."

Katherine gave her head a shake. "I dislike walking onto a ballroom floor in the middle of a dance," she said. At least this was half true. Of the moment, she did not desire to dance with Evan. Some part of her was out of patience with him, perhaps because he had been ignoring her so steadfastly since the race, or perhaps because she believed he was still angry with her because she had suggested he call out Mr. Wooding.

"Then may I offer to escort you about the rooms?"

His expression had softened considerably, which left her feeling confused all over again. She desired to refuse him, but there was some quality in his manner that bade her to accept his request.

"Yes, of course," she said. She took his arm, and together they made a leisurely progress around the perimeter of the chamber toward the entrance.

"Then you are not still angry with me?" she queried as they left the ballroom.

"Angry?" he responded, his brow furrowed. "I do not recall being angry. When was this?"

"Wednesday last, when I suggested you call out Mr. Wooding," she reminded him. "After my race with Miss Kelly."

At that, he chuckled. "I was not angry with you, though I believe you had taken a pet over something I said about one of *your friends*."

"Yes, I certainly had. I only wish I might convince you that there is no harm in Mr. Wooding."

"No, no," he said softly, giving her arm a squeeze. "I

refuse to be drawn into that quarrel again, though I will endeavor in the future not to say provoking things to you about him."

She looked into his eyes and saw that he was both sincere and slightly amused. She could not help but smile. "Do you know, I had begun to think you were so angry that you had taken to avoiding me."

He shook his head. "Not by half. Mr. Keymer and I have been much engaged with the Prince these past three days. If I have been absent from your side, it was not by design."

"I am greatly relieved," she responded.

"Are you?" he said, smiling in a manner that set her heart to fluttering—again.

She lifted her chin slightly. "Yes, for I am never happy when I have caused any of my *friends* to begin avoiding my company."

He smiled in a manner which said he did not in the least believe her platonic rendering of the conversation, and led her on a brief tour of Lady Walford's principal receiving rooms. The house was quite elegant and spacious, for it had been built on property adjacent to the Steyne but not nearly so limited in size as those directly on the Steyne. The lot was fairly close to the ocean, and so it was that when Evan ventured to take her into the gardens, she acquiesced quite readily. "For I wish to hear the waves at this hour."

Once outside, Evan whispered, "We are but a few minutes from the cliffs and the tide is low. Would you care to walk with me on the beach?"

Katherine was shocked and stared at him with a disbelieving smile on her lips. "You would ruin your slippers and I would ruin mine! How can you suggest such a wicked thing?"

An odd smile touched Evan's lips. "Are you game?" he queried, challenging her.

Katherine chuckled again. "You are serious!" she

cried. "No, you cannot be! You would not do anything so wicked."

"I am most serious, and I do not think it wicked by half. If we are missed at all, it shall be for only a brief half hour; then we shall return with none the wiser. See if I am not mistaken."

"I do not believe you are in any manner serious and shall prove it to you by accepting of this ridiculous challenge."

He led her through an arched gate over which a bevy of red roses hung. After a scant few minutes she found herself on a well-used path which led behind several houses directly to the cliffs and to an equally well-used staircase which descended to the beach below.

"Do you still disbelieve me?" he queried as they began descending the stairs.

"No," she said. "But my heart is racing. What if we are discovered?"

"We will not be discovered. No one is about at this hour."

He was right. The beach was entirely deserted except in the distance where fishermen camped all night beside their boats on the shore.

The beach was still sandy at the base of the stairs. Only the areas near the newly constructed groynes were collecting thick deposits of shingle from the relentless tides.

Presently the tide was out, and for quite a distance the beach was a gentle, wet, glimmering pool of shallow lapping waves. Evan removed his slippers and stockings and rolled up his pantaloons to the knees.

Katherine felt like a girl stealing honey from a neighbor's beehive. She giggled nervously. "How very wicked this is!" she whispered.

He laughed at her. "I shall turn around while you remove your sandals and stockings."

"See to it, then," she countered.

When he had turned his back, she quickly removed her stockings, rolling them up carefully and stuffing them into the toes of her slippers. She then caught up the skirts of her gown and slung the unwieldy bulk over an elbow, aware that her legs were exposed almost to the knees just as his were. The circumstance was very strange, yet as soon as her toes dipped into the cold night water and the gentle ankle-deep waves began spilling over her feet, she forgot about her exposed legs entirely. She dearly loved the sea, which was presently lit by a full, glittering moon.

"How beautiful it is," she murmured, looking up into the starry sky.

"Very," he agreed.

In the distance, at the far end of the shore, the fishing boats were resting on the sand and the laughter of the fishermen who traditionally slept on the beach at night, after the day's fishing, wafted toward them. "What a simple life they must lead," she observed.

"A very hard life, but, yes, simple I suppose, though the sea is not always a kind mistress."

"Not by half, I am certain."

He was silent apace, then queried, "Do you approve of Miss Alistair's attachment to Mr. Keymer?"

She glanced at him, surprised. "Why would I not?"

He shook his head. "No reason, I suppose. I fear her mother has greater ambitions."

"A mother may have all the ambitions for her children she desires, but in the end she should wish for a love match."

"Would you be so romantic were he penniless?"

"Now we are discussing a different subject entirely," she responded. "Mr. Keymer is entirely able to support a wife in a marked degree of luxury, or am I mistaken?"

"You are not mistaken."

"Then for Mrs. Alistair to wish for more than that is foolishness if her daughter truly loves Mr. Keymer and if he truly loves her, especially since they seem so well suited in temperament. As for a man who might tumble in love with Miss Alistair and yet be himself impoverished, I daresay Miss Alistair would not be able to engage in such a match herself. She does enjoy the feel of silk prodigiously."

"You are a wholly sensible young lady, Katherine."

"I know I have said as much before, but I will remind you that my eldest sister would not allow any of us to indulge our romantic sensibilities to excess. Even Marianne, who was known to fall in love with all the most ineligible gentlemen, still frequently voiced her intention of marrying a duke if she could get one."

"Which duke?" he queried.

She chuckled. "Now you are joking. She was always very ambitious, but in the end she chose for love."

"Sir Jaspar was also quite wealthy."

"My point exactly," she returned. "She knew her limitations. Marianne could no more have wed an impoverished Major of the Horse Guards than she could the local baker. She, too, preferred the feel of silk."

"And what of you?"

Katherine was silent apace. "Do you mean, why have I never married?"

"Yes, and did you scrutinize all the gentlemen of your acquaintance as Marianne might have, or as it appears Miss Alistair has?"

"Do you mean with respect to rank and fortune?"

"Yes."

She shook her head. "I was never much interested in any of them save the quality of their horses. And I must add that not many of them were at all interested in me, I suppose because the few times one or the other sought a kiss, I was properly shocked and turned them away with a hard shove."

He paused in his steps. "You never did so to me," he stated, smiling.

"I should have, for you are by far the most obnoxious man I have ever known. I do not know why I let you kiss me, but I am grateful you have abstained from attempting to do so again."

She paused, gathering up her skirts a little more, and turned to face the depths of the shallow waves. "I believe the tide is turning," she said, "for the water is up above my ankles now."

"We should return," he said, glancing down at his own feet, which were a shocking white next to the wet sand and black water.

"Yes, I suppose so. The air is wonderfully pleasant tonight. Of course it is nearly August, the hottest month of the year. I vow I could remain here for hours."

"I, too," he said, "but we should return, else our slippers will be washed away by the sea and I do not know how we could explain that to our friends."

Katherine laughed and took up his arm once more, heading back to the cliffs. "I have come to love Brighton more than I ever believed possible. It is the sea, of course. I love the heavy feel of the air; even the dampness pleases me. This time of year in Berkshire, the lanes begin to dry out far more than is truly pleasant. The dust rises in the air, and I find myself sneezing a great deal. But here I am more comfortable than I can say. What is it like in Worcestershire in August?"

"I cannot say," he responded, "for I have not been to my home during the summer routinely since I can remember."

"How many horses do you have in your stables, and is the breeding going as well as you planned?"

He smiled, "Now you are talking on a subject which I fear I could strain for some time. Are you truly prepared to listen?"

"You know I am. This much you must know of me. I could talk of horses for hours."

He chuckled and began by saying that he had just had

a letter from his head groom stating that a most promising mare was in foal by his best stallion. "We are greatly hopeful for the offspring, but one can never tell. It is all a bit of a chance, certainly."

"But you will have years, and many mares to work with, so that this foal will simply be the first of many."

"You understand the process."

"Of course."

He then discussed the various mares he had acquired in the past ten years and his hopes for each one. Katherine listened intently and made pertinent comments, which tended, one after another, either to amuse or interest him. She loved these moments with Evan, when for some unaccountable reason they could actually converse with ease and, yes, even pleasure.

When they reached the cliffs, the slippers were not in the smallest danger of being washed away. The tide, when it turned, rose slowly if steadfastly. Katherine sat on the bottom step of the cliff stairs and began wiping the sand from between her toes.

He leaned over the railing to better see her. The old wood creaked with his weight and wobbled beneath him. "Thank you for coming down here with me, Katherine. This was truly delightful."

"Yes, it was," she said, glancing up at the moon. "Even enchanting. How do you explain that one moment we are brangling and the next we are able to converse so easily, even intelligently?"

"I cannot," he said, smiling warmly.

Katherine met his gaze, and for some reason it held. She knew the strangest impulse to kiss him, to take hold of his neck and to kiss him, if only to express her present enjoyment of his company.

She should not, of course. But then, she should not have walked on the beach with him either.

She rose up suddenly, still barefoot, and approached

him. He rose up as well, and with the railing between them, she leaned up and placed a long kiss on his lips.

That was all she had meant the kiss to be, a long, surprising kiss, designed solely to express her present delight.

Instead, however, his arm slid around her waist, which seemed to prompt her arms to encircle his neck. The kiss deepened, and he searched her mouth with his tongue as though trying to discover why she had kissed him in the first place. There was no answer, prompting him to try a little more and then a little more, to achieve the searched-for understanding.

Katherine received the familiar assault as she had all the others, with astonishing pleasure and excitement. She felt as though she could go on kissing him for hours, or at least until the tide came in and they were forced to desert the beach.

He released her suddenly, but only long enough to round the end of the railing and take her more fully into his arms. She felt the length of him this time—the toughness of his thighs, his chest, the way he bent her backward a little as though unable to draw close enough to her. How her sisters would be scandalized seeing her thus embraced by a man who would never be her husband.

An ache formed in her heart and began to swell within her. She felt her throat constrict with strange tears. Evan would never be her husband.

The poignancy of the thought, so incomprehensible, seemed to stretch itself into every part of her being. Her fingers could not keep from digging into his hair, and her ankle, bare of its usual silk stocking, had wrapped itself almost stupidly about one of his ankles. A thin, gritty layer of sand slid between her leg and his. She heard Evan groan. She was filled with both joy and sadness. She giggled and sighed, and he kissed her more deeply still.

She felt the railing pressing into her bottom. She felt it wobble. Evan became more insistent. She tried to balance herself on her foot, but it was caught behind Evan's ankle. One long shudder, and the railing gave way. Katherine fell with it, fortunately landing upon soft sand which had built up alongside the rail. Evan fell on top of her.

"Good God! Have I hurt you?" he cried, rising up.

She sat up laughing. "No! No! I am unharmed, but is this not the most absurd thing? To be undone by a bit of rotten wood!"

She could barely make out his features, for the cliff had cast his face in shadow.

"You are so beautiful," he said, his gaze raking her face, lit by the moon shining fully over his shoulder.

"And you make very pretty love when you are not brangling with me."

"I would kiss you again," he breathed. He reached behind her and drew away the broken piece of railing. Katherine did not precisely know what he was about until, having thrown the railing behind him, he fell on her, pressing her back into the sand.

She had never been kissed in such a manner. She was reminded of the kiss she had shared with him at the Pavilion. Her thoughts were escaping her one by one. Only images now forced themselves into her mind. Of a bed, of a husband, of being ravaged in the most sensual manner.

The weight of Evan's body was so satisfying, as though the pressure of his chest, his hips and his legs had been designed just for her. She knew all of this to be ridiculous, even as she savored the feel of him, as once more he entered her mouth and assaulted her.

"Oh, dear God," she heard him murmur as he drew back from her, relinquishing his possession of her mouth and instead placing gentle kisses on her brow, her eyes and her lips.

She tried to capture his mouth again. She slid her hands about his neck and attempted once more to pull him down on her.

"No," he whispered. "You are far too innocent to know what we are about."

"Kiss me again, Evan. I enjoy it above all things."

He smiled, and a small chuckle escaped his lips. "I am sure you do, dearest one, but this will not do. Come." He rolled off of her and as he rose, lifted her at the same time to her feet.

He turned her around and began patting the sand from her gown, swiping and rubbing. She giggled, for it was the act of a parent with a small child.

"However are we to get the sand from your hair?" he asked.

"I shall contrive somehow," she said. She tipped her head sideways and began gently to swipe in small motions at her curls. The sand began to fall away. "You ought to put your slippers on," she said. "This will take a few minutes."

After a time, she approached him. "Wipe my back, please, with this kerchief."

He carefully began to run the soft embroidered cambric over her skin. He leaned forward and placed a kiss at the back of her neck.

"Oh, Evan," she breathed. "Your kisses feel just like heaven. I wish you might go on kissing me forever."

"If the sun would refuse to rise on the morrow," he said, again kissing her neck, "I should agree to do just that. Forever."

Katherine again felt an ache in her heart, the presence of which made no sense to her. She could comprehend it completely were she in love with Evan, but she was not.

Thirteen

Once returned to the ballroom, Katherine felt oddly detached from herself. Her thoughts refused to coalesce upon any fixed point, and she found herself exceedingly grateful that the only activity required of her was to dance and dance. This she did with great energy and enthusiasm, even though the hour was well past midnight. Her sole mental effort was to put out of her mind as best she could her adventure upon the beach with Evan, and she succeeded remarkably well, due in great part to the fact that Evan quit Lady Walford's home shortly after restoring her to the ball.

Only in a quiet moment or two between sets, when the gentlemen had set to arguing about who was supposed to dance with her next, would her mind drift to the kisses she had shared with him at the bottom of the cliff stairs. A warmth would invade her in such moments, and her mind would begin to wander in the strangest directions. It was not long before she began to imagine that every man who claimed her hand was Evan. She found herself pretending that Mr. Sawyer had his strength, and Mr. Horsfield his handsome features, and Mr. Raikes his grace when he moved.

She received two offers of marriage that night, which she gently refused. Mr. Kelly, the second of her suitors, begged to know if her heart was already given. For some reason, her mind flitted to Evan and to the wicked manner in which he had pushed her back in the sand.

Mr. Kelly stunned her by saying, "You need say no more, for I see the answer writ in your eyes. Who is the deuced lucky fellow that I might congratulate him?"

"Indeed," she responded, surprised, "there is no one."

"I see," he murmured with a smile. "You mean to keep it a great secret. I only trust he is not an ineligible partis."

"No," she responded, both thinking of Evan yet not thinking of him.

"Never fear. I shall not breathe a word of our conversation to anyone."

Since it was by this time past three o'clock in the morning and she was feeling utterly fatigued, she did not try to dissuade Mr. Kelly from the opinion that she was in love with someone else. Instead, she begged him to take her to Lydia, who she could see was also appearing decidedly fatigued.

Once returned to West Street and after her maid had finished preparing her for bed, Katherine had just laid her weary head on her pillow when Lydia stole into the room. "Are you asleep yet, Katherine?"

"No, though I daresay I will be shortly. I am as tired as a dog after a hunt."

"As am I," Lydia said, carrying a candle. "I have been waiting for your maid to depart, for I have the most exciting news." She skirted the footboard and came to sit on the edge of the bed beside Katherine. Settling the candle on a nearby table, she did not hesitate to speak what was uppermost in her mind. "Mr. Keymer has asked me to be his wife."

Katherine sat up, sleep deserting her instantly. "He did not!" she exclaimed. "This very evening? But it is all so sudden. Whatever did you say?"

Lydia smiled softly. "I accepted him. How could I not when I love him so dearly?"

"Oh, Lydia," Katherine cooed, embracing her friend warmly. "Only tell me . . . when are you to be married?"

Lydia lowered her chin, and only then did Katherine realize her friend was weeping. "I do not know," she said mournfully. "Mr. Keymer means to speak with Mama on the morrow, but I know her opinion of him, that he was certainly suitable enough for Miss Pamberley of Lady Brook Cottage but not for Lydia Alistair. I hope I do not offend you in saying as much."

"Of course you do not."

"But I . . . I know she will forbid the marriage, and then what shall happen to me?" Lydia covered her face with her hands and a sob escaped her.

Katherine patted her shoulder. "Dearest, do but think," she said. "You are of an age to marry whomever you wish. You are one and twenty. If you truly wish to wed Mr. Keymer, she cannot prevent it. Indeed, no one can."

"I do not wish to elope, nor to marry without Mama's support and approval. I love her with all my heart, and the thought of wounding her in such a manner is more than I can bear. We . . . we are not just mother and daughter, but friends as well. Besides, until I met Mr. Keymer I shared her ambitions. Indeed, I welcomed them, for I had always hoped to marry a lord, like your sister Constance."

"There are not so many of them about to be had," Katherine offered in a sensible strain.

"I know, and it is a truly horrible thing to be lying abed at night and wondering when the next peer should die, making his heir the new holder of a title. Really, it is a terrible thing."

"And did you ever make such an effort?"

Lydia smiled ruefully. "Every night during the last season, and whenever a gentleman unknown to me would but enter a chamber I immediately sought Mama out to know if he was a peer or not."

"Oh," Katherine breathed, a little surprised by her friend's former strategies. "But all that is changed now."

"Yes, of course. I see now how silly it was, and I even wonder why Mama permitted me to be so ridiculous. Only—oh, Katherine—what if she will truly forbid me to marry Mr. Keymer?"

"There is only one way to discover her wishes," Katherine, said, drawing up her knees and pushing the covers back. "We must go to her at once."

"Oh, no!" Lydia cried. "We cannot! Not now!"

"Now," Katherine said. "For I know you. If you lose heart, you will never broach the subject. I mean to see that you do not let the night slip by without telling her what is going forward. You would regret it forever otherwise."

"I cannot," Lydia wailed.

At that, Katherine spoke sternly. "Do but think how unfair it would be to Mr. Keymer to allow him to seek an audience with your mother without her foreknowledge of his intentions. I think it would be cruel. If you say you love Mr. Keymer, then you must make a push. You must."

At that, Lydia straightened her shoulders. "You are very right," she said, nodding once firmly. "I had not thought of it in that way before. Only, will you come with me? I vow I shall swoon otherwise."

"Of course I shall."

Katherine slid from her bed and donned a serviceable robe. She hooked Lydia's arm and, taking up the candlestick which her friend had brought with her into the room, she led the way to Mrs. Alistair's bedchamber.

Mrs. Alistair was lying on her side, snoring gently, when Katherine pushed open the door.

"We should retire," Lydia whispered urgently. "See how she sleeps."

Katherine hesitated just long enough for Mrs. Alistair's snoring to stop with a decided halt, and her eyes to pop open. "What is it, child?" she queried, rousing herself and sitting up. "Whatever is amiss? What is the hour? Speak, Lydia! You are frightening me."

Katherine gave her friend an encouraging push. Lydia's voice squeaked as she said, "The hour is a little past four."

"Indeed? Is this true? Then I have been asleep for ten minutes. How very strange, for I feel as though I have been sleeping for days." She gave herself a shake and settled herself back into her pillow. "Only come to me and tell me whatever is the matter. Why are you crying?" She glanced from Lydia to Katherine and back. "Good heavens! Whatever could have happened to have caused you so much distress, for on the carriage ride home you seemed rather exhilarated?"

Lydia let a sob escape her as she fairly ran to her mother, plopping on the bed and falling into her arms. Katherine moved to stand at the foot of the bed and once or twice met Mrs. Alistair's concerned gaze as she comforted her daughter, who quite unintelligibly poured out her history with Mr. Keymer. Most of the circumstances were lost in Mrs. Alistair's shoulder and in the sobs which frequently escaped Lydia.

Mrs. Alistair continued patting her daughter's shoulder and petting her hair. After a moment, she said, "Come. Do sit up, my darling, for I cannot understand all you have told me, though I perceive that Mr. Keymer is somehow involved. Has he taken liberties with you?"

"Oh, no!" Lydia cried. "He would never do so, for he is a gentleman, a very fine, wonderful man. I love him and I wish to marry him."

At this clear confession, and undoubtedy because of the shocked expression on Mrs. Alistair's face, she once more fell into her mother's arms, sobbing even harder still.

Katherine watched Mrs. Alistair's expression fall rather heavily. She knew the older woman was letting go of all of her hopes, all of the plans she had made probably from the time she had rocked Lydia in her cradle. Tears brimmed in her eyes.

Finally, she waved Katherine away with a gentle sweep of her wrist and a watery smile. Katherine might have considered staying to support her friend, but there was just such an affection between mother and daughter which convinced her that only a happy outcome would result from the night's conversation.

She left the candlestick on a table and quit the room, stubbing her toe only once as she made her way to her bedchamber in the dark. She fell into bed with a deep sigh and was instantly asleep.

The next morning, she arose in time to attend church, alone, for she was given to understand that Mr. Keymer would be calling to perform his duty at the same hour as the morning service. Lydia did not seek her out, and Katherine left West Street feeling that she was being of use to the family by absenting herself during a time which could only be a sore trial for mother and daughter, no matter what the outcome.

She had been in hopes of seeing Evan at the Royal Chapel, but he was not present, a circumstance which cast her into such a depression of spirits that she could only wonder at her stupidity. What was Evan to her anyway but a friend who, for whatever reason, she enjoyed kissing? Perhaps it was better after all that he had failed to attend church.

When she returned to West Street, she met a sight which could only bring her the sweetest joy. Mrs. Alistair was smiling and weeping, and Lydia was standing beside Mr. Keymer, who was supporting her with an arm about her waist. She was smiling up into his eyes in the most tender fashion, and he was returning the smile with an equal degree of affection, which could only mean his proposals had been accepted by Mrs. Alistair.

"Katherine," Lydia called out, leaving Mr. Keymer's side to run to her. "Mama has consented. All she requires is that we wait a twelve-month in order to ascertain that ours is a true and abiding love. After that, we may marry with her blessing whenever we wish for it."

Katherine embraced her and afterward hurried to embrace Mr. Keymer as well. "You will both be very happy. No one can be in doubt of that, and what is a year! Scarcely anything. The months will fly as quickly as the seasons rise and fall and give way to the next."

Turning to Mrs. Alistair, she dropped to her knees before her and took up both her hands. "I have known for a very long time that you were all that a lady ought to be. You have been a wonderful example to me, and I have learned so much by observing your conduct. However, this morning you have proved yourself the very best of mothers, and I have learned yet a new lesson at your hand, of grace and of sense. If you have any reservations concerning Mr. Keymer's character, I wish to say that I believe Lydia will be the happiest of women, for Mr. Keymer's advice is sought by a duke and even a prince. Your grandchildren will have every advantage, not just because of his connections, but because of his kindness, his wisdom and the fine scope of his mind. Lydia could not have chosen a better man."

"Praise, indeed," Mrs. Alistair murmured, once more retiring to her kerchief.

"I did not mean to make you cry, ma'am," Katherine said, rising to her feet.

"I know you did not, but you succeeded anyway by speaking so kindly to me and by offering what I believe to be a careful rendering of your opinion of Mr. Keymer." She glanced his direction. "And should he live up to even half of it, I shall be more than content."

Mr. Keymer smiled and responded, "I fear no one

could live up to such an accolade as Miss Pamberley has showered upon me. However, I do mean to make your daughter a good husband, to bring her as much happiness as is in my power, and to make certain that our children will have every advantage within my command."

"Then I can wish for nothing more."

Katherine glanced from one beaming countenance to the next, her heart full yet empty. This is love, she mused, this gentle, purposeful flow between Lydia and Mr. Keymer. Would she ever know such a love?

That afternoon, lounging in his rooms, Evan listened in some wonder to his friend's news as well as to the recounting of how the event transpired.

"You are to wed Miss Alistair," he repeated, stunned. He had never imagined Mr. Keymer would marry. In some part of his thinking, he had always believed his friend was as committed to a bachelor's existence as he was. He had even been considering suggesting to Mr. Keymer that together they form a partnership of horse-breeding, trading and racing, since Mr. Keymer's knowledge of horseflesh nearly equaled his own.

Now, however, that would be impossible, for Lydia Alistair was of an age when all her thoughts would be centered upon first setting up her house in London and, shortly afterward, her nursery. Between Keymer's responsibilities to his wife and to the Duke of Relhan, there would be little room left for a friendship, let alone a partnership in trade.

He said as much.

Mr. Keymer nodded. "It is the way of the world," he stated solemnly, "and I am sorry for it to the degree that our friendship will diminish. However, there is one means by which you might delay such a circumstance."

Evan could hear the teasing note in his voice and did not hesitate to ask, "And what would that be?"

"Well, if you were to marry Miss Pamberley, then I should be obligated to visit Captain and Mrs. Ramsdell quite frequently since Lydia would insist upon it."

Evan was not so amused. "I do not know why you should say anything so ridiculous. I certainly hope you do not mean to recommend the married state to me at every turn as most newly affianced gentlemen tend to do. Once leg-shackled, these same men often pelt me with the advice that I, too, should marry, for then I would be overcome with joy."

"With the right woman, you would be. I have seen you with Miss Pamberley and I am persuaded she is inordinately suited to you."

Evan ignored his friend's broad hint. He was irritated by the conversation as a whole and felt neither like joking about the subject nor pondering any such idle suggestions as marrying Katherine. "How did you win over the mother?" he asked, instead. "She has been in search of a handle for her daughter's name since time out of mind."

Mr. Keymer shrugged. "Lydia spoke with her the night before, at Miss Pamberley's prompting. I believe she was nearly reconciled to our marriage when I begged for her daughter's hand, though I must say, Miss Pamberley spoke so well and so convincingly for me afterward that Mrs. Alistair's reserved manners have all but fled."

"Katherine spoke for you? How is this? Did you prompt her to do so?"

"On no account. The whole of it had the complete air of spontaneity. Even Lydia expressed her surprise that she had done so." He then related Katherine's warm recital of his virtues and her belief he would make Mrs. Alistair's daughter very happy.

"She said as much? She said all this to Mrs. Alistair, on her knees in front of the lady? She made her weep?"

"Yes, it is as I have told you. I owe her a great debt and mean to make it up to her if I can. I tell you again, you would be wise to marry her, for you will not find the likes of her again in another decade. I am convinced of it. The Pamberley ladies have a fine reputation. All of them are spoken of with great respect wherever they go. They have endured much in the past ten years, which I believe has served solely to prove each of their characters, Katherine Pamberley's no less than the others, that much is obvious."

Evan had much to ponder at the end of this speech. Not that he was any further motivated to take a wife, but rather that he wondered how much more he had failed to take notice of generally in Katherine's character. That she had spoken on Mr. Keymer's behalf, in his presence, was a great kindness on her part. But not just a kindness, for it reflected her ability to judge between one man and another. Now, had Mr. Wooding offered for Miss Alistair and she had made such a speech of him, he would have thought less of her—a great deal less! But recognizing Mr. Keymer's value was a stroke of common sense and perception which weighed mightily with him. He found he approved of Katherine now more than ever.

Not that it mattered, of course. She was nothing more than a friend to him and a woman he enjoyed kissing, a great deal too much for either his good or hers. He certainly hoped she was not now entertaining notions of marriage merely because he had coaxed her onto the beach and afterward kissed her while reclining on a bed of sand.

He sipped his coffee and peered out the window, his mind returning to the night before. He had quit Lady Walford's house rather abruptly after presenting Katherine to a besotted Mr. Kelly. Once returned to the ballroom, however, he found he no longer had a taste for dancing or any of the other common antics one might experience at a ball.

He wished to clear his head and had strolled toward

the Steyne, which was quite empty since the hour was midnight. He had walked at length, pondering life, his career as a soldier, his desire to take to horse-breeding full time, his inexperience at flushing out assassins, his almost dogged pursuit of Katherine Pamberley's lips, her forehead, her neck, her eyelids, even her company in general.

He had realized last night that he had never singled out a lady so completely before. He had always enjoyed a flirtation, but he usually handled the duration of the relationship with a great deal more caution and discretion. He could not precisely account for his conduct since his arrival in Brighton.

Of course, he was not the only man in the seaside watering hole who had found her intriguing. Indeed, as the weeks had passed, her popularity had actually grown instead of diminishing as was usually the case.

He could explain none of it. Perhaps he was like all the others and had become enchanted by qualities in Katherine undetectable, perhaps unknowable. She was beautiful, but so were many young ladies. She was conversant with modern affairs, as were a number of other ladies. She was kind, and her kindness did serve to distinguish her from most. She had ordered and sent a great deal of fabric to the workhouse. He knew of no one else of such a generous nature, and she was not so well circumstanced as a hundred Brighton belles. She had gained the Prince's attention. He had actually walked the length of the Corridor with her. An exceptional circumstance, to be sure. She had conducted herself discreetly in a race and lost with utter composure and grace. Now Mr. Keymer was full of her praise, and Evan's mind had grown full of her once more.

Oh, why the devil was he thinking about her so much? He decided then and there to cease such useless reflections. He turned to Mr. Keymer and asked if he had seen much of Wooding lately, or of Miss Page.

Mr. Keymer set his coffee cup on the table. "They are gone to the country, to Lady Beavan's estate, I believe, which as you know is but fifteen miles to the northwest from Brighton."

"Wooding and Miss Page?" Evan asked, startled.

"Mr. Page as well. Why? You look nearly apoplectic. A bit too much of the coffee, old boy!"

"Bah! Do not be ridiculous. It would seem he intends to make a match of it, then, with Miss Page."

"I believe so. Why do you disapprove?"

"Because he is a gamester and she an heiress," Evan stated.

"Is she, indeed? Yet no one here knows any such thing. I was certainly ignorant of it. How is this?"

"Mr. Page wished it kept quiet."

"Then I would presume Wooding is yet uninformed of her propitious circumstances."

"He knows. By God, he knows. I'll be damned if he does not!"

"Harsh words."

"The truth will out. He is after her fortune. Make no mistake."

"Lunsford, on the other hand—" Keymer began provocatively.

"Yes? What have you heard?"

"Only that he is in debt to the cent-per-centers for ten thousand."

"My God," Evan breathed. "How did you learn of it?"

"I made inquiries of Bow Street. It would seem he has worked for the government in the past as an agent provocateur but now appears to embrace the radical causes."

Evan settled his cup on the table as well. "Is he suspected of the recent incident at the donkey races?" he asked.

"As to that, I believe it is too large a leap, but I have a man watching him."

"This man would not happen to dress as a tradesman?"

"No, of course not," Keymer responded, chuckling. "Whyever would you say such a thing?"

"I saw Lunsford arguing with two men on the street at Hove the day of Katherine's race. Men of trade, apparently."

"Arguing?"

Evan nodded.

"Perhaps Lunsford owed each of them," Mr. Keymer suggested. "He is in debt here in Brighton already, though his cousin has settled a number of them."

Evan grimaced. "All the more reason for Wooding to pursue an heiress."

"I do not know," Keymer said solemnly. "He seems to love her."

"Love—bah!" Evan countered.

Mr. Keymer frowned at him, though an amused light glinted in his eyes. "You should not be so condemning, my friend, else later you might be required to eat your words!"

Evan met his gaze and could not keep from smiling. "I do not mean to be so cynical," he said. "And I am certainly not, where you and Miss Alistair are concerned." He lifted his cup to Keymer. "My congratulations and very best wishes to you both."

Fourteen

On Monday evening, Katherine had just entered the Castle Inn ballroom when Miss Kelly, flanked by Miss Framfield and Miss Hill, approached her. "I wonder that you can even present yourself in public," Miss Kelly sneered.

Katherine was stunned and might have answered her immediately, but Miss Hill spoke first. "Indeed, we all wonder at it," she said, her nose tilted upward.

"I think it shames you," Miss Framfield added.

Katherine did not hesitate to engage the battle. "Have your wits all gone a-begging?" she retorted, having grown heartily fatigued with Miss Kelly's ridiculous posturing. "I have done nothing wrong, and well you know it."

Miss Hill, a particular favorite of Miss Kelly's, took a step forward. "How can you speak so, when you have set so many rumors about for the strict purpose of completely reversing Miss Kelly's win at Hove?" She snapped her fan open in a provoking manner beneath Katherine's nose and pretended to cool herself.

Katherine ignored Miss Hill's antics completely, never permitting her gaze to waver from Miss Kelly's face for a moment. "I have done no such thing, and well you know it, though why you have insisted otherwise I cannot begin to imagine. Do you wish for a second match in order to prove your prowess? Is that what this is about? Or if you like, I shall proclaim here and now, in a very loud voice, the victory which was indeed yours at Hove and which I have never disputed. If you recall, I congratulated you more than once on the accomplishment."

Miss Kelly drew in her breath slowly. There was no evidence that Katherine's words had made the smallest impression on her. "I do demand a second contest, as it happens, but this time on the racecourse, beneath the stands, for all to witness. You robbed me of the first race, and I shall not be robbed of the second."

Katherine narrowed her eyes. "I robbed you of nothing."

"So you say," Miss Framfield interjected. "In which case, why would you not wish to enter into a second race in a more formal setting?"

"Because the setting is not in the least appropriate. Are you not aware how many of our hostesses would be unable to forgive such an action?"

"Not if several ladies entered the race and Mrs. Nutley sponsored it on behalf of the poor through the sale of tickets. I believe even the Prince Regent would attend such an event."

"You would sell tickets to the race?" Katherine asked, dumbstruck.

Miss Kelly lifted a brow, sneering once more. "I knew you had not the bottom for it. I have known it these many weeks since you first arrived in Brighton. You have a well-enough seat, but I have never before seen such a heavy-handed whipster."

"I am no such thing!" Katherine returned hotly. "If you wish for a race, then you will have it. Arrange the matter with Mrs. Nutley, inform me of the date, and I shall present myself, astride Prince, prepared to race anew."

Miss Kelly smiled with so much satisfaction that Katherine felt certain she had been tricked in some manner.

"It is already arranged," Miss Kelly stated confidently. "Mrs. Nutley agreed to it several days past for Monday next, in the afternoon, if that would please you?"

"Yes, Monday would be acceptable, only tell me, did Mrs. Nutley truly arrange the race?"

"Yes, but you know what she is, how fond she is of entertainment particularly if an excellent wager might be involved."

Both of these elements were certainly true of Mrs. Nutley.

"Then it is as good as settled?"

"Yes," Miss Kelly stated. "You may speak with her if you like. We were only awaiting your acquiescence. Now that we have it, I shall see you on the racecourse."

The ladies inclined their heads and moved away, leaving Katherine with the sensation that she had been run over by a mail coach. How in the world had she ever agreed to such a wretched scheme? And did Mrs. Nutley truly intend to sponsor the race? And why had she so lost her temper that Miss Kelly had actually got command of her?

Regardless, she was now committed to the race, so long as it was approved by Mrs. Nutley. She decided to search out that good lady and discover the particulars of the scheme. She still could not credit that any of Brighton's leading hostesses would condone such a race, yet Miss Kelly had spoken as though the matter was of little consequence.

She found Mrs. Nutley at cards and waited until her game of whist drew to a close. She then begged a word with her.

"I learned from Miss Kelly a short time ago that you were arranging a horse race next Monday, on the racecourse itself."

"Why, yes, I am," she said, beaming. "We intend to sell a great number of tickets and distribute the profits to the poor. Is it not a remarkable idea? It was Miss

Kelly's, after all. I think it shall be vastly amusing, with all female riders. Do you mean to join in the festivities?"

"Of course," Katherine responded, relieved. "I should be happy to oblige, particularly since the proceeds will relieve the sufferings of the indigent."

"You have a great heart, Miss Pamberley. Ah, but do forgive me. Lady Chiltingham is signaling to me and I did promise to be her partner for the next round of whist. She is an excellent player, and we intend to win a few pounds of Lady Walford and Mrs. Hill before the ball is through."

"Of course," Katherine responded. She watched Mrs. Nutley go, the dear lady scratching at her turban of yellow silk. She was still slightly bemused that Mrs. Nutley did not seem in the least concerned that she and Miss Kelly would be two of the riders in the race. However, Mrs. Nutley had greatly enjoyed the Hove race even though she lost her ten-pound wager. Whatever misgivings she might be feeling were laid to rest upon the sure knowledge the event would be properly sponsored.

With a faint shrug of her shoulders, Katherine returned to the ballroom, where Mr. Sawyer claimed her hand for the minuet.

On the following morning, quite early, Katherine emerged full-clothed from the sea-bathing machine and much to her surprise found Evan waiting to speak with her. She had not seen him since Saturday night, and over the past two days a terrible longing for his company had crept into her soul. How her heart strained toward him as images of the kiss she had shared with him, not so very far from where they stood even now, pressed into her mind. She found she could not think very clearly and seemed to have only one thought of the moment: how to find her way back into his arms.

But this was ridiculous! What could she ever achieve

by following such a course? Nothing but an increasing ache in her heart.

Fortunately for the hapless nature of her ruminations, she found that Evan was sadly out of temper. He did not seem in the least enamored of her, and she could only wonder in what way she had offended him this time. If she felt a certain disappointment, she refused to dwell on it. Yet, to greet him now, when he seemed all out of patience with her, dampened her spirits.

"Whatever is the matter, Evan, for you seem in the boughs?" she asked softly. She did not immediately descend the steps, but waited for him to answer her.

He threw his hand in the air. "What the devil is this nonsense I have heard that you mean to ride Prince next Monday afternoon in Mrs. Nutley's charity race?"

"Oh, I see. Then you have heard already."

"It is spoken of everywhere."

She watched him for a moment, then slowly climbed down the three steps to the sandy beach. He appeared desirous of brangling with her, but she was not of a mind to do so. She determined to answer him carefully and sensibly. "I was given to understand that the race was arranged entirely for the benefit of the poor, in which case why would I not wish to race?"

"You cannot be serious!" he returned adamantly. "No lady of quality would acquiesce to take part in such a scheme—for the poor or not! Can you honestly tell me that this was, indeed, Mrs. Nutley's idea that you should race?"

"Yes, absolutely," she returned, turning the brim of her bonnet away from the strong sunshine. "Although Miss Kelly provoked me into the contest in the first place, later I confirmed for myself Mrs. Nutley's approval of my participation. She seemed quite enthusiastic, I assure you."

Some of his temper cooled. "This is all very odd," he

remarked, his brow split with a frown. "Very odd. You must in some manner be mistaken."

"I am not. I made certain to speak of it to Mrs. Nutley within the hour after agreeing to Miss Kelly's scheme. She assured me that she thought very highly of my willingness to participate. She was rather delighted with the notion that the race would involve only female riders. Even had I wanted to withdraw, how could I have refused Mrs. Nutley?"

Evan shook his head, clearly bemused. "What, then, does Mrs. Alistair say of the race?"

"As to that, I do not know. I have not had an opportunity to speak of it to her. She is much occupied in Lydia's recent betrothal, and I must say I am come to believe she intends to relent of her original request that the couple wait a year. She is already discussing the cake for the wedding breakfast." She smiled at Evan, hoping he would take up her hint and change the subject.

His countenance lightened for a moment. "Mr. Keymer is *aux anges*. He seems very, very happy, and for his sake, I hope Mrs. Alistair will change her mind. Which puts me in mind of something I wished to say to you. According to Keymer, you spoke very forcefully and kindly on his behalf to Mrs. Alistair. He was infinitely grateful to you, as am I."

"I spoke from my heart," she stated, feeling shy suddenly.

He held her gaze for a very long moment. Her skin prickled with the pleasure of seeing a warm smile in his eyes.

"You performed a great kindness," he said.

She was surprised. "I am happy to hear you say so." Feeling a trifle embarrassed, she gestured to the bathing machine. "Do you mean to bathe this morning?"

He shook his head. "No. I mean to escort you to West Street, for I still hope to persuade you from racing on Monday week. Come." He offered his arm, which she took quite happily since it was always difficult to walk in sand.

As she headed in the direction of the cliffs, Katherine once more felt completely at a loss. "Then, even though I have Mrs. Nutley's patronage, you are opposed to the race? I do not understand you, Evan. If Mrs. Nutley approves, why would your sensibilities on the subject be more refined than hers?"

"I simply cannot like it," he stated. "This manner of exposure will open you to every sort of unfortunate remark. Surely you are aware of that."

"I will admit I thought as much at first, but Mrs. Nutley's enthusiasm changed my opinion. Besides, I am looking forward to laying to rest all the terrible rumors which have flown about Brighton since last week to the effect that I won the race at Hove. Miss Kelly is become quite piqued by the continued gabblemongering."

Evan frowned. "I have heard nothing on that score," he stated.

"It is not necessary that you have heard the rumors, only that Miss Kelly has, and that she has become quite offended. Indeed, she believes I am the author of them, even though I have assured her a hundredfold I am not. Mrs. Nutley's race is meant to put an end to all this nonsense."

"But there will be other competitors?"

"Yes, or so I have been given to understand, though I have no idea who they are. Mrs. Nutley said 'female riders.' "

Reaching the cliff stairs, she gathered up the skirts of her gown and began her ascent. "Who told you I was racing?" she asked.

"Mrs. Hill. I met her near Fisher's a little while ago. She was appalled to learn you had agreed to the scheme."

Katherine frowned. "Did she mention Miss Kelly in your discourse? No other competitors?"

"No, only you."

"And you say she was appalled?"

"Quite. I was not mistaken in that."

"How very odd," she returned. "Well, I daresay I should lay the matter before Mrs. Alistair. Mrs. Hill is a friend of hers, and I would not wish for her to meet with Mrs. Hill and discover what might be unhappy news from anyone but me."

She paused near the middle of the staircase and turned back to him. "Do you truly think it an entirely bad notion—the race, I mean?"

"Of course," he cried, quite astonished. "A public race?"

"Evan, I confess I fully concur with you."

At that, he smiled rather crookedly. "Is it possible we have actually agreed on something?"

Katherine giggled. "So it would seem, but I do not mean to make a habit of it." She turned back and continued climbing the stairs.

Evan followed her, his chest strangely tight. Her nose was a little pink again from having been in the sun. Even her arms were rather brown. She was, he thought, the picture of health and vibrancy. He realized she frequently surprised him. When he expected her to throw a tantrum, as a dozen other females might, she was uncommonly reasonable. When he thought his words might startle her, she would only lift a brow in response. When he was certain she would quail beneath his temper, she gave him word for word entirely.

And she was game for any lark——like walking on the beach in the moonlight. Desire took strong hold of him as his mind became filled with images of lying in the sand with Katherine. In the three days since he had last kissed her, she had rarely failed to be far from his thoughts.

If only she were not quite so pretty and her lips such a lovely shade of rose, else he might not be feeling as he often did in her presence, as though no pleasure on earth could be greater than taking her into his arms.

Reaching the top of the stairs, she turned toward him, a warm smile on her face. Faith, but she was so beautiful. His desire for her sharpened, and had they not been at the top of Russell Street, where the traffic was quite thick, he might have cast all caution to the wind and kissed her yet again. As it was, he had to be content in escorting her back to West Street. He offered to fetch a sedan chair for her, but this she waved aside. "I shall do no such thing. I enjoy walking. Perhaps it is not wholly fashionable, but I benefit so greatly from the exercise."

"I did not know you were in the habit of walking."

"When I am alone, always. Lydia is not so great a walker, and when she comes with me, we generally send for the carriage."

The conversation turned to many subjects after that, as she once again took his arm and he guided her to Mrs. Alistair's home. When the subject came round to Waterloo, she presented many questions which he was more than happy to answer.

"Does the battlefield always fill with dense smoke?"

"Of course, unless there is an inordinately strong wind. Between the cannons and the rifle flintlocks, which both discharge portions of gunpowder, a great cloud swells over the terrain."

"Much like after a display of fireworks."

"Only infinitely thicker."

"Were you much in Wellington's company?"

"On occasion, but he is a very great man, a duke now, of course, and his attention was always for men of greater rank whether in the army or among the *beau monde.*"

"I should like to meet him one day. From all the accounts in the newspapers he seems to me a most remarkable man. Only, how was it possible he did not perish at Waterloo? I have come to understand that he rode before the army across the line of regiments, encouraging the troops, throughout the entire battle."

At that, Evan smiled. "His fate, I would say. Providence would not have it otherwise, else we might have been brought into the French Empire ourselves."

"Impossible!" she exclaimed.

"Not so impossible as you might think. Bonaparte was a man of great brilliance, and had he not bungled his advance into Russia, the entire affair might have turned out quite differently."

"I cannot but shudder when I think of Russia and so many lives lost."

"Nearly half a million on that disastrous campaign." He turned to her and offered a sympathetic half smile. "You have a good heart, Katherine. I admire that about you."

"And you do not speak nonsense, at least not very often."

He chuckled at her teasing tone.

By now, he stood at the entrance to Mrs. Alistair's house. Katherine offered him her hand and he took it, but instead of responding with a friendly shake, he lifted her fingers to his lips. He could not help but place a lingering kiss on her gloved hand.

He heard her sharp intake of breath, and when he released her hand he was not surprised to find that a flush was upon her cheek and a familiar glitter in her eye. He felt again a powerful urge, which he had experienced so many times before, to kiss her. The street, however, was quite full of persons going hither and yon. He could do little else but bid her good-bye and watch her enter the house.

Evan returned to North Street shortly afterward and spent the next hour pondering the forthcoming race. He felt so certain she should not engage in the event that he soon took up a sheet of paper and a pen and addressed a letter to Lady Ramsdell, his sister-in-law. Constance might be able to intervene.

On Saturday evening at the Marine Pavilion, Katherine saw Evan for the first time since he had escorted her home from the beach four days earlier. Her attention became quickly fixed on him, on the dashing figure he cut among Brighton's *beau monde.* He was dressed fashionably in a coat of black superfine, an embroidered white waistcoat and black pantaloons. His shirtpoints were a moderate height and were not wilting as many were in the overly heated rooms. She felt her heart swell with affection as he caught sight of her and acknowledged her presence with a quick, warm smile. He made his excuses to Lady Chiltingham and began crossing the room to her. Did he know how handsome he was? He gave no evidence of it, for he was not a vain man by any means.

She felt an odd sensation of pride as he made his way toward her. She truly admired him and valued that he had singled her out. She had missed him very much, she realized, in the days since she had last seen him. Her fingers began to tremble, and only then did she realize how rapidly her heart was beating.

Was this love, she wondered, *to be missing someone so much after only a few days apart? To be trembling? To have one's heart feel as though fireworks were exploding from within?*

It was all such a mystery, but did she love him?

When he arrived to stand before her, he complimented her on her violet gown and the manner in which her maid had dressed her hair in a knot of curls atop her head.

"Thank you," she responded softly. "And may I say how dashing you appear this evening? Brummell's fashions agree with you quite handsomely."

"As an arbiter of fashion, Beau Brummell is not only

unequaled, but has my undying gratitude. You cannot imagine how relieved I am that a gentleman no longer must needs appear in society in heavy brocades, powdered wigs, and stockings sporting the figures of clocks."

Katherine chuckled. "I cannot imagine a soldier, like you, dressing in such a manner."

"Nor can I," he agreed. His expression grew somber suddenly. "I was hoping this evening that you might give me a little relief and tell me you are not racing on Monday, though I must say all the gossip still tends to lead in the opposite direction."

"I have not had occasion to speak yet with Mrs. Alistair," she said. "She is presently much consumed with Lydia's wedding, which, as you must know by now, is to take place in a month, after all."

He nodded. "Mr. Keymer smiles all the time. Really, he has become unbearable."

Katherine laughed.

Evan took a step closer and lowered his voice. "I must beseech you again, Katherine, to leave off racing. It is madness. Surely by now you have received some criticism for your involvement."

"Yes, from Mrs. Hill and Mrs. Framfield. I do not, however, pay either of them a great deal of heed. I told them both that unless Mrs. Nutley wished it otherwise, I would not disappoint her, for she was expecting me to take part in her charity event."

He frowned. "I think there is something I should tell you. I chanced upon Miss Kelly last night, just after the Promenade, and I asked her if she was racing on Monday. She held my gaze rather contemptuously and said that of course she was not, that her mother would never permit her to engage in a public race."

Katherine was stunned. "But she arranged it! I do not understand." She thought back to the moment at the Castle Inn when Miss Kelly provoked her into the race. At the time she had felt tricked in some manner, and apparently she had been, but she could not understand why, to what purpose.

Evan glanced about the chamber. "Mr. and Mrs. Nutley have just now arrived. Come. Let us ask Mrs. Nutley what she desires you to do."

"I think that would be best," she said.

He took her arm and guided her slowly across the Red Saloon.

Mr. Nutley was already mopping his brow, for he was always hot at the Pavilion. When he eyed her, he immediately broached the subject before Evan could bring it forward himself. "What is this I hear that you mean to race on Monday," he queried, "at m'wife's races?"

Katherine shook her head, greatly confused. "Miss Kelly desired me to do so," she explained. "She had come to believe, however erroneously, that I had told everyone I won the contest at Hove, and she wanted a second race in order to prove that hers was the better horse."

He scowled in some concern. "I may not be conversant with every nuance of polite life," he said, turning to his wife and addressing her, "but I cannot believe it would be at all the thing for Miss Pamberley and Miss Kelly to engage in such a race. Am I mistaken?"

Mrs. Nutley shook her head. "No, of course not," she stated emphatically. "My dear Miss Pamberley, I cannot imagine how you came to believe Miss Kelly meant to take part in my charity race. I promise you, she would never do so, being as elegant a young lady as she is."

"I am very confused," Katherine admitted. "I could not have been mistaken in Miss Kelly—she was adamant in challenging me to a race. However, if you will recall, ma'am, I sought you out most specifically to inquire whether you wished for me to race. You approved of me, of that I am certain."

"I did no such thing," she responded, quite shocked.

"I remember the conversation most distinctly and I said nothing . . . that is . . . oh . . ." She broke off suddenly, her features now pinched with a frown similar to her husband's. "Are you saying that when you said you meant to participate in the race, you meant you intended to actually ride your horse?"

"Why, yes, because I believed that was what Miss Kelly intended."

Mrs. Nutley opened her eyes very wide. "I thought you meant to purchase a number of my tickets!" she exclaimed. "Nothing more, I assure you."

"Oh," Katherine responded, completely dashed.

Mr. Nutley crimped his lips together and narrowed his eyes. "Miss Kelly, eh? I never could abide that young lady. Too snippety by half, and as jealous as a green bean on a squash hill."

"Whatever do you mean?" Katherine queried.

"He means," Mrs. Nutley continued, "that you have been tricked, my dear. Miss Kelly only wanted you to either enter the race or be known to have entered the race, that you might incur some disfavor of our hostesses. You must admit you have stolen any number of her beaux from under her nose since your arrival, and she was the acknowledged belle of Brighton before you came. It is only natural she might wish to give you . . . what is it you always say, Mr. Nutley?"

"A leveler."

"That's it! She has given you a leveler. But pay no heed, for I shall make it widely known that it was all a hum, that you never intended to race."

"Thank you," Katherine returned, utterly stunned. "Only tell me, ma'am, who are the female riders then, the ones racing on Monday?"

"It is the most famous thing, though I am keeping it a great secret—performers from Astley's, in London! Is it not a fabulous notion!"

"Indeed, it is," Katherine cried. "From Astley's! I have

long desired to visit the amphitheater and see all the extraordinary riding feats."

"You would be vastly amused!" Mr. Nutley cried. "Ah, but I see Lady Chiltingham is waving madly at us. Come, my dear, it would not do to keep Her Ladyship waiting."

"Upon no account," Mrs. Nutley agreed.

With that, the pair excused themselves and left Katherine alone again with Evan.

"You were so right," she said. "I feel quite foolish to have believed Miss Kelly, but why would she go to such lengths to harm me?"

Evan chuckled. "I tend to think Mr. Nutley had the right of it. She has been as jealous of you as a green bean on a squash hill."

Katherine laughed. "It is all such nonsense, after all."

"Indeed it is," he responded.

Evan watched her for a long moment, light from the lustres overhead playing on her brown curls. Some thought rose in his mind, a compliment he wished to pay her, yet it would not form on his tongue. He did not seem to have the words with which to tell her exactly what he was seeing in her.

His mind wandered to the drawing room of Sir Jaspar Vernham's home, The Priory, in which his brother and Constance Pamberley were joined in matrimony. He had seen the light in his brother's eye as he gazed upon his bride, as though he were seeing so many things hidden from everyone else. A lover's eye.

Was that how he was seeing Katherine right now, through eyes filled with love?

"Miss Alistair is waving to me," she said, interrupting his thoughts. "Would you excuse me, Evan?"

"Of course," he said. He watched her go, enjoying how she carried herself and that she seemed so unaware of her beauty and elegance. Good God, was he in love with her?

He turned away, uneasy with such thoughts, and bent his mind toward the distressing message he had received from the landlord of The Ship Inn at Hove but a few minutes before departing for the Pavilion. A rumor had surfaced, a terrible one to the effect that another attempt would be made on the Prince's life, this time at Monday's horse race involving the female riders. The publican had been unable as yet to obtain any helpful details but hoped that very soon he would have more information to communicate.

When Evan had spoken earlier with the Prince's men, he had learned that the rumor had already been conveyed to His Royal Highness. Beyond acknowledging that, yes indeed, the Regent was aware of the seriousness of the information The Ship Inn publican had provided, Prinny refused to forgo the pleasure of seeing the race on Monday.

As he reached Mr. Keymer, he turned back to take one last look at Katherine and he withheld a deep sigh. An odd ache had developed in the vicinity of his heart which he could not explain.

As Katherine crossed the room, she noticed that Lydia was conversing with Miss Page, who appeared decidedly, and rather strangely, somber. She could not help but wonder if the young lady was well, for her complexion was quite pale and there was a pinched look about her eyes.

Miss Page smiled rather falteringly as she said, "Miss Alistair was just telling me about the gown she is having made up for her wedding."

"Satin!" Lydia cooed, "and as much lace as I can manage without appearing as though I am having a court dress made up for the occasion."

"Whether a mountain of lace or none at all," Katherine offered, "you will be a beautiful bride."

Lydia giggled and sighed and giggled a little more. "I

have never been so happy," she murmured, glancing from Katherine to Miss Page. Her gaze caught on something across the chamber. "Oh, I see Mrs. Nutley is waving to me. I must go to her, for she had some notion or other about a veil I ought to wear with my gown. You will excuse me?"

"Of course," Katherine said. She could not help but smile as she watched her friend leave, for it would seem that Lydia had forgotten entirely that it was she who had summoned her from Evan's side but a moment ago.

Katherine turned to Miss Page. "I have never seen her happier," she said.

"She is to be married," Miss Page said. "She has the very best of excuses for being a trifle forgetful."

"The very best." Katherine would have asked Miss Page concerning her opinion on the subject of wedding veils, but the waifish young lady had suddenly paled even further. Her gaze was fixed on a point past Katherine's shoulder on the opposite side of the entrance.

"I cannot believe *he* is here—that he is allowed to cross these portals," Miss Page murmured enigmatically.

Katherine wondered to whom she might be referring and glanced in the direction of Miss Page's gaze. She saw Mr. Wooding conversing with his cousin Mr. Lunsford.

Katherine did not understand Miss Page's statement. She had supposed Miss Page was nearly betrothed to Mr. Wooding, for she had come to understand that her father had accompanied the interesting pair to Lady Beaven's home only a week past. Had something occurred to disrupt the courtship? "Why should Mr. Wooding be unacceptable to the Prince?" she asked. "He has always been a favorite of His Royal Highness."

"He still is, I . . . I am sure of it," she stammered. "I was speaking of . . . of Mr. Lunsford. But I mean to say no more. It is merely that . . ."

Miss Page's eyes filled with tears and she began to tremble.

Katherine caught her arm and begged her to move into the Chinese Corridor. "Just until you are more comfortable," she said. She could not imagine what was going forward to have so deeply overset Miss Page.

Fifteen

Once in the corridor away from listening ears, Katherine addressed Miss Page. "You are trembling," she stated softly. "Whatever is amiss, for I have never seen you so distressed before?"

"I cannot say," she whispered in utter anguish. "If *he* should discover it! Oh, Miss Pamberley! I am so frightened."

"Let us continue to walk down the hall as though we came here for no other purpose. In that way, if anyone should come upon us, we would appear as two ladies bent on having a comfortable coze."

"Yes, yes, that would be best," Miss Page responded hurriedly. "Only, do you think anyone can hear us?"

"Not if we talk as though telling secrets, keeping our voices very low." She whipped her fan open in a theatrical manner and held it against her cheek as she leaned toward Miss Page. Deepening her voice, she added, "What do you say?"

The silliness of Katherine's antics caused the young lady to finally take a deep breath as she, too, unfurled her fan. She even ventured a half smile.

"Better?" Katherine asked.

"A little, thank you," she responded.

"Then tell me what has troubled you so deeply."

Miss Page, anxious to be rid of the news which was

keeping her in a state of severe agitation, poured the history forth with rapidity. She had been returning from sea-bathing yesterday morning and had decided to complete the morning's exercise by walking the length of the beach to the groynes near the stairs. "For the tide was not so high as to be bothersome, and I have always enjoyed long walks in Worcestershire."

She had come to rest at the base of one of the embankments, before climbing the stairs, when a familiar voice had assailed her. Here, she paled anew. "Mr. Wooding's! At first I was *aux anges,* Miss Pamberley, for it cannot have escaped your notice that I have become sincerely attached to him. But when the next voice to intrude was that of his cousin's, I felt compelled to keep my presence quiet. Mr. Lunsford quite frightens me. I have heard his temper twice since his arrival in Brighton, and I do not know how Mr. Wooding bears his company, especially since . . . that is, he said . . . oh, dear, I am feeling faint again."

"Come," Katherine commanded her. "Let us sit down, only do keep your voice a little lower."

"Yes, of course."

After taking her seat, she continued. "Mr. Lunsford was saying something to Mr. Wooding about how he was being a coward, that all was settled for Monday and that he would receive his prize for his part in the matter once the dog was *despatched.* Yes, those were his words—*once the dog was despatched,* which of course means killed! Well, at first I thought he was referring to Mr. Wooding's dogs, or one of them, for he has a fine tack of hunters in Lincolnshire, but Mr. Wooding responded that he had never agreed to a prize, or any of it, and that Mr. Lunsford would settle nothing by engaging in an activity which could only bring him to grief."

Katherine shook her head, perplexed. "But what do you believe it all means?"

A tear suddenly rolled down Miss Page's cheek. "Mr.

Lunsford is an acknowledged Jacobin. I believe when he speaks of a dog, he is speaking of the Prince of Wales."

Katherine gasped. "The Prince? You mean as in 'The prince must die'?"

"That is precisely what I believe. I have heard Mr. Lunsford speak of Prinny in the most hateful of terms. At times his language is vile. I have pondered what I heard yesterday a hundred times and I have concluded . . . oh, how am I to even speak these words aloud?" She drew breath and forced herself to continue, "I believe he means to injure the Prince at the races on Monday."

Katherine felt ill and could understand completely why Miss Page was so distressed. "Did either of the gentlemen say as much, specifically?"

Miss Page's lips quivered. "No. I could not bear to hear more on the subject. I was trembling from head to foot and nearly swooned twice upon retracing my steps up the beach. I have spoken to no one save you."

Katherine frowned, "Did Mr. Wooding hint you away from the races?"

She shook her head. "No . . . that is, not precisely. He did wonder that you had entered the race, for it is not at all the thing. I believe he had some concern on that head, but he said nothing to me about not attending the races. Miss Pamberley, you must not think ill of Mr. Wooding. It is merely that he is become ensnared by his cousin. He grew up with Mr. Lunsford, you see, for Mr. Lunsford was an orphan. Wooding's father permitted him to live in his home, to be educated by the same tutors Mr. Wooding enjoyed. I believe Mr. Wooding sees him as a brother more than a cousin."

"As I expect anyone would under such circumstances," Katherine responded sincerely. Her mind then drifted to the gathering in the red drawing room as she wondered just what she ought to do with the information Miss Page had shared with her. She felt certain she should tell Evan not only of her conversation with Miss Page, but also of Miss Page's knowledge of Mr. Lunsford's character and attitude toward the Prince Regent.

She said as much to Miss Page.

"On no account!" Miss Page cried, horror-struck.

"I feel I must, for at the very least, Captain Ramsdell would be able to detain Mr. Lunsford during the race tomorrow and perhaps thereby prevent a second assassination attempt."

Miss Page's lower lip trembled. "I fear for Mr. Wooding," was all she would say in a woebegone fashion.

Later, after supper had been served and the guests were gathered about the pianoforte listening to Lydia play, Katherine drew Evan aside. She carefully explained what Miss Page had told her. When she was done, she queried, "Do you believe the Prince is in danger?"

He nodded, his gaze shifting to locate Mr. Lunsford. When he found him conversing with Miss Framfield, his features hardened. "The government is well aware of his Jacobin activities. If his conversation with his cousin does indeed reflect an intention to harm our Prince, then Miss Page has done well to reveal her terrible secret. Besides, more than one of the Prince's own spies have received information to the effect that an attempt will be made on his life on Monday."

Katherine drew in her breath slowly. She found she was trembling. Then it was truly possible that Lunsford was the assassin after all. "What will you do?" she asked quietly.

At that, he lifted his brows. "Why, I shall have a conversation of my own with Mr. Lunsford." He then turned to her more fully. "Will you promise me this much, Katherine—will you refrain from attending the races, you and Miss Alistair? The rumors have been rife for so long that I could not be at ease knowing you were present at the racecourse."

"I could not agree with you more," she said, greatly

subdued. She had come to believe that she could have been killed during the donkey races—that a small step in the wrong direction at the wrong moment might have easily ended her life.

"And now," he said, drawing a deep breath, "I must speak with Keymer."

The next day, Sunday, Katherine received a brief billet from Evan to the effect that both he and Mr. Keymer were having an extended conversation with Mr. Lunsford and that he expected to be fully occupied through the rest of the day and possibly the night discussing several pertinent matters with the man he now referred to as a *completely hardened gamester.*

Unfortunately, gaming is all he will admit to, his letter read, *that and concerted praise for his cousin who he confessed frequently paid off his gambling debts. You may have been right all along, Katherine. It would seem Wooding is not so bad a fellow as I had first thought, and for all my harsh opinions regarding him, particularly as a friend to you, I do apologize. As for Lunsford, given all that Miss Page was able to reveal concerning his professed dislike of the Regent, as well as Mr. Keymer's knowledge of his Jacobin activities, we are expecting to eventually learn the truth about his intentions.*

Katherine felt utterly sobered by the letter. The very notion that someone with whom she was acquainted could actually plot and attempt an assassination so filled her with horror that she could do little else but sit in quiet reflection and hope that the entire matter would be settled before the next day. She was content to finally be in agreement with Evan concerning Mr. Wooding's character, but the circumstances were so distressing that she could not be happy.

That night, as she lay in her bed staring up at the shadowed canopy, her mind soon became overrun with thoughts of a possible assassination of the Regent at to-morrow's races, as well as with the earlier attempt. She considered Mr. Lunsford and the possibility that he was the assassin, or in league with a group intent on revolution.

Something nagged at her, however, so much so that for hours she tossed upon her bed like a rowboat on a windy lake, bouncing and wondering and worrying. She reviewed everything Miss Page had told her. *Once the dog was despatched.*

Why did that sound so familiar to her? *Despatched.* Was the reference truly to murder? She thought of messengers sent between regiments bearing despatches. Was Lunsford a messenger of some sort?

She recalled the first attempt on Prinny's life, over a fortnight past. Her mind cast about for the details of the horrifying event—the donkeys; the girls racing for gowns and bonnets; the muscled footmen; the firecrackers; the gunshot; Evan leaving her in the crowds; Mr. Wooding holding Miss Page; being pushed, shoved and bruised on her leg; Mr. Lunsford on the ground with his head cut open. Could an assassin have been injured in the affray? Possibly. When a crowd panics, anyone might be hurt, even an assassin.

She slept poorly that night. Her dreams were filled with images of armies and terrible battles, of Evan lying wounded on a field, of Mr. Lunsford laughing, of Miss Page weeping. She awoke the following morning with a dull headache.

Yet once more, her mind became seized with images of the assassination attempt at the donkey races. She knew something was amiss, that some piece of the puzzle was trying to work its way to the forefront of her mind. Her thoughts turned, oddly enough, to the evening of Mrs. Nutley's ball when she had allowed Evan to escort her to Mr. Nutley's billiard room. She had spent her time agreeably throwing dice for all the gentlemen gathered about the green baize table.

What was it Evan had said about false dice?

Despatchers.

That was it!

She sat up in bed abruptly. Mr. Lunsford had not been speaking of murdering anyone when Miss Page overheard his conversation with Mr. Wooding, but of making use of *despatchers,* a vulgar term for false dice. Lunsford was a gamester, not an assassin; of this she was convinced.

Still, her mind was restless, hurrying from one thought to another. She could not rid herself of the images of the panicky crowds during the donkey races. If Mr. Lunsford was not the assassin, then who was?

She closed her eyes and tried to bring forth more images of that day, but the sequence of events had occurred so swiftly—the exploding firecrackers, the gunshot, the charging crowds—all seemed to be a blur. Try as she might, nothing of use would come forward.

She decided she must inform Evan of her suspicions concerning what Mr. Lunsford may have meant by saying *once the dog was despatched.* She quickly penned a letter to that effect and sent it by way of one of Mrs. Alistair's footmen.

She rang for her maid, ready to begin dressing for the long morning which would be spent with Lydia. She paced her bedchamber floor, a supreme restlessness at work within her. She considered the many wonderful hours she had spent in the Prince Regent's company at the Pavilion. The thought that he might be harmed today at the races worked in her miserably. The very idea of it plagued her until by the time Marie arrived, she was nearly in tears.

"Yes, the lavender muslin will serve," she stated absently to her maid's query about which gown she desired to wear.

She turned abruptly to her wardrobe. "No, not the lavender muslin!" she exclaimed suddenly. "My light blue habit. Yes, that is what I must wear today."

"Miss Pamberley!" Marie cried. "Do you mean to race, then? After all that has happened?"

Katherine nodded. "Yes, for a life—a very important life—is in danger, and I must do what I can to intervene. Please hurry, though. We have not much time. The hour is approaching nine and the race is at ten."

Katherine was about to pen a second letter to Evan explaining her change of mind about racing, but at that moment the door opened, and instead of Lydia appearing in the reflection of her looking glass, another lady entirely strode into the room.

"Constance!" she cried. "Whatever are you doing here?" She rushed forward and embraced her eldest sister. "What an extraordinary surprise."

"Katherine, darling. Oh, how beautiful you are, and what a fashionable habit."

"Thank you, only do but look at you!" Her gaze swept over her sister's swelling figure. "I had almost forgotten you were increasing."

"Six months now," she said. A stricken look entered her eye. "Do I assume by the habit your maid is holding that you intend to race after all?"

"But how did you know?" she asked, shocked.

"Ramsdell and I had a letter from Evan several days past. He was greatly concerned that you had agreed to take part in a race that would put you beyond the pale. I believe he desired our presence hoping that one or the other of us might be able to dissuade you."

Katherine took Constance's hands in hers and led her to the chaise longue. "There is so much I must tell you," she said. She told her about Miss Kelly's initial challenge and how it had been all a hum, for Miss Kelly had never intended to race. Then she discussed the rumors rampant about town concerning a second assassination attempt on the Prince's life, as well as the most recent situation with

Mr. Lunsford. "Who I have come to believe is precisely what he professes to be, a gamester only. I am convinced I saw the assassin that day at the donkey races, but I cannot say which of the many persons rushing around madly he might have been."

Constance appeared grave as she settled herself on the comfortable couch. "Then it is true that Prinny's life is indeed in danger?" she queried. When Katherine nodded, her sister continued, "Ramsdell has been deeply concerned these many weeks and more for the Regent's welfare. Now, however, I begin to fear for your safety equally as much. Do you say that on the day of the donkey races, you might have been killed as well?"

"I believe the assassin was standing very near to me at the moment he fired his weapon."

Constance pressed a fist to her breast. "Pray, do not go to the races today, dearest. If anything should happen to you—!"

Katherine's eyes filled with tears. "I must race," she said quietly. "I must do all that I can to avert so heinous a crime. I know it makes little sense, since I will be racing very hard about the course, but I am persuaded that I shall be able to scrutinize the crowds in a manner none of the Prince's men will be able to. Also, I have a nagging sense that I truly do know who the assassin is, and should I chance to see this man, then I will be able to act quickly. You know what Prince is, how swiftly he responds to my commands. Oh! I just realized that my horse bears the same name as the Regent!"

Constance suddenly embraced her. "You were always the bravest of us all, Katherine. Nothing ever seemed to be too daring or bold or impossible that you could not accomplish the feat. I will not forbid you to participate, nor even attempt to persuade you to do other than what you think best. Indeed, how could I possibly succeed when I can see that you have grown into a young woman

with a mind of her own? Only, pray take the greatest
care throughout."

"I will," Katherine said, her heart filling with determination.

Evan was exhausted. Mr. Lunsford had proved intrac-
table through a long night of arduous questioning. All
that he would say was that Miss Page had misunderstood
the exchange, that he and Mr. Wooding had been referring to a wager only, not an assassination attempt on the
Prince.

"If you will recall," he had repeated endlessly, "I was
wounded the day of those ridiculous donkey races. I had
to go to the infirmary, or have you windmills in your
brain-box?"

Evan in turn had repeatedly reminded Mr. Lunsford
of his Jacobin associations and philosophies.

Mr. Lunsford had been adamant. "I have never coun-
tenanced violence. Besides, of what use would it be to
wound a prince, particularly this prince? He is a fop,
nothing more."

"Do you have associates who desire his death?"

"Any number, for he is a flagrant extravagance in the
face of the people's suffering. Have you never been to
the East End?"

"Of course I have."

"Then you know they . . . we . . . have cause to be
outraged."

"The Prince is our future sovereign and as such de-
serves our loyalty and support."

"Then you are a fool, for he is a spendthrift and robs
his kingdom of her future bread."

His arguments were not without merit, but Evan was
determined to wear him down. "What of the race tomorrow? You spoke of the Prince being wounded tomorrow
at the races."

"Wooding and I were entering into a wager, nothing more. It had nothing to do with the Regent. The dog being despatched was a metaphor only, for a . . . a wager."

"According to Miss Page, Mr. Wooding was reluctant to, er, *wager* with you, and he felt the whole scheme to be injurious to yourself. Why would he think the scheme to be a bad one?"

"Miss Page misunderstood the entire conversation. There were merely some debts to be paid, and I suggested a gaming venture, in which my cousin was disinclined to participate."

All this sounded quite reasonable. Evan narrowed his eyes at Lunsford. "Will you swear to this?"

"I will."

Since the hour was well past midnight, Evan was unwilling to summon Mr. Wooding in hopes of having the wager illuminated for him. He felt there was something Lunsford was not telling him, but he no longer sensed that the gamester was interested in risking his neck at Tyburn Tree by plotting to assassinate the Prince.

By four in the morning, he and Keymer concluded there was nothing more to be done except to keep Mr. Lunsford under arrest until the races concluded sometime after ten o'clock.

He returned, therefore, to his home in North Street, climbed wearily into bed, and within a minute or two drifted into a profound sleep.

Sometime later, he awoke with a start as a rough hand shook him firmly by the shoulder.

"What the devil!" he cried, sitting up abruptly.

"You look like the devil," his brother said, smiling at him from the side of his bed.

"Ramsdell! Good God, what are you doing here? What is the hour? I feel as though I just tumbled into bed."

"By the look of you, I would say you did. It is nearly nine o'clock."

Glancing at the clock on the mantel, Evan shifted his legs over the edge of the bed. "Nine o'clock! So it is! I need to be at the racetrack by ten." He turned toward his brother, "I say, I am glad you are come, though I must presume you have seen Katherine and know that she intends to remain at home with Miss Alistair until the races are concluded."

Ramsdell cleared his throat. "When I left Mrs. Alistair's home, Katherine was wearing a lovely blue velvet riding habit, and a hat with a white ostrich feather which I am persuaded my wife admired excessively, and I had already sent word to the stables to have her gelding sent to the racecourse."

"What?" Evan thundered. "But she promised! We were agreed on her remaining in West Street. Why could she not, just this once, do as I bid her!"

Lord Ramsdell smiled crookedly. "She is a Pamberley, I will give her that. If she is half as stubborn as my wife, you waste your breath, my good man. Don't worry. I have a hackney waiting."

Evan pressed the heels of his hands to his tired eyes but shifted his gaze abruptly to the doorway at the sound of his valet's voice. "Captain Ramsdell?"

"What is it?" he queried.

"These came for you while you slept." He held two letters aloft.

"Come," Evan said. He took them and bade his man to prepare his shaving gear.

Evan saw that one of the notes was from Katherine and the other from The Ship Inn at Hove. The innkeeper must have learned something after all! His heart began thumping against his ribs. He read Katherine's missive first, however, and said aloud, "I believe she has the right of it. She thinks when Lunsford spoke of *despatching* the dog that he was talking about having *despatchers* made up."

"False dice? Whatever for? And who the deuce is Lunsford?"

"It is a long story, but I will tell you all in the hackney."

He broke the seal of the second letter and read the contents quickly. "Good God," he murmured. "Worse and worse, but I believe this is what we have been hoping for."

One of the landlord's many friends had overheard several threats against the Regent's life made by a former British soldier wounded at Salamanca and now forced to earn his living by selling trifles to children, like hoops, sticks and slingshots. The fellow apparently had flown into a rage upon hearing the Regent praised. He vowed to put an end very soon to his extravagance, for it was a crime that decent Englishmen who had served in His Majesty's Army struggled to keep flesh and bone together while Prinny had enough gold in the Pavilion to build a hundred hospitals for the suffering.

When provoked to set an hour for accomplishing this feat, the fellow had had just enough ale to pronounce the Monday races the right sort of opportunity he required.

Evan knew that a large number of returning soldiers, particularly those who had been crippled in battle, had little to look forward to from their country except encroaching poverty. He had great sympathy for the plight of his fellow soldiers but could not countenance the use of murder to attain better conditions for England's indigent. At the same time, Evan could not help but wonder what the Prince might think, if anything, of the assassin's complaints. He would be a wise ruler to contemplate the severity of the grudge a disabled soldier held against a man who had pillars of solid gold in his dining room.

"Read this," he commanded his brother, handing the letter to him. "Here, I believe, is the information you wished me to unearth all these many weeks. Our assassin has an even stronger motivation for harming our future sovereign than I might have guessed, something for which I have a great deal of sympathy. It would seem he once served in His Majesty's Army."

While Lord Ramsdell consumed the contents, Evan shaved quickly. A few minutes later, the brothers were pounding down the stairs together and fairly leaping into the waiting hackney coach.

"It is imperative, Mrs. Nutley. I must and I will race." Katherine stood staunchly against the flustered lady who was trying to impede her progress onto the racecourse.

"Oh, but Miss Pamberley," Mrs. Nutley fairly wailed, wringing her hands. "You will be lost to all polite society in Brighton if you choose to race this day. Surely you must know as much. I thought we had settled this terrible business at the Pavilion. How disappointed Mr. Nutley will be!"

"No, he will not!" a voice boomed out.

"Mr. Nutley!" Katherine cried, turning toward the deep, masculine voice.

Mr. Nutley's expression was quite serious as he approached her. Taking both her hands in his, he addressed her like a kindly father. "My dear, I could never be disappointed in anything you set your mind to. I have not known you these many weeks and more without having learned a degree or two of your character. If you feel you must race, for whatever reason, then I trust your judgment implicitly."

"Mr. Nutley," his good wife interjected strongly, "your wits have gone a-begging!"

Katherine bit her lip to keep from smiling. She looked into Mr. Nutley's eyes and said, "You have made me very happy today. Believe me when I say I had much rather not race, but I feel compelled to."

"Then race you shall." With that, he took the reins of

her horse and led her to the riding block which she used to swiftly mount her horse. Mr. Nutley would not permit her yet to take the reins, but instead led her onto the racecourse himself.

The closer she drew to the starting line, at which the four female Astley riders were already assembled, the louder the whispering and hushed cries arose in the stands. From the ropes, however, where the ordinary folk of Brighton were gathered, she heard nothing but applause and more than once the comment that she "were the young miss wat gave the girls the fabric at the poorhouse."

"You are one of the bravest men I have ever known," Katherine whispered, "to be supporting me in this fashion."

Mr. Nutley glanced back at her, smiled and winked.

She was greatly encouraged by his aplomb. For someone she admired to express so much confidence in her was so generous an act of kindness that she found tears starting to her eyes. Knowing that he had probably saved her from being completely ostracized, while at the same time opening himself up to all manner of criticism, deepened her devotion to him.

Once at the starting line, he gave her the reins and. clasping her hand, said, "Cross the finish line first, Miss Pamberley!"

If only that were my true object, she thought as she in turn squeezed his hand. "I shall do my best," she promised, then watched him retreat swiftly toward the stands.

She glanced up in the stands and saw that the Prince Regent was just now arriving, which at least had the benefit of distracting the crowd from her scandalous presence on the racecourse. He was, as always, groomed to perfection even though his girth made him an almost comical character. He waved to the crowds up and down the course, which set the multitude cheering happily. It seemed so impossible that someone present at the race-course was actually intent on harming him.

Katherine turned her attention to her competitors.

The Astley riders, four in all, sat astride fine horses obviously groomed for show. Together, the riders made an admirable assemblage, costumed identically in fine black hats, sporting enormous yellow ostrich feathers and long black riding habits, the skirts of which hung nearly to the ground. Katherine felt cast into the shade in her pale blue habit with but a small white plume atop her hat.

The ladies had been surprised by her presence, but she had explained that she was merely fulfilling her part in a wager she had lost, which seemed to satisfy their joint curiosity.

Katherine's gaze became fixed on Mrs. Nutley, who had in great excitement elected to be the race's starter. The lady, however, no longer seemed so content with her position as she met Katherine's gaze. Katherine offered her a tremulous smile, then shifted her attention to the kerchief in the good lady's hand.

"Ladies, are you ready?" Mrs. Nutley queried in as strong a voice as she could manage. The crowd grew hushed in anticipation.

The moment the kerchief left her fingers, Katherine's whip touched Prince's flank. He lurched forward and within two seconds was flying down the course. The air was filled with a thousand voices screaming at a feverish pitch. The shouts of the other riders spilled over Katherine, who was positioned in the middle of them. She held Prince back, even though she could sense he desired to burst ahead of the Astley horses. Soon the four riders had passed her.

She maintained a small distance between herself and the professional riders.

The racecourse became a strange, slow-moving blur before Katherine's eyes. She could see people waving their arms, but the sound which met her ears was muffled and dim. She pressed Prince forward, all the while her gaze scanning the depths of the crowds, particularly those gathered across from the Regent.

Children playing horse and rider.

A man selling slingshots, limping.

Three pretty young women, heads together, ignoring the race entirely.

A man, limping.

Katherine eased Prince around the final bend. Her mind whirred and bumped as Prince pounded ever forward, continuing to lead his competitors. Her mind reached back to the day of the donkey races.

Her leg ached suddenly.

A man had bumped her. A limping man. Something so hard had struck her thigh that she had been sore for days. A firearm! Yes, that was it!

She understood then that she had actually touched the assassin that day. The man who had shot at the Prince was the toy-seller! Her sudden disquiet communicated itself to Prince, who galloped harder still.

Her gaze found the man selling slingshots. The boys around him were now picking up stones and beginning to practice with their new toys. He turned away from the crowd of children and drew a rifle from the bulk of his long coat.

Katherine did not hesitate, but began drawing rein, much to the disappointment of the crowds. Her gaze never left the face of the assassin, who was completely unaware of her deviation from the course. She began to shout and wave an arm about wildly. She suspected she had the appearance of being unable to control her mount, which had the happy effect of sending the crowds flying out of her way so that in the end she was able to charge toward the toy-seller. He in turn was so intent on his business that he neither saw nor heard her.

* * *

Evan had watched Katherine for several moments of the race and knew she was holding Prince back. He noted how she was constantly surveying the crowds and knew she was hunting for the assassin as steadfastly as he and the Prince's men were.

When she pulled up and charged into the crowds, he knew she had located the toy-seller.

Following the line of her charge, he saw that she was heading directly for a man who was now holding a rifle aimed into the galleries opposite.

He was not far from the man and ran hard in his direction.

Battle—ready, he lunged toward the assassin, reached him seconds before Katherine did, caught the rifle and averted the aim. The gun discharged. The crowd nearby, already in disorder because of Katherine's charge, was flung into a complete chaos of screaming and running.

Evan subdued the man easily, for though he might have desired to kill a Prince by means of a weapon, he had no strength in his limbs. Mr. Keymer was beside him swiftly, along with several of the Prince's men.

Evan stood up, his heart pounding in his chest. "Is the Prince all right?" he shouted to Keymer.

"Yes. Perfectly well."

"And Katherine?" He looked around and saw her horse being held in check by a frightened boy who kept pointing to the ground nearby.

Time slowed for Evan.

He understood what had happened before he actually saw her crumpled form on the ground.

Sixteen

"Katherine!" Evan cried in a hushed voice, kneeling beside her and gathering her in his arms. Blood from the wound had soaked her habit and was now seeping into his coat and neckcloth.

He felt ill, the horror of what had happened, what he had done in attempting to keep the Regent from getting shot, striking his heart like a blast of cold wind. His gaze raked her still, pale face for any sign of life. He leaned his ear to her mouth and felt her breath in small puffs upon his cheek. She was not dead!

Gaining his feet, he lifted her up and headed in the direction of the coaches. Keymer was beside him instantly. "Is she alive?" he asked.

"Yes, but barely," Evan responded.

"Do you mean to take her to the infirmary?"

"No. To Mrs. Alistair's."

"I shall fetch the surgeon at once."

Evan glanced at his good friend. "Yes, please," he said. "And do hurry, Keymer. I vow we haven't much time."

Keymer took off at a run.

The crowds parted for Evan. Only vaguely did he see the assassin being bound and led away, or the crowds which were gawking at Katherine as he passed by.

His brother hurried up to him. "My God! I had heard

a lady was wounded but I did not think it was Katherine. Oh, my poor Constance. Come, Evan. My coach is just here."

Evan followed his brother blindly. His heart was aching desperately and a great pain burned behind his eyes. *How will I bear it if she dies?*

He understood something now, something terrible: *He loved Katherine Pamberley more than life itself.* He had been fooling himself these many weeks, perhaps even last summer when he had ignored her so pointedly.

He looked down at her briefly. How infinitely dear she had become to him in just a few blazing seconds.

Arriving at the coach, he handed her up to Ramsdell, who settled her in Constance's strong, capable arms. Evan mounted the stairs and took a seat next to his brother.

Ramsdell shouted for the coachman to return to West Street. The coachman, who had been in Ramsdell's employ forever, began shouting for the crowds to disperse, showering any number of gawkers with a string of invectives which indicated some practice of the art.

The coach could not move quickly enough.

"Keymer is fetching the surgeon even as we speak. I daresay he shall have the physician awaiting us when we arrive."

Constance nodded, but her face was pinched and tears had filled her eyes. "I tried to dissuade her, but I saw it all and I believe she was right to try. I believe she saved Prinny's life."

"I am in no doubt of it," he said, gripping his knees as he let his gaze drift to her face. Her complexion was the color of the cliffs along the Kentish coastline near Dover.

Will she live? The question filled the air of the coach, but no one dared to speak the words.

The trip to West Street normally required twenty-five minutes. The coachman, shouting the entire distance, made the trek in fifteen. And yet, Evan felt as though an hour had passed.

When the coach drew up before Mrs. Alistair's house, the surgeon was standing on the step in his shirtsleeves, his expression grim. Keymer hurried to open the door of the coach. Evan bounded out, and Ramsdell, his strength superior to two men, easily handed Katherine into their joint arms. Together, they hurried her into the house.

"To the morning room," Mrs. Alistair commanded. "All is ready."

Once within the chamber, Evan and Keymer settled her on a table covered with several sheets.

"You must leave us," the surgeon stated in a voice brooking no argument. Three women in crisp, black gowns quickly took Katherine's still form in hand. Even as Evan reluctantly quit her side, they were cutting the fabric of her riding habit, peeling it away from her and the wound which had torn her shoulder.

He did not get farther than three feet out the door before he sank to the floor and buried his face in his hands. The tears flowed so quickly that he could not have stemmed them had he wished to. He felt his brother's presence before he saw him, and was not surprised when Ramsdell sank to the floor beside him where together they waited. And waited.

Katherine felt light as a feather and happy beyond words. Her eyes seemed to flutter open all by themselves, and she found herself staring up into the canopy of her bed. The hour was late, for the only light was the flickering of a single candle. She tried to turn her head but found the effort almost impossible. She knew someone was in the room with her. She wanted to see who, and why a candle had been left dangerously alight at her bedside.

She heard the clacking of knitting needles. What a comforting sound.

Finally she was able to turn her head, and her gaze met a most welcome sight. She tried to speak her sister's name but could only utter the faintest moan. Whatever was wrong with her?

Constance must have heard her, however, for her gaze jerked from the blanket she was knitting. "Dearest," she murmured, rising sharply, the blanket and needles falling to the floor.

Katherine tried to smile, tried to ask a question, but failed in both efforts.

"No, do not try to speak. You have been very ill. Do you know where you are? Nod, if you can."

Katherine dipped her chin and Constance smiled, saying, "You are at Mrs. Alistair's."

Katherine dipped her chin once more. Her mind suddenly flitted to her mother, who had been able to communicate for so many years with only blinks of her eyes. Here Katherine was able to do but little more. She understood now in the worst way how horrible those years had been for her dear parent.

"Are you thirsty?"

She dipped her chin again.

Constance raised her up with one arm and tipped a little water down her throat. Katherine could hardly swallow and ended up choking.

"My darling!" Constance cried. "I am so sorry."

"More," Katherine said, some of her strength returning.

"Yes, of course."

Constance helped her swallow the cupful, and afterward Katherine felt much better. She sank into the pillows, her eyes closing as though they had been working far beyond their usual capacity. She could feel Constance take her hand and pet it. She felt droplets of water striking her hand and arm. She wondered if it was raining.

She remembered something. She opened her eyes. "The . . . Prince?"

"He is perfectly well." Tears ran down Constance's cheek. Why was she crying?

"Evan?"

"Unharmed, I promise you."

She smiled and fell sound asleep.

When she awoke again, the sun was pouring into her room. The window was slightly open, and the muslin curtains billowed like sails on an open sea.

She breathed deeply, feeling unutterably peaceful and content. All was well; Constance had said so.

"Are you hungry?"

Katherine glanced over to see who had spoken and saw Lydia sitting in the chair beside her bed.

"Hallo," Katherine said.

Lydia promptly burst into tears and called for Evan.

Evan entered the chamber, his face drawn and wearied as though he had been marching with Wellington's army for days. She smiled at him. "What happened?" she asked. Only then did she realize how badly her shoulder ached.

Lydia fled the room, but Evan took her place. "Water?" he asked.

"Yes, please."

He lifted her as Constance had. When she had had her fill, she thanked him. "Only . . . tell me why you are so tired."

He chuckled, but his eyes filled with tears just as Lydia's had. Finally Katherine comprehended what must have happened at the racecourse. "I was shot," she stated.

He nodded. "Deep into your shoulder. You bled badly. We were not sure for a long time . . ."

He could not continue, but looked down at the floor.

So that is why I feel like a feather, she thought. She had almost danced with the angels; she could sense it now, as though somewhere in her dreams she had met at least one of the celestial beings. She giggled.

"I must not have been wanted in heaven just yet," she said, reaching her hand toward Evan.

"What?" he asked.

She could only smile. "Nothing to signify." She met his gaze fully and could see that his eyes were full of tears. "Are you crying for me?" she asked.

"I think, for myself," he said enigmatically. He took her hand and squeezed it softly. "I do not know what I would have done had you perished." His gaze was forceful, and she felt him willing her to understand him.

"You would have been sad?" she queried.

"More than I could ever express."

"Do not blame yourself, Evan," she said, thinking he must in part feel guilty about what had happened.

He shook his head. "You mistake me, Katherine. When I picked you up from the racecourse, I felt with every drop of blood being spilled onto the grass that my heart was being drained of its reason for living. I thought I would die with you had you left this earth."

Katherine struggled to understand him. He was rubbing her hand and arm. He leaned over and kissed the palm of her hand, then each of her fingers.

"You love me," she stated, a sublime wonder filling her.

"Yes, my darling, I love with you all my heart. I have become so sincerely and completely attached to you that I cannot imagine life without you. My heart is yours, and will always belong to you, if you wish for it."

"If I wish for it," she returned softly. She was feeling very light again, as though the angels were tiptoeing quite close to her once more, only this time with something else in mind. "Oh, Evan. I wish for it more than anything else on earth!"

He rose up and placed a kiss on her lips. Even in her weakened state, she could feel his kiss to the tips of her toes. The lightness of her being vanished, and in its place was a desire that the moment never end, that Evan go on kissing her forever and ever, the way she always felt when he kissed her.

He drew back. "Have I hurt you? I thought I heard you moan."

She smiled, grateful he had not released her hand. "I did moan, but it was not from any discomfort. Evan, you have made me the happiest of women."

"Then make me the happiest of men, and marry me."

She could only smile. "I shall not be willing to wait a year," she said, closing her eyes. How tired she was. As she drifted off to sleep, she heard Evan say, "As soon as you are able to walk down the aisle, we shall be wed, my darling."

Several days later, Katherine reclined in the drawing room of Mrs. Alistair's home, watching the Prince Regent bow over her hand. "I have thought a thousand times how I might repay you for risking your life for me, and after begging of your relatives what might please you most, I have two offerings to make to you. First, that a school might be established in your name for female orphans of Brighton to learn the trade of sewing. What do you think of that?"

Katherine gazed into the florid face of her future sovereign and smiled. "You have read my heart exactly. I could wish for nothing more, I promise you."

"Your example was my inspiration. I heard of your wonderful generosity in providing fabric at your own expense to the young ladies who raced so many weeks ago."

"I have since heard they are each excelling in the art and are grateful for the opportunity to better their lives."

"Excellent, excellent," he murmured softly. "Now. I have a second gift, which I am hoping will bring you true delight." He seemed almost gleeful as he smiled at her. "There is a certain horse in my keeping, a mare with an excellent lineage for breeding, that I wish to bestow upon you. I have long since comprehended your love of horseflesh which I believe is nearly equal to my own, and for that reason I became convinced this would be the right gift for you. What do you say, Miss Pamberley?"

Katherine stared at him blankly for a long moment. She could not comprehend how he could part with any of his beloved horses. "You cannot be serious?" she blurted out afterward regretting her words instantly. "Pray do not take offense, but I am convinced you will come to regret such a decision. I know quite well how one becomes attached to one's horses."

He could only chuckle. "I have over two hundred, Miss Pamberley. I daresay I can relinquish one with but the smallest qualm."

The entire chamber broke into a roll of chuckles. Even Katherine smiled. "Then I most happily accept of your gift, and I promise to keep you informed on how well your mare thrives in my stables. You may rest assured that I shall care for her extremely well."

"I have no doubts on that head."

He drew back, and Mrs. Alistair begged him to take the seat next to Katherine. He remained for a very polite quarter of an hour, inquiring after everyone, in particular Lord Ramsdell. When he left, a round of lively chatter ensued about how gracious he was, how handsome he had been as a youth, and each wondering which of his mares he meant to give her.

Katherine said very little but watched everyone with gratitude and happiness. Lydia stood beside her betrothed, listening intently to a conversation between Mr. Keymer and Evan. Lydia's wedding was but two days away. Katherine's illness, having kept her in a state of delirium for days, had collapsed time for her. Already it was the middle of August.

Several important events had transpired in the days before Katherine had finally made her way down to Mrs. Alistair's drawing room today. Mr. Lunsford had left town several days ago, having been released shortly after the race since there was no evidence of his involvement in the attempted assassination. He finally admitted that, yes, he had procured a pair of false dice, which, just as Katherine had suspected, was what his conversation with Mr. Wooding had been about. There was no question that he was no longer welcome in Brighton's polite circles.

The toy-seller who had been captured in his attempt to harm the Prince Regent had been taken up to London and was held in the deepest bowels of Newgate Prison awaiting trial. It was expected he would die by way of Tyburn Tree. At least twenty-five persons had come forward desirous of bearing witness not only to his part in the horrible event but to many hate-filled speeches he had made during the preceding year against England's royal house.

Mr. Keymer had been released from service as secretary to the Duke of Relhan since he was to be married so very soon. Mrs. Alistair was probably the happiest of the three and even now was telling Constance that though they had debated a lemony Queen cake, she had settled on the traditional Bride cake for the wedding breakfast.

Constance was a welcome presence in Brighton during her convalescence, and every day seemed to increase her motherly appearance. Ramsdell stood next to her, and Katherine had the distinct impression he had grown quite protective of her, and of the child she was carrying. Her heart warmed to the thought, for together they were the perfect picture of happiness. His Lordship might have sensed her thoughts, for he suddenly turned and met her gaze, a smile suffusing his face.

He crossed the room and took a chair beside her,

which prompted Mrs. Alistair to excuse herself to join her daughter and Mr. Keymer. Lord Ramsdell queried, "And how do you fare this fine morning, Miss Katherine?"

"Very well indeed. I was not so dizzy as I have been. I barely needed Constance's arm when I descended the stairs earlier."

"Does your shoulder give you much pain?"

"Only a very little, but the doctor has told me it is because I lost so much blood." She wondered if she should not have spoken so openly about her brush with death, but he did not seem perturbed in the least.

"You have been through a difficult ordeal," he said kindly, "but we are all so very proud of you."

"Thank you, Ramsdell. Now tell me, do you intend to be a very strict parent?"

He smiled crookedly. "On no account. Your sister will be a veritable dragon, as you must know already, so I intend to spoil them all when she is not looking."

Katherine could only laugh. She admired and respected her brother-in-law prodigiously and had little doubt he would make an excellent father.

Evan joined them and begged to know what his brother had said to make her laugh. "Nothing to signify," she said; "just a ridiculous whisker."

Ramsdell pretended to be shocked that she would dare believe him capable of anything so unvirtuous, but after congratulating her again on her improving health, returned to Constance's side.

Evan took his brother's place and did not hesitate to possess himself of her hand. "Do you think we should tell everyone we are to be married?" he asked.

"Do you really think no one suspects when you are forever taking up my hand in public when you know you should not, and when you tend to ignore everyone in company when we are together?"

He lifted her hand to his lips and kissed her fingers

tenderly. "I shan't attempt to justify holding your hand, but as to ignoring everyone, I have good cause to do just that. You nearly slipped from my life, and I intend never again to take your presence for granted."

She thought it a noble notion but doubted that once they had marked a second or third anniversary, and the nursery became filled with all manner of happy noises, he would find many excuses to steal away from her side. For the present, however, she chose to bask in the warmth of his affection.

He cleared his throat and without ceremony promptly announced their betrothal. He did not receive the enthusiastic response he had hoped for. Instead, everyone merely regarded him as though he had just announced very old news indeed. "Will none of you offer a well-wishing?" he queried.

At that, Mr. Keymer stated, "The deed should have been done many weeks past, my good friend. I consider what you have just said to be long past due indeed, and can only wonder at your look of surprise. Or did you not know that you and Miss Pamberley have smelled of April and May since you first arrived in Brighton?"

Evan's mouth fell agape. Katherine could only laugh, for she knew it was very true. It was she and Evan who had been beetle-witted, kissing at every turn and yet somehow believing they were not headed for the altar.

Everyone laughed at poor Captain Ramsdell, including his bride-to-be.

Shortly afterward, a welcome visit was paid by Mr. and Mrs. Nutley. Mr. Nutley approached her bearing both an enormous bouquet of roses and a smile to match.

"Seeing you relieves all my unhappy fears!" he cried as he laid the flowers gently in her arms. "And my sincerest congratulations for your blooming health. I was so terribly worried!"

"Mr. Nutley," she said, her eyes swimming with sudden tears. "You are the dearest man. Thank you for the flowers, and even moreso for escorting me onto the race-course that day."

He shuddered. "Pray, do not remind me!" he cried. "I can still see you falling from your horse. I . . . oh, dear!" He grabbed for his kerchief and mopped his eyes.

Mrs. Nutley, who was beside him, patted his arm. "There, there, Horace, you can see she is perfectly well and . . . and you did right that day." She turned to Katherine. "We saw the whole of it from the stands. Had you not acted, either the Prince would have been killed or perhaps other innocent people around him. You were very brave, and I wish you to know that I will not permit anyone to disparage your character for having raced as you did, particularly when you had such a heroic intention in mind. And you did, did you not?"

Katherine was overcome with so much emotion, so much gratitude at their joint support of her, that she could barely speak. After a moment, she recovered herself enough to say that she had indeed been in search of the man intent on harming the Prince.

Mr. Nutley bobbed his head several times, his eyes still watery. "I knew you had a mission that day," he said, his words choked.

"Dear Mr. Nutley," she returned, taking his hand and pressing it warmly. "But let us not dwell, either of us, on the terrible events of that day, for you are come in time to offer a little well-wishing. Captain Ramsdell and I are to be married."

At that, Mr. Nutley chuckled and blew his nose. "You finally came to your senses, the pair of you, eh?"

Because Evan scowled in disbelief at him, the entire room erupted into another roll of laughter.

A sennight later, Katherine walked along the sandy beach with Evan beside her. She was much recovered and took in the healthful smell of the damp sea air with great pleasure.

Constance and Ramsdell had returned to Bedfordshire, to Ramsdell's home, where her sister would remain until her confinement. Keymer and Lydia had spoken their vows four days earlier and were presently enjoying their honeymoon on a cousin's estate in Hertfordshire.

Katherine smiled up at Evan, leaning heavily upon his arm. The sun was setting, casting a brief pink glow on the waves which lapped gently nearby. "So you mean to make me your wife," she said teasingly. "Yet you had always seemed to me a confirmed bachelor. I often wondered whether you would ever marry."

"I had been merely waiting for you, my love," he said. She thought he might be teasing in response, but the look in his eye was a warning that his love for her would not be trifled with at present. She understood him. He was still too close to having lost her to be entirely comfortable.

He stopped her in mid stride and turned her suddenly in his arms. "My dear Katherine, have I told you today how much I love you?"

"Only a dozen times, dearest," she responded, her eyes filling suddenly with tears.

"Not nearly enough," he responded, his lips forcefully upon hers in a kiss that was as urgent as it was needful. She kissed him warmly in response, her heart beating strongly in her breast as though straining to join with Evan's heart. She loved him so dearly.

When he drew back, she queried, "Have I told you today how much I love you?"

He surrounded her with his arms once more, holding her tightly against him. His smile was soft, the expression in his blue eyes warm and inviting as he gently pushed a strand of hair off her cheek. "Only a dozen times," he responded quietly.

"Not nearly enough, my darling, not nearly enough," she said.

He held her for a long time, and if there were eyes observing them from the cliffs which would be shocked at the intimate embrace, Katherine did not care, not one whit. She had been given her life anew, and in that giving had been granted the husband of her dreams. She would set aside propriety for the moment to receive again his declarations of love and as many kisses as he would bestow upon Katherine Pamberley of Lady Brook Cottage.

More Zebra Regency Romances